Trebled Waters

Books By Leah Dobrinska

The Mapleton Novels

Love at On Deck Cafe

Good To Be Home

Together With You

Choosing Love

The Larkspur Library Mysteries

Death Checked Out

Mayhem In Circulation

A Killer Hold

The Fall In Love Series

Friends Don't

Enemies Don't

Exes Don't

Pros Don't

The Songwriter Sleuth Mysteries

Trebled Waters

Trebled Waters

LEAH DOBRINSKA

Editing: Caitlin Miller, CM Editorial

Cover Design: Melody Jeffries @whimandjoy

Author Photo: Beth Dunphy

Library of Congress Control Number: 2025916417

ISBN: 979-8-9885978-6-5 (paperback) | 979-8-9885978-7-2 (ebook)

For Grandpa Jerry, with love.

1

Nashburg, Tennessee, wasn't called "crazy town" for nothing. In this city of neon lights, big hair, and bigger dreams, the highs were atmospheric and the lows were, well, bone-crushing. The country music industry was cutthroat.

Still, I hadn't expected to have a knife stabbed into my metaphorical back by a colleague I'd come to know, trust, and call friend.

Cal Dutton was a star—a country music rising star, to be exact.

Me? I'm a songwriter.

The two of us have collaborated on countless projects. He knows my talent. I know his. I thought I could trust him. But now I know otherwise.

"What did you just say?" I stared Cal down, and at the same time, mentally told my central nervous system to take a chill pill. Maybe I'd misunderstood him. Maybe he wasn't completely sabotaging my dream job before I even had a chance to apply.

Cal finished scratching out a few notes on a blank piece of sheet music at the piano before he glanced up at me. "I, uh—" He looked away ... *the coward.* "I told them you probably wouldn't be a good fit."

I tipped my head back and pinched the bridge of my nose, blowing out a deep breath. This couldn't be happening.

"Let me get this straight." I glowered at him. "You heard about a career-making job opportunity—a chance for me to get a contract as a staff writer with Red Vector Publishing, one of the hottest, up-in-coming music publishers in Nashburg. The very job I've been looking for, what I've been *clawing* toward, and you went and told your contact I wasn't a good fit?"

"I know it sounds bad, but I need you to trust me on this one, Leigh." Cal's tone was dismissive, and he still wouldn't meet my eye as he continued to scribble notes on the sheet music. Which was odd. Cal was self-centered to a fault, but he usually owned his decisions. If he was messing with my life, I expected him to at least look me in the eye and tell me why. "You should just stay independent. Or wait for another music group to offer publishing contracts."

"Oh, of course." I huffed out a maniacal laugh, turning to my pet beta fish, who was swimming circles in his bowl atop the piano. "You hear that, Phelps? I should just wait around. Because jobs like this pop up all the time. You know, the ones that promise a steady income, some stability, and the opportunity to make a living doing what I love." I closed my eyes. All I've ever wanted to be is a songwriter. I've been busting my chops, grinding it out in any writing room I could get my big toe into. This could be my chance to get a legitimate, well-paying gig.

Before Cal dropped this bombshell, I had assumed he would help pave my way. I've been writing with him since we met in music school. If one of the songs we've co-written gets picked up for his debut album, that could be a huge break for me. Even if it doesn't, given his position, he has the power to put in a good word on my behalf. I trusted him to do that, and he went behind my back and did the exact opposite.

"You told them I'm not a good fit!" I jabbed Cal in the shoulder. "How could you?"

"Ow, Leigh. Watch it." Cal rubbed the sore spot. "I've got a show tonight."

"Exactly! *You've* got a show. You get to go out there and do your thing. What about me? You just undercut what could have been a huge break for me."

"Leave it alone, Leigh." Cal shook his head at me, his expression not revealing even an ounce of remorse, which made my blood come to a spluttering boil.

I balled up my fists at my sides. "Screw you, Cal. Get out of my apartment."

He opened his mouth, and for a split second, I thought maybe he was going to walk it all back, say something that made this situation make sense. But he clamped his jaw shut and schlepped together the sheet music we'd been working on at my apartment. He shoved the pages into his messenger bag and went to the door, swinging it open. He paused, glancing at me over his shoulder. His movie-star good looks were on full display with the sun acting as his own personal backlight, making his sandy blond hair glow. "Things aren't what they seem. Forget about this job, Leigh. I promise it's for the best."

The absolute audacity.

"Get out," I seethed.

He didn't argue. He disappeared down the exterior stairs that would take him to the alley behind my building.

I stared at the closed door for a solid three minutes, and then I turned to my fish. "Can you believe him?"

Phelps didn't respond. Naturally. Though when I let loose a string of curse words, I'm pretty sure my magenta beta-fish blushed a deeper shade of red.

If only Emma, my roommate, was home. She was Cal's sister, and she would totally commiserate with me about her brother. Emma and Cal had a tenuous relationship. Usually, I was the one to remind her of his positive qualities. Not today. Today, I'd gripe right along with her.

I had to do something productive. Cal and I had been in a writing groove, penning a chorus that had promise, until he casually dropped the bomb on little ole unsuspecting me about the job opportunity. There was no way I could write anymore. Not now. I needed to clean something. Work out some aggression.

I donned my rubber gloves and headed to the tiny bathroom in our apartment.

Forty-five minutes later, the grout was bleach-white, and the seafoam-green tiles were shining. The toilet was clean enough for Phelps to safely swim a couple laps in the bowl. Not that I'd subject my fish to such an environment. That would be too much like what Cal just did to me ... all but flushing my chances down the toilet.

From the bathroom, I moved to the kitchen and proceeded to do a number on it. By the time I wrapped up, a person could just about see their reflection in our glass stovetop as if it were a mirror.

But almost two hours of cleaning had done nothing to make me feel better about what Cal said. I stared around my spotless apartment and let a hiss of air escape from between my clenched teeth. There was no way in honky-tonk I was going to let Cal cut my legs out from under me before I even had a chance to apply for this gig.

I ditched my rubber gloves and grabbed my phone off the kitchen counter, shooting off a message to Cal.

Leigh: Can we talk?

I said a silent prayer that whatever he had said to his contact at Red Vector wouldn't put me out of consideration before I had a chance to show them what I was made of, what I was made for—writing music that moved people.

My heart did its own version of a two-step in my chest as bubbles appeared on the screen a second later. They disappeared and reappeared twice more before a message came through.

Cal: At the Banta Bowl. No time.

I let out a growl. If Cal thought I was going to let this go, he had another thing coming. He didn't get to tell me what to do—or speak for me—without explaining himself.

Sure, Cal was under a lot of pressure, especially lately. I knew that, and as a result, I let his arrogance, sulkiness, and mood swings slide most of the time. He was on the cusp of a huge career break. The dream was so close, he could taste it. Heck, I could taste it.

Was that why he sabotaged this job opportunity? Did he want to keep me under his thumb, exclusively writing with him?

I shook the thought off. For all of Cal's faults, he wouldn't be so cruel ... would he? This was the country music industry. In a lot of ways, it was everyone for themselves.

I swallowed down the ball of emotion that rose in my throat. I would not cry over this. I didn't cry. Ever. I locked down my feelings a long time ago, and they'd stay that way, thank you very much.

I snatched my keys from the music-note hook to the side of the door. "He'll get his, Phelps. You wait and see."

I took the steps two at a time, flying down the narrow staircase that anchored the back wall of our apartment and the café below. I squinted against the harsh Nashburg summer sun and typed out a quick reply to Cal.

Leigh: Im coming ocer theere.

I didn't even bother to correct my typos. For someone who made her living—or at least hoped to make her living—as a wordsmith, that said something about how frazzled I felt.

The Banta Bowl, where Cal was performing, was the same place Emma worked. It was a free show, but I knew from Em that they presold ticket vouchers to keep attendance numbers within the fire code limit. I didn't have one, but I'd weasel myself in somehow. I needed to talk to Cal before he went on stage. I couldn't explain my urgency, except that it felt like with every minute that passed, my chance at this job slipped farther out of my grasp.

I shouldn't have let him leave without getting more information from him. I shouldn't have spent the last two hours cleaning. I should have gone after him right away.

Would've, could've, should've.

I cursed the precious extra seconds it took me to ease my truck forward and back enough to angle it out of where I'd wedged it in between a Prius and a Toyota Camry. I was accustomed to the cramped street parking in the Village, an eclectic borough right outside downtown Nashburg. On the sidewalk next to where I'd parked, a couple of fellow villagers, as we called ourselves, waved and smiled at me. Their good humor and neighborly cheer stood out in stark contrast to my stormy mood, but I faked the best return smile I could before pulling out from the curb. You didn't want to burn bridges in Nashburg. Everyone could be a potential connection.

I rolled my shoulders and told myself to relax as I navigated my route, merging onto the interstate. The dashboard on my old truck was lit up like a Christmas tree, which wasn't unusual. I put my foot on the gas and unmuted the radio—the last time I'd been in my truck, I had my own melody in my head and wanted silence as I tried to remember it until I could voice message it to myself.

Now, when the signal came in, Pita Paige and Penn Stewart crooned a searing duet through the speakers. I grunted in disgust and jabbed at the dial, silencing their perfectly harmonized voices. I wanted nothing to do with the reigning king and queen of country music right now. You want to talk about this industry being every person for themselves? You won't get a better—or should I say worse?—example than these two self-serving, cunning, toxic superstars. You'd think since they were in their late forties, maybe they'd be mature enough to see the err in their ways, but I haven't been approached with any sort of apology or explanation for the way they used me. So ... guess not.

Let's just to say, they aren't my favorites.

I snagged the closest parking spot I could find to the venue, but I had a half-mile walk to the Banta Bowl. The bars in this part of town weren't as massive as those lining Boardwalk Way, but they were still hopping. The strains of country music wafted out from open doors, but I hardly registered them. I dodged tourists and carefree locals who were enjoying the warm early evening air as I strode onward, planning my second inquisition as I went.

The Banta Bowl was pulsing with energy. Cheers rose from the back of the building, where a full-scale baseball diamond hosted regular games for the local minor league team. Ticket-less folks like me milled around the front entrance, trying to figure out a way into the main event. Smiles lit every face in the crowd as, concert or not, the promise of a fun evening hung around everyone's neck like a locket full of possibilities.

Women wore bold-colored crop tops and high-waisted jeans, their platform sandals completing the look. Some men wore pastel board shorts and polo shirts. Others were in skintight jeans and cowboy boots. Nashburg was a melting pot. Folks dressed how they liked and made any statement they wanted in doing so. I loved that about this place, how it let everyone be themselves and welcomed each individual brand of funky, traditional, cutting-edge, or crazy. At the moment, though, I wasn't in any mood to wax poetic about how incredible Nashburg was. I needed to focus on getting backstage and finding Cal.

In the past, that would have been no problem, but now, he was sort of famous.

Two months back, Cal signed a deal with Red Vector Records—AKA the recording wing of the music group that also housed Red Vector Publishing. Red Vector was the big league here in Nashburg. Sure, they were a relatively new group, but their label was fresh, their songs pushed the just-right boundaries, and they'd already made a name for themselves, especially since they signed Jace James, an undeniable music superstar with a killer vibrato and other-worldly range, a few years back. Now, anyone who was anyone wanted to be under Red Vector's umbrella.

Cal was pegged as its future break-out star.

Based on the crowds tonight, the future was now.

I elbowed my way to the front entrance of the Banta Bowl and through the swarm of fans, only to be stonewalled by the bouncer, whose nametag read "Ted." He reached for my arm and yanked me back just as I attempted to slide through the entryway with a group of three women who'd scanned their e-vouchers.

"You got a code?" he asked.

I glanced past him into the oversized bar, and almost said, "I'm with the band," but decided I'd rather not be a complete cliché.

"Full house tonight," Ted said, drawing my attention. I met his gaze and he shook his head. "No ticket, no entry. Move on back."

Okay, Ted. Reciting a line from "The Wheels on the Bus" just added insult to injury, thank you very *little*.

I begrudgingly stepped aside as the groupies, better known as *Cal's Crew*, pressed their way forward. Each of them wore a pin with a number in the center. They literally had a limit for how many of Cal's most loyal fans earned the pin. *Barf.*

Cal called them job security. To Emma and me, they were more like a pain in the butt. Granted, my annoyance at their antics paled in comparison to Emma's complete and utter disdain for her brother's fan club, but I had to agree with her in part—their obsession with Cal was borderline creepy.

I scanned the contoured faces of the mostly female fans and, for a moment, felt self-conscious about my own appearance. I was wearing my scuffed white cowgirl boots and cutoff jean shorts with a plain black tee. I left the apartment without so much as applying a swipe of lip gloss to my barely made-up face. Not to mention the fact that I probably smelled like bleach from my cleaning frenzy.

Next to their shimmering skin and lengthened lashes, I was sure I looked like a pale peach shower curtain.

I ran a hand over my short, box-brunette hair. I wasn't here to impress anyone. I had a job to do.

Or, rather, a job opportunity to defend.

As I swung my attention back to Ted, the burly bouncer, to plead my case, Whitney Allerow, the unofficial leader of Cal's Crew, strode toward the group from the backside of the venue. She shoved a strand of her perfectly curled auburn hair behind her ear and repositioned her Cal's Crew pin, sparkling with a giant #1 in the center. Her eyes darted around, taking in the scene, and our gazes connected. She stuck up her nose and looked away, but not before a panicked look crossed her face.

Whitney clapped her hands. "Dutt, Dutt!"

The posse of Cal's fans responded in kind. "Dutt, Dutt!"

Gag me.

It was their rally cry—a play on words of a quarterback's "hut, hut," snap count, of all things—and it was as annoying as having popcorn kernels stuck in your teeth.

Bouncer man Ted had his hands full with one of the members of Cal's Crew who couldn't get her voucher to scan, so I ducked and skirted the crowd, sneaking in on the far side of the door. I'd lived in and around Nashburg my entire life. I had a pretty good feel for how things worked in this town, and while I'd like to say this was my first time entering (or leaving) a concert venue unnoticed, that would be a lie.

No matter. Mission number one, accomplished.

My eyes took a second to adjust to the hazy light of the bowl-ing-alley-turned-hot spot for up-and-coming and established country music stars alike. A cover band was on stage singing a rousing rendition of "Friends In Low Places."

The clank of glasses on granite rang out as bartenders mixed drinks and shoved them into the open hands of thirsty patrons.

I pulled out my phone and fired off a quick message to Emma.

Leigh: At the Banta Bowl. Need to talk to Cal. Where are you?

I expected an almost immediate response. When Emma wasn't working, she was always on her phone—updating her social media accounts, listening to hotel and restaurant management podcasts, or catching up on the Printer's Alley Press news. She was the poster child for our generation—a girl in her early twenties, glued to her device.

When bubbles didn't appear on the screen right away, I pocketed my phone and scanned the crowd. Across the room, I spotted Zac Gaffedab, the president of Red Vector Records. He was huddled with a man I didn't recognize, but judging from his black polo shirt with the neon green BB embroidered on the pocket, he was a Banta Bowl employee. His frown deepened as he listened to whatever Zac was saying.

The two turned and walked toward the bar.

And I was thrown completely off balance when a shoulder suddenly knocked into mine from behind.

"Hey!" I barked. "Watch it!"

My annoyance fizzled as I looked up into the moody, hazel-colored eyes of the one and only Jace James. His face was shaded by a baseball cap, creased and pulled close to his temples, but there was no question I was standing next to the biggest country music star in recent history.

"Completely my fault. And also ... sorta intentional." He rocked back on his heels and shot me a smile. "Good to see you, Leigh Notrap."

Jace was teasing me, intentionally pronouncing my last name as *Not Rap* instead of *No Trap*. It was an inside joke that went back to our time at music school together.

I unstuck my tongue from the roof of my mouth and tipped up my shoulder—the same one that was still prickling at the contact it just had with Nashburg's heartthrob. "You know, I could beat you in a rap battle any day, Jace James."

Mirth danced in his warm eyes. "Name the time and place, and I'll be there."

"Don't know about that," I hummed. "Let's be real. Between the two of us, you've been harder to get a hold of recently."

Jace's laugh was as smooth as butter sliding over warm pancakes. "True. I'd say it's my own loss." His gaze held mine, and flecks of green glittered like emeralds in the dim light. This was new. Jace never flirted with me. I'd been firmly friend-zoned by both him and Cal, which was fine by me. A relationship with either of them was not on my radar. But now, something passed behind his eyes that I'd never been on the receiving end of before.

I swallowed. "Haven't lost your charm, have ya?"

His foot on the gas grin was all sorts of dangerous. "Not even a little bit."

I shifted my weight, not sure what to do with his undivided attention. "You in town for a while?" I asked him as we moved closer to the bar.

"Break in the tour. I'm around until the festival. Good chance to catch up on all the housekeeping stuff I let fall by the wayside when I'm on the road. So far, I've accomplished my yearly physical, got some new glasses, and went to a dentist appointment."

"So glamorous." I laughed. When Jace talked about his life like that, it almost made him seem normal.

Almost.

He grinned before casting a look over my shoulder. "I was hoping to catch Zac before the show, but also not be recognized by anyone in the crowd. What do you think my chances are?" He jutted his chin to the fans packed like sardines.

I shrugged. "I'd say slim to none."

It was only a matter of time before the people here to see Cal realized Jace was in the house and jumped him for an autograph or a photo op. I winced on his behalf. I knew how it felt to long for a fleeting moment of privacy. At least, I used to.

"Zac was over there. If you hurry, you might be able to catch him—" I swung my gaze toward where I had last seen Zac, only to find him striding away and ducking down the hallway on the far side of the stage. "Then again, maybe not."

Someone pointed, and a collective squeal rippled in our direction.

"Help an old friend out, would ya?" Jace aimed a disarming grin at me, and the entire room quieted—at least to my ears. The only sound I could hear was my own heartbeat as he reached out his hands, calloused from strumming a guitar six out of seven nights each week, and squeezed my shoulders, positioning me directly in front of him, pretending to use me as a human shield.

My chuckle came out high and pitchy at the same time as my phone buzzed in my back pocket. I pulled it out, grateful to have something to focus on besides Jace's dancing, jewel-infused eyes, and opened a text from Emma.

Emma: Get backstage now. It's Cal. There's been an emergency.

2

In songwriting, timing is everything. It's all about picking your moments. Go full throttle with words that require a dictionary, and you wear people out. Use overly simplistic rhyme schemes, and you lose their interest. Songwriting has to be nuanced. The best lyrics and melodies sneak up on you and knock you on your butt—in the most satisfying way.

Emma had yet to master the art of nuance. She tended to be all drama, all the time—the human equivalent of a song that thrashed and yelled for its entire three-and-a-half minutes of airtime. I loved her for it, but to Emma, an emergency was a stain on a t-shirt or a low cell phone battery.

Still, I sucked in a hard breath when I read her message.

"What is it?" Jace dropped one of his hands and cupped my elbow, turning my body so both of our backs were to the stage and, by extension, his horde of fans.

"Emma says there's been an emergency." I rolled my eyes, letting him know I wasn't too worried, because this was Emma we were talking about, but then I shrugged. "I should go check it out. She's backstage."

"I'll come with you. Hopefully I can catch Zac."

Together, we crossed the hall, the floor already sticky with spilled beer and glitter. Jace kept his head down, and I plowed through the masses of chatty fans, trying to pave a way for him. A buzz of anxious anticipation zipped like lightning through the crowd. Cal was supposed to take the stage in less than ten minutes. Whatever this so-called emergency was, hopefully it would be easily assuaged.

Security tried to stop us at the backstage entrance. Fortunately, I was with Jace. He took off his baseball cap and didn't even need to show an ID. The guard stumbled over his words, then immediately let us pass. Lifestyles of the rich and famous and all that jazz. Usually that would annoy me, but in this case, I was grateful.

Jace took my elbow again and steered me ahead. "His dressing room is probably this way."

We picked up our pace, but when we turned a corner of the labyrinth of backstage rooms, I pulled up short. Ahead of us, Zac Geffadab stood stiff, his tanned face streaked with pensive lines. Someone else was sobbing from inside the nearest room.

Jace reacted first, urging me forward with a palm on my lower back. "What's going on?" He directed his question to Zac, who shook his head slightly.

I peered into the open door of the dressing room on the left. I caught a glimpse of a name placard that read 'Cal Dutton' before my attention was completely taken up by Emma. She was standing at the foot of a charcoal-gray leather couch. Cal's long limbs were all I could see. His face was blocked by a woman kneeling at his head. Her body shuddered with her wails.

Emma turned to me, her mouth hanging open and her eyes the size of watermelons. I hesitated for the briefest second, not certain I should enter the room, but my concern for Emma won out. She was like a sister to me, and my protective streak kicked in.

I strode to her side and pulled her into a tight hug. She didn't say a word, but she gripped me as if her life depended on it.

"What's going on?" My voice was muffled, the words caught up in Emma's golden hair.

"Cal." Emma said her brother's name in a hoarse whisper. "H-he's non-responsive."

I reared back, keeping hold of Emma's forearms. "What are you talking about? He just texted me thirty minutes ago." He'd been plenty responsive then—so much so that I'd wanted to stuff a sock in his mouth.

I turned and eyed the couch. Autumn Silver, Cal's long-time girlfriend, had her nose pressed into the front side of his shirt, sobbing. When she shifted to lay her head flat against his heart, I caught my first glimpse of Cal's face. His eyes were closed, and his right arm hung limp at his side, his knuckles grazing the low-ply carpet on the floor. His bare left arm was unmoving on his chest.

Two EMTs shoved their way into the room. One of them, a young woman dressed in blue slacks and a blue-collared shirt, approached Autumn. She eased her away from Cal's immobile body so her partner, a middle-aged male, could complete an evaluation.

"I think he's dead, Leigh. I couldn't find a pulse," Emma whispered, as if terrified that saying the words aloud would make them true.

For one of the first times in my life, I was at a loss for words. Cal? Dead? There was no way. And yet, my own eyes didn't lie.

The dejected way the male EMT sat back on his heels, not even bothering to administer any type of resuscitation, didn't lie.

Autumn's screams didn't lie.

My stomach gave an uncomfortable lurch, and I scanned the room, not able to look at Cal. Two mugs sat on the end table on the far side of the couch. Along the wall on the inside of the hallway, a sink and countertop were littered with snack packages and a bouquet of red roses. Off to one side of the sink was a basket containing Cal's vitamins and medications. He was notorious for carting around a medicine cabinet's worth of drugs to keep his vocal cords in tip-top shape.

Zac and Jace hovered outside the door. Jace was frowning and shaking his head. The shocked expression coloring his features made him look less like a country music superstar and more like the guy I met at music school, who was still trying to figure life out just like the rest of us.

"Yeah. We're going to need the medical examiner."

The sound of the male EMT's voice ripped my attention from Jace. I cut a glance at Emma. Her mouth was agape in fresh horror.

The EMT hung up his cell, turning to Emma and—by extension—me.

Emma swallowed and took a small step forward. "Is Cal really—I mean, he can't possibly be? But..."

I grabbed her hand and clutched her fingers. She was trembling.

"I'm so sorry, Miss...?" The EMT flicked his gaze from Emma to me.

"Dutton," I supplied. "Emma Dutton. She's Cal's sister."

His eyes softened, the edges of his mouth lowering into a frown. "I'm sorry, Miss Dutton, but there's nothing we can do for him. I'm so sorry for your loss."

Emma opened her mouth to speak but closed it again, firming her lips. She nodded. She wasn't crying, but she continued to shudder.

Two uniformed police officers joined us in the room, and the EMT huddled up with them, giving a brief run-down of the situation. I could only hear bits and pieces.

Cal Dutton. DOA. Cause of death unknown.

That about summed it up.

One of the cops pulled out his phone and tapped the screen before holding the device to his ear. "We're going to need your unit here at the Banta Bowl." He paused. "Right outside. Good. See you soon."

"How does someone just die like that?" Emma's question drew my attention. She blinked but didn't seem to really be seeing anything. I wondered if she was going into shock.

I continued to grip her hand in hopes of anchoring her. "Usually they don't." My voice was gruff, matter of fact.

Emma flinched, and I chided myself for sounding so cold. I tried softening my tone. "I guess people's hearts give out, but—"

Shouts in the hallway cut me off.

"I don't like you people just storming in here through the front doors! I have a business to run! How's it going to look if cops are swarming around?"

The sound of the irritated voice snapped Emma out of her stupor. We exchanged a knowing glance. That was Willie Davis, the owner of the Banta Bowl and Emma's boss. Zac and Jace stepped aside, and two more law enforcement officers appeared in the doorway, followed closely by a very agitated Willie. One of the cops was older, probably in his late fifties, with thinning brown hair. The other looked young and fit. His dark skin was smooth, and his black hair was cut in a close crop. I'd peg him to be in his early thirties.

The older officer was trying to placate Willie. "Look, sir. I've got a job to do just like you do. I assure you we'll be sensitive to your situation, but I'd hate to have to write you up for police interference."

The younger cop wedged his way into the crowded dressing room. He had the look of someone who knew exactly what he was doing. Like, I had seen the guy for all of ten seconds, but I would already trust him with my life. His black eyes took in everything as he made a thorough sweep of the room—Cal on the couch, the mugs and the messy kitchenette area, Autumn in the arms of the female EMT who, honestly, deserved a prize for her compassion at this point, and finally, Emma and me.

As for me, my gaze dropped to the blue jacket he wore, and my heart skipped a beat. I saw the yellow stitching on the cop's breast pocket: Nashburg Metro Police Department Homicide Unit.

There was a very good chance Cal's death wasn't an accident.

3

The younger detective didn't try to speak to anyone right away. He nodded at us before approaching the male EMT. They conversed in hushed tones, and I couldn't make out a word they said. The only person I could hear was Willie, and I was ready to shut him up myself.

"What are we going to do?" Willie flailed his arms around from where he stood in the hallway. "I've got a full house expecting to see Cal Dutton"—he glanced down at the watch on his wrist and groaned—"five minutes ago!"

The outburst caught the young detective's attention. He glanced at his partner, and they nodded at each other.

The older detective turned to Willie. "Sir, this is an active police investigation. Obviously Mr. Dutton will not be performing tonight, but we need to keep the details of the scene and the case private for the time being, so you're going to need to come up with an excuse."

"Willie—" Emma stepped toward him, but he cut her off with a look.

"An excuse?" Willie's voice was dangerously high. Beads of sweat formed along his slicked-back hairline. He narrowed his eyes at the cops. "What would you have me say?"

Zac stepped forward, placing a hand on Willie's shoulder. "Jace will perform." He turned back to Jace. "Won't you?"

Jace's jaw dropped. "Are you kidding me? You want me to sing at a time like this? To go out there and pretend everything's fine? Cal is—was—my friend."

"Then you can and should do it to honor him, right?"

Jace squirmed, his gaze flitting to Emma and me before he sighed. "Sure. You're right. Okay." He turned to Willie. "I'm going to need at least ten minutes to warm up. It'll have to be an acoustic show. Buy me a few, yeah?"

Willie slapped him on the back, suddenly all smiles.

Ugh.

"You got it, Jace. You're a lifesaver." He took off to find one of his Banta Bowl minions who'd alert the crowd of the change of concert plans and hype them up for a surprise Jace James performance—not too difficult of a job, all things considered.

Jace looked dazed, as if he'd just come off a rollercoaster and was trying to reorient himself. When we were in music school together—Jace, Cal, and me—I didn't think it was possible for Jace to get any better looking, but I was wrong. Time had been good to him. The mixture of vulnerability, pain, and resolve that splashed across his face in the last several moments was all sorts of attractive.

He gave me one last look, and I tried to offer him a reassuring smile but couldn't get my mouth to lift in time before he disappeared down the hallway.

"Well, now that the most important business of the hour is taken care of..." The older detective entered the room, his sarcasm as thick as the three-stacked rolls on his neck. "We can get to work."

He stopped in front of Emma and me. The female EMT steered a hiccupping Autumn in our direction, and the detective nodded at her. "I'm Detective Keith Ottom. This is my partner, Detective Isaiah Yance." He motioned a beefy hand toward the younger guy. Detective Yance's gaze bounced from Autumn, to me, and settled on Emma for a beat longer before he crossed his arms and tipped his chin in acknowledgment of Detective Ottom's introduction.

"Can we get your name and your relationship to Cal, please?" Detective Ottom pried a spiral-bound, pocket-sized, flip notebook from his back pocket.

Emma squared her shoulders and took a step forward. "I'm Emma Dutton, Cal's sister."

Detective Ottom nodded as he jotted down a note.

"I'm Autumn Silver." Autumn blew out a shaky breath. "I'm Cal's girlfriend."

Detective Ottom did a double take, his eyes widening as he blinked at Autumn before scribbling something on the page. Autumn was a renowned singer herself, but her usually porcelain face was blotchy and her eyes bloodshot, so I could see how Detective Ottom hadn't recognized her at first.

Next to him, Detective Yance didn't bat an eye. I had no doubt he knew exactly who Autumn was the second he entered the room. He seemed to know everything.

The detectives looked to me for my introduction.

"I'm Leigh Notrap." I swallowed down the surge of panic that always catapulted into the back of my throat when asked to identify myself. Fortunately, the detectives had more pressing things to concern themselves with than who I was, and like Emma, my identification didn't make either of them think twice. "Cal and I write music together," I added.

Detective Ottom jabbed his pen at the notebook page before swinging his gaze over the three of us. "We're going to need to ask y'all a few questions."

Across the room, the EMTs pulled a tarp from their bag, and they solemnly covered Cal's body. Reality crashed down on me, pressing into my skull like the disorienting weight of the stack of books I used to walk around with to perfect my posture.

I hated those books.

I hated this moment.

To my right, Emma nodded. To my left, Autumn blew her nose.

"Who was with Cal this evening?" Detective Ottom asked.

"I was." Autumn cleared her throat, but her voice still came out raspy. "He picked me up, and I rode with him here ahead of his show."

"How had Cal been acting? Was he behaving unusually?"

"Not really." Autumn cocked her head to the side. I could almost see her reliving the past couple of hours, and my heart broke for her. Cal was not an easy person to get along with, but somehow, he and Autumn made a relationship work. I'm not sure how or why she put up with him, but they seemed to have a true partnership.

"He was excited to perform tonight. Maybe a little more fidgety than normal. But otherwise, he was his usual self." Autumn shrugged.

Emma snorted. "Which means he was grumpy and a pill to anyone whose name wasn't 'Autumn'. No offense," she added, nodding at the popular singer.

Autumn raised a shoulder, a sad smile on her lips. "You're not wrong."

Between Cal's ego and his mood swings, there wasn't a lot of room for anyone else's feelings. I knew that firsthand.

"I overheard Cal and Willie arguing when Cal got here," Emma offered.

"You were here?" Detective Yance spoke for the first time to clarify Emma's point.

She nodded. "I work here. I'm Willie's site manager. I was headed back to his office to do our nightly check-in, but when I got to the door, it was cracked open, and I heard fighting."

Detective Ottom made more notes. Detective Yance stared at Emma.

"Anyway," Emma continued, "Cal left the office before I could hear what they were saying. He blew by me in the hallway without a word." Emma kept her voice level, which wasn't always easy for her. Most of the time, Cal acted like Emma didn't exist, and she took it personally that he held himself in such high regard above her.

When Cal signed with Red Vector, he hosted a huge party out at his parents' mansion. The Duttons were an old-money family, and Cal and Emma's parents pulled out all the stops. Professional catering, the backyard expertly decorated. It was a stunning event, and Emma had overseen it all, making sure it came together seamlessly. All sorts of friends, neighbors, colleagues, and the Who's Who of the music industry descended on the place, and Cal got up and gave a speech where he thanked everyone for coming and started crediting those who helped him get to this point. He made a big show of talking about family and how important family was to him. How he couldn't wait to carry on his parents' legacy. He gushed about how much his mom and dad had done for him, both in general and that party in particular.

He didn't say a word about Emma. Completely ignored that she was standing right there. That she was the reason there was a chocolate fountain and a life-sized ice sculpture of Cal himself in the backyard. That even though she always showed up for him, he never gave her the time of day.

She'd locked herself in her room for the rest of the night.

Detective Ottom clicked his pen. "We can talk to Willie." He pointed his writing utensil at Autumn. "So, you weren't with Cal the entire time he was here, then?"

Autumn shook her head. "I had to call my manager to sort out a few things for the Country Music Festival. I was supposed to meet with her in person, but I wanted to come with Cal. I ducked into an open room shortly after we arrived to take care of my business. After my call, I came in here, and Cal was already here. Alone."

"What time was that?" Detective Ottom asked.

Autumn checked her phone. "Just after six."

I slipped my hands into my back pockets and bit my lip. That was around the time he would have been texting me.

"Can you describe what Cal was doing before he lost consciousness?"

Autumn pursed her lips, fresh tears welling in her grassy green eyes. "He ran through his voice warm-up exercises, and then we sat down to have a cup of tea and some cookies. My manager called me, so I stepped into the hallway to take her call. When I came back, Cal was mad because he said his tea tasted awful. It was too bitter. He added three extra spoonfuls of honey before drinking the rest. He wanted to have a word with management here. Said they should know how he liked his tea by this point." Autumn shot an apologetic look to Emma, whose face was set like flint.

Detective Yance walked over to the end table where the two mugs were set.

Autumn eyed him warily before taking an audible breath and continuing. "A little after that, he turned bright red. He gasped, said his heart felt like it was going to explode, and then he started talking gibberish. I told him to lie down. He was burning up. Before I could even call anyone for help, he started convulsing, and then he lost consciousness."

Autumn started sobbing, and I reached over and put a hand on her shoulder. I wasn't really the touchy-feely type, especially with people I wasn't close to, but I powered through my awkwardness. Though I didn't know Autumn well, we'd always had a relationship of mutual respect, and offering her some show of comfort felt like the least I could do.

"So you didn't drink any tea?" This came from Detective Yance, who had donned gloves and moved to sniff the abandoned mugs.

Autumn sniffled. "I didn't eat or drink anything in this room."

Detective Yance crossed over to the kitchenette area and, with his gloved hands, started examining Cal's medications and supplements.

"Then what happened?" Detective Ottom prompted.

Emma raised her hand like a student in a classroom. "That's when I showed up. After seeing Cal so agitated in the hallway, I figured Willie would need some time to cool off. So instead of going to his office for our check-in, I went out to see how the stage looked. I came back a few minutes later and had my meeting with Willie, and then came here. I found Autumn with Cal. She was standing over him, screaming for him to wake up. She started CPR, and I called 911."

Detective Ottom swung his gaze to me. "And you?"

For a half second, I debated telling the detectives the reason why I'd showed up. It all seemed so insignificant now, but I didn't want to withhold information from law enforcement. If they obtained Cal's phone records, they'd find out anyway, so I decided to be completely honest.

"I got here after Emma called the paramedics. Zac Gaffedab was standing in the hallway when Jace James and I arrived." I glanced behind me to find that the label president had left. In his place, uniformed officers continued to flit about. One of them was talking to Phil McMann, Cal's manager, who must've caught wind of what was going on.

I faced Detective Ottom again, straightening my spine. "I wanted to talk to Cal about a conversation we had earlier today."

One of Detective Ottom's eyebrows arched in question.

My heart stuttered in my chest under his appraising glare, but I refused to cower. "He told Red Vector Publishing I wasn't a good fit for a staff writing job with their label."

Emma and Autumn gasped, which was satisfying. I resisted the urge to say, *I know, right?*

"Why would he do that?" Emma said at the same time as Autumn said, "That doesn't make any sense!"

Their confusion and outrage made me feel marginally better, but none of it mattered anymore. Cal was dead. His reasons for sabotaging my chances of getting the Red Vector job died with him.

Thunderous applause reached my ears. Somewhere outside this room, the venue's deejay was announcing Jace. "Ladies and gentlemen, country music fans of all shapes and sizes, put your hands together for the one and only Jaaaaaaace Jaaaames!"

The crowd went wild, and the room we were in vibrated. I recognized the plucking of the opening chords to Jace's current hit song, "Heartbreak High," but then all the outside noise turned to static.

Phil McMann stepped toward us and stood next to Autumn. The four of us stared at the detectives. Detective Ottom made another notation and flipped the notebook shut as Detective Yance rejoined our circle.

"We need to secure this room." He dropped his voice to a whisper, but his words carried, managing to cut through the hum of concert noise. "I think I know what killed Cal Dutton."

4

When I parallel parked my truck in the Village two hours later, my body felt like it was full of heavy, wet sand. The kind that filled the bags stacked up along the coast during hurricane season.

The Village's nightlife didn't hold a candle to the neon lights and bad decisions of downtown Nashburg. There, the streets were packed and loud. It was quieter here. But that didn't mean that the sidewalks were empty on a summer Friday night. Groups of friends were out and about, laughing before they ducked into the bars that punctuated the corners on each end of Crowbar Road, the main thoroughfare through the Village. Twangy live music spilled out from the bars' open doors, and I could actually hear the song lyrics because there weren't so many bars with different bands competing for my attention.

The warm, glowing lights of Java Flo's blinked at me from a block ahead. I picked up my pace, glanced left and right, and jaywalked across the road, doing a courtesy jog when a car approached.

The second I yanked open the coffee shop door, the bungee cord belting my rib cage together and cutting off my air supply snapped. I took what felt like my first worthwhile breath since Cal was at my apartment this afternoon.

A couple of the worn, wooden tables around me were littered with the remains of the day—straw wrappers, condensation rings from water glasses, and crumbs. That mess wouldn't last for long. Not at Java Flo's. The owner of this fine establishment—and also, as it were, my landlord—ran a tight ship. Her name was Agnes, not Flo, as one might assume. Agnes bought Java Flo's from a woman by the name of Flo, but, as she told me in her no-nonsense way when we were first getting to know each other, 'Java Agnes's' didn't have the same ring to it.

I didn't care what the place was called as long as I could always count on it being here, with Agnes behind the register or in the kitchen. Sad as it may sound, Java Flo's was the closest place to *home* I'd ever known. The eatery also helped me keep a roof over my head. When songwriting gigs were scarce, I worked behind the counter to earn extra cash.

I nodded at one of the busboys as he bustled out of the swinging door from the kitchen. He'd have the dining space cleaned up in no time.

A smattering of patrons sat around the coffee shop. Nat and Daren, a young couple who moved to the Village last month, were sipping on iced drinks in the corner. Daren was an Emergency Medicine doctor at the nearby Memorial Hospital. Nat worked for the city of Nashburg's Chamber of Commerce. I didn't hold the fact that they were madly in love against them, even though their heart eyes made me want to gag.

They spotted me and waved me over, and I headed in their direction.

"Leigh, how goes it?" Daren raised his cup to me in greeting.

"Been better," I said.

Nat's eyes pooled with concern. "Is everything okay?"

"No." I glanced over my shoulder. No one was paying us any attention, but I still dropped my voice. "You know Cal Dutton?"

The couple nodded.

"Emma's brother," Daren supplied.

"I just heard his song on the radio today," Nat added. "He's going to be a star."

"Yeah, not anymore." I winced. "He passed away tonight."

Nat covered her mouth with her hand. Daren grimaced.

"Oh my gosh. What happened?" Nat gasped.

"Not really sure." I shrugged. The pair looked horrified, and I felt a twinge of guilt for ruining their picturesque evening. "Sorry to dump that on you."

Nat shook her head. "No, it's okay. Is Emma alright?"

"Is there anything we can do?" Daren offered.

"If there is, I'll be in touch. Thanks, y'all." I left them to their drinks and each other's company.

Straight ahead and to the left of the front counter, a guy I had never seen before sat at a table for one. He had a sleek laptop open, wireless headphones planted over his ears, and he slurped one of Agnes's famous frozen cappuccinos. Bold choice for this late in the evening. He must've felt me staring because, from behind his dark-rimmed glasses, his eyes rocketed up to my face. Our gazes locked, and he offered me a closed-mouth smile before dipping his chin and refocusing on his screen. He wore a t-shirt that read, *Never trust an atom, they make up everything*. I huffed a small laugh in spite of myself.

On the other side of the dining room were more regulars. Suzan had her long blonde hair blown out in beachy waves, which made me think she must've had a celebrity come through the salon and was trying to make a good impression as the owner. She sat chatting with Kristoff. He was usually staffing the front desk at Nashburg's swankiest downtown hotel, The Burg.

I waved to them, trying to act normal. But how was I supposed to do that when I'd spent my night at a crime scene?

I made my way to the counter, and since it was absent of all signs of human life, I dinged the tiny silver bell Agnes had set up for just such moments. I pressed the dinger a couple times, making the bell sound in the same pattern as "da, da, da, da, da, daaaaa, charge!"

Agnes came out of the kitchen butt first, her arms laden with a plate of cookies and two ceramic mugs filled with some type of steaming drink. My heart swelled in my chest. I had texted her an undetailed synopsis of what went down at the Banta Bowl, and told her I was coming. This was her response—to ply me with comfort food. I loved this woman something fierce, and all I wanted to do was bury myself in her chest and have her tell me it would all be okay. But I didn't make it a habit of melting down or showing weakness, so I gave her a brisk nod in greeting.

"Leigh, baby. You made it. How're you doing?" Agnes gave me a quick once-over as if assessing for signs of injury. She wouldn't find any ... at least, not on the outside. But my nerves were shot.

I shrugged. "I'm fine."

Agnes cocked her head to the side, the disbelieving look on her face telling me she didn't believe me for one second. She motioned with her elbow to an empty table for two just this side of the register. "Come, sit. Let's talk."

Over tea, I told Agnes the entire story, starting with my songwriting session with Cal this afternoon and ending with how we left things at the Banta Bowl.

"Emma went to her parents'. The detectives had to break the news to them." I popped the last bite of my third cookie into my mouth. "I cannot even imagine how they'll take it."

Agnes frowned. "Cal was always the golden child. They'll be devastated. How's Emma holding up?"

I shrugged. "Shocked. Confused. I don't think any of it has sunk in yet."

Agnes crossed her toned arms over her bosom, smushing the crucifix she always wore around her neck into the front of her flowy, eye-lit shirt. "Yet that detective already thinks he knows what happened? How is that even possible?"

"Based on what Autumn described, he says Cal's death has all the markers of being the result of fast-acting poison. He deduced the poison was in Cal's pre-concert tea."

My voice sounded distant to my ears as my mind took me back to this afternoon, when Cal was alive and well ... before he dropped the bomb about the job thing. He'd been intent on trying to write a love song. A sort of timeless chart-topper like Brad Paisley's "Then." I told him we couldn't force something like that. That sort of song would have to come to us organically.

Quite frankly, I had a difficult time writing love songs because I don't really believe in love. Sometimes, if I put myself in the head of a fictional character or imagined the backstory of a cute couple I saw walking down the street—a couple like Nat and Daren, for example—I could get there. Otherwise, I had about as many lovey-dovey feelings in my heart as the frog I saw trampled on the walking path in Millennial Park the other day.

Then again, my reaction to Jace James tonight told a different story—but now was not the time to dwell on that.

Cal had been adamant about the love song. We played around at the piano for a bit, tossing out ideas. Eventually one stuck, and "Here to Catch You" was born. We had the chorus written, and it was pretty good, actually. That was as far as we'd gotten.

As far as we'd ever get.

My mind flashed to Cal, sipping the tea he had no clue would end his life. I swirled my own mug of tea, staring into the cloudy depths before slowly pushing it to the center of the table, suddenly not in the mood for what was normally a comforting beverage.

"So what's next?" Agnes's question broke into my thoughts, puncturing them like a needle to a balloon.

I shook my head. "I don't know. The detectives said there would be an autopsy and they'd run a toxicology screen. They're going to put a rush on some more specialized tests to verify the poison. They want to confirm Detective Yance's suspicions."

"There are a bajillion poisons. How will they know where to begin?"

"They're going to look into how much Belladonna tincture was in his tea, for starters."

"Bella-what?" Agnes frowned.

"Belladonna tincture." I sighed. "It's not widely accepted as safe, but taken in small doses, it's not lethal. Cal swore it helped him when his asthma flared."

Agnes stuck her nose in the air. "He was self-medicating? Doesn't surprise me. That boy always acted like he knew best."

Didn't I know it?

"Yeah, well, Detective Yance has some sort of biochemistry background, and when he found the nearly empty bottle of tincture in Cal's dressing room, it jumped out at him. He said one of the chemicals in it, atrop-something, would cause the symptoms Autumn described."

Agnes frowned. "Who would do this to Cal? I know most people don't like him, but jumping from dislike to murder? Crazy!"

I sighed. "That's the million-dollar question, I'm afraid."

I shifted my weight, trying to stuff down a thought that'd been niggling at me since Detective Yance surmised that Cal had been poisoned.

Agnes studied me from across the table. No matter how much I tried to keep my thoughts masked, she saw right through me. "What is it?"

Dang it.

Keeping secrets from Agnes was futile.

I rested my forearms against the wood table, clasped my hands, and leaned in. "The detectives didn't come right out and say it, but if a fast-acting poison killed Cal, then their suspects are going to be people who were with him in the last couple hours of his life and had access to his dressing room."

Agnes blinked in quick succession as she processed the implication of my words.

We both said two names out loud at the exact same time.

"Autumn and Emma."

5

Everyone processes traumatic life events in different ways. Some people journal. Some people talk things over with a friend or therapist. Some people go shopping or lose themselves in books or movies. Some people binge eat.

Me? I'm a swimmer.

On Saturday morning, less than twelve hours after Cal's death, I eased my way into the pool at Hooks High School, home to the Honeybears and the closest public school to my apartment in the Village. I worked part-time as an assistant custodian, and I had a deal with my contact at the school to get access to the pool. Since I had been vetted for my own key fob, I was free to come and go as I pleased and use the lanes in the swimming pool when students weren't present, as long as I cleaned up the locker room after myself.

I much preferred the solitude of the high school pool to the crowded workout venues around town. The fitness clubs in Nashburg were a little too judgmental and opinionated for my taste. Not to mention the membership fees.

I secured my goggles firmly over my sockets before submerging my head. As the water rushed over me, so did a sense of peace. When I resurfaced, the pool area was quiet—the only sound bouncing off the vaulted ceilings was the trickle of water cascading from my body. Black conference championship swimming banners hung flat against the cream-colored walls, immobile. The air was thick with stagnant chlorine. I loved being alone here.

Using my feet to push off from the side of the pool, I took off toward the other end of the lane in a slow front crawl. I focused on my breathing—steady and constant.

In and out. In and out In and out.

I did some of my best thinking—some of my best songwriting—in the pool. Anytime I was stuck on a particular song or idea, I ended up in the water, and I would inevitably figure it out. The rhythmic breathing required for my front stroke mirrored the type of innate rhythm—a feeling that was as one with a person's soul as the air they breathed—I tried to capture with my songs.

This morning, I couldn't focus on songwriting. The lyrics I'd been workshopping last week blurred together and sank to the back of my mind. My focus was preoccupied with thoughts of Cal.

And Autumn.

And Emma.

As I swam, my mind snagged on Emma and Cal in particular. Their relationship was rocky, to say the least. They were only eighteen months apart in age, and two years apart in grades, but where Cal was always a shining star, Emma was more like a black hole—even though, based on their personalities, you would have imagined those two descriptors to be flipped around.

Cal was petulant, prideful, and independent to a fault. He was also driven. He always knew he wanted to be a singer. A rockstar. He was one of the hardest workers I knew, and he earned what he got, but I often thought he would do well not to make so many enemies or be such an island along the way.

Emma was effervescent, and what her brother lacked in friendliness, she made up for in spades. Everyone who knew Emma loved her, but she was sort of like a hummingbird, fluttering about all fast and frantic but never landing. In fact, until she fell in love with hotel and restaurant management in the last year, she was always adrift. Now, opening her own venue in Nashburg was her singular focus.

I met Emma through Cal. She and I immediately clicked, and when I was looking for a roommate after music school, she was an obvious choice. We meshed. Cal and I meshed, too, but in a different way. I was sort of a go-between for the two siblings. They both had good relationships with me, but not with each other.

Which made me wonder why Emma was in Cal's dressing room before his show, or why she would want to see him at all. They weren't close. Of course, there was absolutely no way Emma could have killed Cal, but if the police learned about their no-love-lost sibling relationship, they'd have questions for Emma, no doubt. The thought made my stomach roil.

I pushed it aside and focused on my stroke, willing my mind to go blank as I churned through the water. My muscles were loose now, and I executed a perfect flip turn on the near side of the pool, pulling my head in and mimicking kissing my knees before rocketing off the wall and submerging for a couple meters.

When I surfaced to take another breath of air, a door slammed.

6

Startled, I dragged in a mouthful of water. I spluttered, looping my arm around one of the lane lines and trying to clear my lungs. With my free hand, I peeled off my goggles. The hair on the back of my neck stood up, and I dipped my head halfway under the water, leaving just my nose above the surface as my gaze darted around. Shadows lunged at me from the four corners of the large open space, but after panning back and forth twice, I was certain the building was empty. At least it was now. Still, my heart hammered, and I had to give myself a stern talking to.

No one was here.

I had nothing to worry about.

I was afraid of shadows.

I gave my surroundings one last survey before I kicked into a tentative stroke again, but I'd lost my rhythm, and my breathing was all off. I did a couple more lengths, trying to get back into the groove, shoving unnecessary thoughts out of my brain in an attempt to recapture my calm, but it wasn't happening.

I cut my swim short, hoisting myself up and out of the pool. Even as I toweled off, I couldn't shake the creepy-crawly feeling that someone had seen me and knew I was here. I didn't linger and take my usual post-swim shower. Instead, I slipped on a pair of athletic shorts over my swimming suit, pulled a t-shirt over my head, palmed my keys, and headed for the exit. I'd shower off at home.

When I pushed open the heavy exterior door and walked into the Saturday morning sunshine, the tension in the back of my neck eased, and my muscles seemed to relax.

I crossed the empty parking lot to my car, and just as I was sliding behind the wheel, my phone pinged with an alert. I glanced at the screen to see a notification from the Printer's Alley Press app.

I tossed my bag in the backseat and clicked on the app. When it loaded with the day's news, all the blood rushed to my head, and my limbs tingled as a picture of Cal took up the screen. It was taken at a concert earlier this year. Cal was onstage with his guitar slung over his shoulder and his hand on the mic, mesmerizing the crowd like he was Johnny Cash himself, signature grin on his handsome, full-of-life face.

I blew out a breath and scrolled through the headline article titled "Murder on Music Row." My vision tunneled as all of the facts of Cal's case were laid out for everyone to read.

Cal Dutton, unresponsive in his dressing room before his show. Jace James steps up. Cal's death ruled suspicious—maybe a poisoning? Persons of interest include Cal's sister, Emma Dutton, and his girlfriend and fellow country music star, Autumn Silver.

In Nashburg, Printer's Alley was an actual place. It had been the epicenter for the city's printing and publishing houses in the early twentieth century. Both *The Tennessean* and the *Nashburg Banner* had offices on Printer's Alley once upon a time. Later, it housed saloons, which turned into speakeasies during prohibition. Now, it was a popular nightlife destination, filled with bars, restaurants, and hotels, bursting at the seams with Nashburg residents and visitors eager to take in everything Music City had to offer.

The Printer's Alley Press, better known by its initials as PAP, was sort of a Nashburgers secret—a source for local news and media. Not that it wasn't up for general public consumption, but people outside of Nashburg probably didn't care about it as much as locals did.

Despite its less-than-endearing name that conjured up images of both a female reproductive health annual exam *and* the paparazzi, I was not ashamed to say I was a committed subscriber, and the rundown of area happenings was something I looked forward to reading. Things like who was seen out with whom at an area establishment, and what the status of the Bachelorette peddle taverns were. It was always good to have that intel so locals knew when to avoid Boardwalk Way.

The news the app featured wasn't always hard-hitting stuff, but everyone read and followed it. The stories were entertaining and dry and obviously written by an insider. Nobody knew for sure who ran the app. The intrigue surrounding the PAP added to its allure. Whoever was behind it had built a sort of modern-day media empire.

Which meant news of Cal's death was currently circulating faster than lice in a kindergarten classroom. My head fell back against the headrest, and I cursed at the roof of my car. This was bad. All the information the police wanted to keep quiet so they could more easily do their jobs was wrapped up in a nice, neat, PAP-shaped package.

Oh, gosh.

Emma.

She'd texted me last night that she was staying at her parents' house, so I hadn't seen her at our apartment. Hopefully she was so preoccupied with them that she wasn't keeping up with the media.

Doubtful, knowing her.

As if she could tell I was thinking of her, a message banner slid down from the top of my phone screen.

Emma: At the police station. Called in for further questioning. Can you come?

My heart started pounding. Yep. Definitely not good.

I pulled up our message thread to reply.

Leigh: Don't answer questions without a lawyer. I'm coming now.

I stuck my phone in my cup holder and pulled out of the parking lot. As soon as I started driving, I realized I had no idea where the police department was, or at least where Emma had been taken. There was a police station in Midtown and a South Precinct building. There were probably others that I wasn't even aware of.

I pulled over to the side of the road and grabbed my phone.

Leigh: Which station are you at?

Emma: Headquarters. Hurry. I see Detective Ottom. I think they're getting ready to take me back.

Leigh: On my way.

I pulled up the address for Nashburg's police headquarters and let the robotic voice lead me to where my best friend was being questioned about her brother's murder.

When I arrived, I snagged a spot close to the entrance and scanned the exterior of the hulking, impressive building. It was all square angles and mirrored windows on the outside.

The door swung open without warning, and Autumn Silver, her phone to her ear, walked into the parking lot. She looked as put-together as you'd expect a music superstar to be—shoulders back, hair blown out in beachy waves.

I slunk down in my seat and observed her as she walked past my driver's side window. I couldn't see a trace of the tears that had flowed so freely from her eyes yesterday, which struck me as odd. How does a person go from being completely torn up to completely shut down in less than twenty-four hours?

"Not cool, Leigh," I scolded myself. I shouldn't judge Autumn for how she was grieving.

Autumn, who was being trailed by a middle-aged man I didn't recognize, crossed to a black suburban with tinted windows. The driver got out of the front seat and opened the back door for her to slide inside, and she disappeared from my view. The man who was with her, his business suit and briefcase screaming "lawyer," climbed in behind her.

The engine revved, and then they were gone.

So, the police were questioning both Autumn and Emma again. I was a little surprised I hadn't been called in, but I didn't really have much to add to the events of last evening. I could only hope Emma had heeded my advice and gotten a hold of an attorney.

I took a steadying breath before opening my car door and marching inside.

The vestibule of the department headquarters was cool. The air smelled of harsh industrial cleaner and leather seats.

I walked into the lobby and got a couple funny looks from the uniformed officers who were milling about. The smattering of other civilians seated around the room assessed me with arched eyebrows and darting glances. It was only then I realized I was still in my swimming suit and athletic wear. There were wet spots on my t-shirt from where the water had soaked through the material, and a quick brush of my fingers through my hair revealed that my short locks were matted to my forehead after being tucked under my swim cap.

If only my mother could see me now.

I shoved all self-conscious thoughts aside. Easier said than done, considering I was raised to look my best at all times and only attract the right kind of attention. But I was working on owning who I was, flaws, quirks, and all. Besides, it didn't matter what I was wearing. What mattered was what was happening to Emma.

I approached the front desk with my spine straight and my chin held high.

A pretty woman with her hair pulled back into a low bun and a crisp blue officer's uniform smiled up at me, and to her credit, she didn't bat an eye at my appearance. The more I thought about it, the more I figured these people had probably seen worse.

"Can I help you?" she asked.

"My friend is here. Emma Dutton. I'd like to see her."

The woman behind the desk clicked around on her computer screen. "She just went in with the detectives. They're back in an interrogation room. You can take a seat, and they'll be out when they're finished."

I shifted my weight. The thought of Emma in an interrogation room sent a fresh wave of nerves rolling over my skin, triggering another batch of goosebumps. "I can't see her now? Does she have her lawyer with her?"

"I'm sorry." The female officer gave me an apologetic shrug, not offering any more information.

I thanked her and sat down. I shot off a quick text to Agnes, letting her know what was going on. She asked that I keep her posted and insisted that she'd whip up brunch and have it ready for us when we got back to the Village. I hoped she wasn't being overly optimistic about the proposed meal. I had no idea how long the detectives would keep Emma.

About thirty minutes after I arrived, the door to the vestibule blew open again, and Willie Davis marched inside, standing close by a woman in a pencil skirt and blazer.

The woman's firm tone carried across the lobby. "Just follow my lead, and don't answer any questions unless I say it's okay, you understand?"

I turned my back before Willie could see my face as he paced to the desk. I wasn't sure if he would even recognize me, but I didn't want to take any chances. I didn't know him well, but based on what Emma told me, the guy was a jerk. He acted like he was God's gift to this earth. Emma had only started working under him at the Banta Bowl when the opportunity arose because he had years of experience. No one could argue with the business he'd built—he'd taken the old bowling alley from decrepit to one of Nashburg's hottest venues—but as a person, Willie's demanding nature and arrogance were insufferable.

I clicked around on my phone screen, pretending to be occupied. I pulled up the PAP's article on Cal. Now that I thought about it, I wouldn't be surprised if it was Willie who blabbed. He'd been worried about the venue's reputation, but if he found a way to frame Cal's death and have it draw attention to the Banta Bowl, I wouldn't put it past him.

I listened as his lawyer spoke to the officer staffing the front desk.

"My client doesn't appreciate being summoned here, and I'd like the record to show that he's here of his own accord to try to *help* the detectives, though he doesn't owe them anything."

"Miss?"

"Banks. Camilla Banks. I'm Mr. Davis's attorney."

"Right. Miss Banks, I assure you the detectives are only trying to do their jobs, and I'm only trying to do mine, so please, take a seat, and someone will be with you shortly."

I covered up a snort at the desk officer's delivery. I liked that woman.

I peeked over my shoulder as Willie and Camilla found chairs on my side of the lobby.

"I don't like this," Willie muttered. His eyes darted around, taking in his surroundings.

I turned my back before his gaze made it to where I was, leaning against the rail overlooking a staircase.

"It's fine, Willie. Trust me. This is all very normal. Keep your mouth shut, and we'll get out of this unscathed."

I chanced another look and saw Camilla typing away on her phone.

Willie's face was a putrid shade of green, and his next words came out sounding strained. "What if they ask me about the fight? What am I supposed to say then?"

Camilla stiffened and jutted her chin toward him. "I said keep your mouth shut! You have no idea who's listening to you right now. A little discretion would serve you well. I hope you're getting these nerves out of your system before we're with the detectives." Camilla tucked a strand of black, chin-length hair behind her ear, and before I could avert my eyes, she caught me staring.

She leaned toward Willie and motioned toward me.

Shoot.

Willie stood, and my pulse popped with adrenaline. I gulped, trying to collect myself to have a conversation with him. I plastered on a calm smile, but Willie didn't get more than two steps in my direction when Emma appeared with Detective Yance from a hallway behind the desk.

"Emma!" I breathed a sigh of relief. "Excuse me." I nodded to Willie and cut right past him, my flip flops squeaking on the linoleum tile floor. I hugged Emma tight, whispering directly into her ear, "Are you okay? What happened?"

She pulled back, keeping a hold of my upper arms and shooting me her signature grin. "I'm fine, Leigh. Don't worry. The detectives assured me they weren't accusing me of anything, and as long as I told the truth, I'd be fine. Now I'm free to go, right Detective Yance?"

The quiet, stoic younger detective gave Emma a firm nod. "We'll be in touch if we need anything further, Ms. Dutton. Thank you for your cooperation."

Without another word, he turned to the female officer. I couldn't catch their muted conversation, but the clerk motioned to Willie.

Detective Yance pivoted and called out across the lobby. "Mr. Davis. Right this way, please."

"Willie's here?" Emma's eyes widened at the sight of her boss. We stepped off to the side to allow Camilla and Willie to pass. For a moment, Willie looked flustered, but he schooled his features. He nodded at Emma and scowled at me before straightening his shoulders and sauntering down the hallway behind the detective.

"Let's get out of here. Agnes is making us food." I grabbed Emma's hand and tugged her toward the exit.

"Oh, goodie!" Emma started gushing about how she hoped Agnes had her famous French toast on the menu and how she could really go for a shot of espresso. She didn't sound like a person who had just been interrogated.

I squinted as we stepped out into the late morning sun. "Seriously, though, Em. Everything went okay in there?"

She shrugged. "It's fine, Leigh. No biggie."

Well now, I wasn't sure that was true. A police interrogation wasn't anything to downplay, but this was typical of Emma. Carefree and naïve. I meant that in the best possible way, but the point remained. Also, her brother was dead. As much as I prided myself on bucking the universal trend in this town of caring way too much about optics, even I had to admit that saying anything was "no biggie" right now looked extremely callous on Emma's part.

"Did you see the PAP?" I asked.

"No." Emma frowned. "I haven't checked my phone this morning. Why?"

"There was an article in it about Cal." I cringed. "You're, uh, listed as a person of interest."

Emma actually laughed at that. "Are you serious?"

"You think I would make something like that up?" A twinge of annoyance made its way into my voice, and I didn't bother trying to hide it. I needed her to take this seriously.

She sobered. "Well, no. It's just ridiculous, you know? It's not like the PAP is a hard-hitting news source, anyway." Emma waved a hand in front of her and started for the parking lot. "I'm not too concerned. Who would think I would want to hurt my brother?"

I had a few thoughts ... starting with anyone who spent any time with the two of them and listened to how they antagonized each other.

I bit back the comment and settled for a simple, "I don't know." I hurried to match her pace, wishing I could be as nonchalant about it all as she was being. "What did they ask you about in there?"

Emma held up a hand. “Agnes is going to pepper me with this same sort of question. Why don’t I save my breath and tell you both over our meal. Come on, French toast is calling. I’ll follow you home and give you all the juicy details there.”

7

"I've got you set up in the kitchen." Agnes shooed us out of the packed dining room before we had even stepped foot in Java Flo's. The coffee shop was much more crowded on Saturday mornings than on weekdays.

I wasn't complaining about the special treatment. Emma and I wove through Agnes's patrons. I kept my head down, not really in the mood to make small talk with any of our friends and neighbors. If they'd read the PAP, they knew about Cal, and I was still in my swim gear, and while I was working on owning my own image and imperfections, I wouldn't choose to walk around looking as disheveled as the guy in Luke Bryan's "All My Friends Say" music video.

Agnes held open the swinging door behind the bar, and Emma and I stepped into the kitchen. The sound of sizzling bacon greeted us as Dot, one of the two chefs Agnes had on staff, glanced up from the industrial stovetop. "Hey, you two." She waved before expertly flipping an omelet in one of her cast iron skillets. I noticed she was favoring her right leg today.

"You okay, Dot?" I asked, motioning to her knee.

She huffed a mirthless laugh. "Right as rain. Just getting older."

"You're aging like fine wine." I carried a bar stool from the corner of the kitchen and set it closer to the range. She hated making a fuss, but her career as a high school and collegiate basketball player a few decades back had left her with stiffness in her knees, and when her pain flared, it was tough to be on her feet all day.

She shot me a flat look, which I ignored.

Emma shook her head at me as I sunk into my seat at the table for two Agnes had set up just inside the kitchen door.

"How did you even notice her limping?" she whispered. "She wasn't even moving!"

I shrugged. "She was acting off."

"I'll grab you girlies some coffee." Agnes bustled out through the kitchen door and returned in a minute with two piping hot mugs. She dragged a folding chair out of the storage closet and plopped down. "Now tell me what's going on, Em. You okay?"

"Another interrogation, Agnes?" Emma joked. "Before I get some food in my belly?"

"Oh, pish posh." Agnes waved her off. "You know darn well I'll feed ya—put some meat on those bones of yours. I just want to make sure you're doing alright."

For the first time since I'd seen her this morning, Emma's smile faltered. Her shoulders rolled forward, and her entire body sagged into her chair. A small part of me was relieved to see this display of emotion. It humanized my best friend in the wake of what happened. But I hated it too. I didn't want her to be in pain.

"I'm okay, but my parents aren't," she told us. "They're distraught."

"Poor dears." Agnes clucked. "I'm so sorry for all y'alls loss."

"Me too." Emma sighed and glanced at me out of her peripheral vision. She twisted up her mouth so she could chew on the corner of her lip.

"What is it?" I asked.

Emma shifted her jaw back and forth before speaking. "This is going to sound awful." She hesitated, tracing her finger along the lip of the table before bringing her gaze back up to mine. "It's almost like even in death, Cal is getting all the notoriety. Like, *of course* his death would be suspicious, and *of course* there would be a whole investigation surrounding it. He never could do anything in the normal way like the rest of us."

Maybe I should have been shocked by Emma's take, but I wasn't. Because what she said was the truth. Cal was bright and beloved—by his family and fans alike. Emma lived in his shadow. When it came to the two of them, Cal was always the crisp hundred-dollar bill. If you found it on the street and picked it up, you felt like the luckiest person in the world. Emma was like the penny that you barely even noticed.

"Now, now. Cal was your brother. I'm sure this has all come as quite a shock." Agnes set her hand on Emma's arm, and Emma covered it with her own.

"It *is* a shock, Agnes. But Cal and I were more acquaintances than friends. You know that. Am I sad he's dead? Of course. No one deserves to die like that, and he had so much more life in front of him. I'm sad we won't have a chance to get to a good place with our relationship. But also, I'm not as sad as everyone expects me to be. That's all Detective Yance kept asking me about." Emma frowned.

I saw my opening, even as the pit re-formed itself in my stomach. "Yeah, tell us what the detective wanted, Em."

Emma shrugged. "We walked through the events of last night. I had to sign my official statement. He asked me about my relationship with Cal."

"Did you tell him what you just told us?" I shot a concerned look at Agnes.

"In not so many words, I guess I did." Emma took a sip of her coffee. "I can't lie and say Cal and I were close. We just weren't."

Agnes nodded. "Best to tell the truth, indeed."

She was right, but I still didn't like the impression the detectives likely had of Cal and Emma's relationship. I knew Emma. I knew how she and Cal were. They'd never hurt each other. But the detectives had no way of knowing that.

"What else did the detectives ask?" I picked up my mug and took a tentative sip, careful not to burn my mouth on the hot coffee. I had some studio time lined up this week, and I didn't want to try to sing and record a demo with a blister on my tongue.

"He asked me about Autumn and anyone else who was a constant in Cal's life." Emma snorted and rolled her eyes. "I told him about Cal's Crew."

I set my mug down. "That reminds me. Whitney was hurrying around outside the Banta Bowl last night when I got there. It looked like she was coming from behind the building, which I thought was weird. Did you see her before Cal's set?"

Emma tipped her chin up. "I don't think so, but maybe. You know it's darker in there, so unless someone is right in front of you, it's tough to make out faces."

I nodded. "I just thought it was weird that she wasn't leading the pack of fans like she usually is, you know?"

"Maybe she was at that baseball game or something." Agnes stood from the table. "You want your usual brunch? I'll put your orders in."

"Yes, please. Come back and chat with us if you can sneak away," I said as Agnes tore off an order form and stuck it up for Dot to prepare.

"Will do." She left the kitchen, and Emma and I sat in silence, nursing our coffee.

"Thanks for coming to the station," Emma said after a minute. "I felt better knowing you were there. I didn't want to call Mom and Dad because, well ... yeah."

I cocked my head to the side, watching the emotions of pain and uncertainty flash in my best friend's eyes as she tried to come to terms with living in her brother's shadow.

"You know I'm always going to be there for you, right, Em?" I said quietly.

"I know." She sighed and blinked a few times. "Sometimes it just doesn't feel like I even matter at all. My parents—" Her voice cracked, and she pressed her lips together to regain control. This was the most emotion I'd seen her display since Cal's death, and it was coming not over his loss but because, yet again, she was being flattened to the ground while an idol of Cal was erected on top of her.

"I'm sure they took the news hard."

"That's an understatement. Mom fainted. Detective Yance had to help me get her to bed. I waited on her for the rest of the day. I may as well be the hired help as opposed to their own daughter."

My heart broke for my friend. No one should have to feel like that in their own home, regardless of the circumstances.

"They're not in good shape," Emma went on. "They asked me to collect some things from Cal's condo for them since they're not up to it."

"I'll help you," I offered. "We can go together this afternoon. Or tomorrow."

Emma blew out a breath. "Maybe tomorrow? I'm emotionally spent today."

Agnes bustled back in and plopped down at the table. "Food should be read in a jiffy." She looked at us. "What did I miss?"

"Nothing other than me complaining about my family," Emma said wryly before shooting me a grateful look.

I smiled at her before sobering. "I want to know what you said to the detectives about Whitney."

Emma frowned. "I told them she was a stage five clinger, and she could probably tell them every one of Cal's most recent movements because she was always around."

I cringed inside, but managed to school my features so it didn't show. If Emma had said it like that, she'd have come across as spiteful and petty. "What did Detective Yance say to that?"

"He's going to talk to her." Emma shrugged. "Apparently, he's talking to Willie, too. I wonder who else he's getting statements from."

I filled Emma and Agnes in on how I'd seen Autumn when I arrived. "I also overheard Willie in conversation with his lawyer.

He's concerned about being asked about the fight you mentioned between him and Cal."

Emma frowned. "Why would he be concerned? Willie is always picking fights."

"Don't know, but I definitely heard the strain in his voice when he was trying to figure out a game plan for addressing it. His lawyer told him to let her handle it."

"Weird." Emma looked thoughtful, but then her eyes bugged. "Wait, do you think that had something to do with Cal's death? Could Willie have poisoned his food?"

I held up my hands, palms out, making two stop signs. "I have absolutely no idea. That's just what I overheard. I'm sure the detectives will get it sorted out."

Agnes clicked her tongue. "I'm sure they will. I don't want you two doing any snooping, ya hear? Someone had it in for your brother." She tapped Emma's wrist with her pointer finger. "We don't know who that someone is. I shudder to think of you going to work with Willie if he was behind Cal's death. Maybe you should take a leave of absence."

Emma was shaking her head before Agnes even finished speaking. "Can't. Our schedule is packed. It's festival week."

The Nashburg Country Music Festival was set to begin in a few short days. It would mean extra tourists in town to take in the myriad of concerts being offered by the who's who of Music City, which also meant a huge boom for all local businesses.

"I don't think you need to stay away from work." I sided with Emma on this one. Agnes pouted. "But," I added. "It wouldn't be a bad idea to keep your eyes and ears open around the Banta Bowl. Just to be safe."

"I can do that." Emma pinned me with a steely gleam, and I waited, knowing she was about to say something I wasn't going to like. "Now it's time to address the elephant in the room."

I blinked, giving a dramatic look to my left and right. "I see no elephant."

Emma jutted her chin and frowned. "You know what I'm talking about. Cal ... basically hijacking your chances for a job with Red Vector Publishing. We all know how much you want a position like that. Why would he do that?"

I reached my fingers up to massage my suddenly aching temples. "I have no idea."

"Maybe you could talk to Autumn. She might be able to shed some light on Cal's headspace before he died." Emma's voice rose on the last word, making her statement sound more like a question.

"Autumn has more to worry about than me and my career." I was programmed to be hesitant when it came to asking for help. Trust didn't come easily to me, and the last thing I wanted was to be in someone's debt.

"Still, it couldn't hurt to talk to her."

"Maybe." I sat back in my chair and tried to ignore the panic twisting my stomach into tight knots.

I was young by industry standards. To get a publishing contract for a staff writing position at a major publisher at the age of twenty-three would be a huge feat. I had what it took. I knew I did. Cal knew it, too. So why did he tell Red Vector I wasn't a good fit for the job? I might never know, and I'd never be able to confront him about why he'd speak for me without my consent ... without consulting me. My voice and my words were all I had, but they were my greatest weapons, and the only things that were truly *mine*. One of Cal's final decisions in this life was to silence me. Maybe not directly, but it certainly felt like it.

Insecurity bubbled up from my veins and flowed hot underneath my skin. This was going to eat away at my confidence like a tapeworm. Didn't he think I was good enough?

Emma and Agnes had struck up a conversation about Agnes's fall menu offerings. Emma had some ideas—pumpkin pancakes made with hot cocoa powder, for starters.

"Come on! It would be delicious," Emma insisted.

Agnes snorted. “I am not using store-bought cocoa mix in my home cooking!”

I didn’t know the first thing about cooking or owning a restaurant, but I was grateful to sit back and listen. I let the comfortable familiarity of their conversation wrap me up in a blanket of security. The only blanket of security I ever really allowed myself. I was much better at white-knuckling my way through life, doing it all by myself. Since I emancipated myself from my parents at age sixteen, Emma and Agnes were the only two people who I had let in.

And Cal.

Dot swung over and delivered our food. She was definitely limping, and I made a mental note to research some at-home natural remedies to ease arthritis pain. She caught me staring and scowled. “I’m fine, Leigh. Mind your business and eat up. No one likes a nosy nelly.”

I held up my hands, appropriately chastened, but then Dot shot me a smile over her shoulder, and I knew she appreciated my attention.

We dug in. I added about a cup more pure maple syrup to my plate than usual and ate with gusto. With each bite of custardy, sweet French toast, I relaxed. Maybe I was just being lulled into a sugar-induced state of comatose, but at this point, I didn’t care.

Emma lobbed out an idea for campfire-flavored cookies.

“I’m not even going to give credence to that with a response,” Agnes said dryly.

I smiled. It would all be okay. I needed to remember an important lesson I’d learned over the years: trust wisely.

I had trusted Cal, and maybe that was the wrong call, but I was in charge of my own choices. If I wanted the job with Red Vector, I could still apply for it—regardless of what he’d told them.

Letting anyone else control me was a sure-fire way to get burned.

8

Sunday morning, after going to sunrise Mass with Agnes, Emma and I headed to Cal's place.

"I feel like an intruder." Emma cast a wary look down the wide, airy hallway. Cal's condo was on the eleventh floor of a fancy, high-rise building, and you could have fit our entire apartment in just the bathroom off the lobby.

"It's fine. You have a key." I had been to Cal's condo several times, but this felt different. What before had been a normal hallway now seemed darker and spookier. Was someone hiding behind the faux fiddle leaf fig tree in the corner up there? I couldn't be certain.

I told myself to stop letting my imagination get to me. I would never let Emma know I was entertaining such thoughts. Between the two of us, I was the model of rationality. The unflappable one. Besides, she was already out of sorts.

Emma scoffed. "Only because my parents gave it to me."

"Well, they asked you to be here, so quit worrying about it."

"I know, I know." Emma blew out a breath as we came to a stop at Cal's door. She flashed the electronic key fob in front of the sensor, and the lock clicked. "Here goes nothing."

Emma pushed open the door, and we stepped into the foyer. The lights were off, the curtains drawn. A sliver of light from the floor-to-ceiling windows on the far wall shone through the gap in fabric, illuminating dust particles floating lazily about the room. The air smelled faintly of scrambled eggs.

A pang of sadness hit me square in the chest. We used to make scrambled eggs with extra cheese the morning of our showcases in music school. I hadn't realized Cal kept up the tradition, but he must've had eggs for breakfast on Friday morning. His last breakfast ever.

I batted away the morbid thought, trying to focus on something else, but that didn't help. My skin prickled with a sense of impending doom, but I couldn't quite place the origin. The foyer was dark and still. It was wide enough that Emma and I could stand side to side, but neither of us had moved past the front door.

"Detective Yance said we could take whatever we needed. They have everything they wanted for the investigation," Emma whispered. She, too, must have felt hesitant to disturb Cal's space. But then she cleared her throat and stepped toward the windows. "You want to hit the lights?"

I nodded and flicked on the light switch—and a person in a mask and wearing a dark hoodie and baggy sweatpants barreled toward us.

Emma screamed, and glass shattered as she collided with the narrow entryway table.

"Emma!" I lunged for her, only to collide with the intruder, who shoved me to the floor and fled out the door.

I scrambled to my feet.

Emma was still sprawled on the ground, cradling her left arm.

"Em! Are you alright?" I rushed to her side, crouching down beside her.

"Fine, I think. Freaked out, but fine. Who the heck was here?" She looked over my shoulder, and I turned and followed her line of sight.

I stood, crossed to the door, and peeked out into the hallway. Empty.

I closed the door and blew out a breath. "No clue. We need to call the police." I pointed to her hand. "You're bleeding."

She grunted. "I couldn't avoid landing on the remains of Cal's crystal. Thing was probably worth a fortune. Not anymore," she added ruefully.

"Let's get you cleaned up." I led her into Cal's kitchen and dialed the authorities. After giving the rundown of what happened to the operator, who promised to send the cops our way, I hung up.

Emma was doing her best to sift through Cal's medicine cabinet with her good hand. "Can't find Band-Aids," she muttered. "He's got all this crap in the way."

"Here." I nudged her aside and started setting medication and vitamin bottles on the counter.

"Detective Yance asked me about these," she said off-handedly.

"What about them?" I stood up on my tiptoes, trying to find a first-aid kit.

"What I knew about what Cal was taking. If he'd had any issues with addiction, depression, that sort of thing."

I turned to face her. "Do they think he OD'd or something?"

"No." Emma shook her head. "I think they were trying to get a handle on his meds. Cal took a lot of different things." She motioned to the stack I'd set out. There were the usual ibuprofen and acetaminophen bottles, Cal's inhaler for his asthma, and several multivitamin and supplement containers.

"I don't see any of his belladonna tincture," I said, recalling the supplement Detective Yance isolated in the dressing room.

Emma shrugged. "I'm guessing the detectives took it. They were very interested in what I knew about it."

"What did you tell them?"

"Just about its uses, where you can purchase it, and how it can be dangerous if you don't take the right dosage. I told them that I introduced Cal to it years ago when I was dating that herbalist. Remember him? Wiltmore Bentley. Guy was a tool. He was eight years older than me but broke up with me over text, like a teenager." She snorted.

I found a box of Band-Aids, some antiseptic ointment, and a stash of gauze in the back of the cabinet. I motioned for Emma to hold out her hand. My stomach churned. "That's not good."

"This?" She pointed to her wound. "It's superficial. Nothing major."

"No, I'm talking about Wiltmore." I set to work cleaning the cut.

She scoffed. "It's fine, Leigh. That was years ago. I'm over him, and I'm better for it, believe me."

"That's not what I'm worried about."

Emma sucked in a breath. "What then?"

"You basically informed the detectives that not only do you know what belladonna tincture is used for, but you also know where to get it, and by virtue of knowing its risks, you could exploit it." I stuck the Band-Aid on her palm and met her eye.

Emma's mouth had formed a perfect circle. "I mean, I guess. When you put it like that." She frowned and studied her hand, flexing her fingers to check the adhesive. "They weren't asking me about that stuff to accuse me, though. They were genuinely interested, and I thought I was being helpful." She shrugged.

I groaned and let my head fall back. "Of course that's how they seemed, Emma. And of course you were trying to be helpful. That's just so ... so ... you!" I started pacing.

"You really think they'll use that information to-to ... what, build some sort of case against me?"

"I don't know," I admitted.

Her eyes filled with tears. "What if they charge me with murder? I didn't do anything. I swear to you, Leigh, I would never hurt my brother."

I put both of my hands on her shoulders and waited for Emma to look up at me. Her chest heaved as she fought to regain control of her emotions. Finally, she met my gaze.

"Emma, I didn't think for one second that you did."

She offered me a wobbly smile. "But you think the detectives do?"

I glanced away.

"Leigh?"

I sighed. "You had access to Cal in the hours before he died. Given your position at the Banta Bowl, you could tamper with his food and drink. If it was a fast-acting poison that killed him, you could have administered it."

Emma paled. "So I'm just supposed to sit back and wait for them to accuse me?" Her voice broke, but then she straightened her spine. "No way. I'm not about to play defense. I need to be proactive."

I cocked my head to the side. "How are you planning to do that?" Wariness crept into my tone.

"I need to figure out who killed Cal. Then I can clear my name and get justice for my brother. It's a win-win."

I closed my eyes and counted to ten. This was classic Emma. Impulsive and slightly delusional.

"Emma, sweetie. That sounds like a wonderful plan, in theory, but amateur detectives are only in books or movies. We're talking about a murderer on the loose. Look at what happened here today. It could have been worse." I darted a look toward the doorway that led to the front hall, saying a silent prayer the intruder wouldn't come back and finish whatever they were here for.

"You can't be going after whoever killed Cal on your own," I added.

"Good thing I won't be on my own, then, huh?" She waggled her eyebrows at me.

"Emma Marie Dutton." My tone held the same warning that I used to scold Phelps when he swam directly into the side of his glass bowl.

"Please, Leigh. We could do this, and you said it yourself. I can't do it alone. Besides, let's face it, between the two of us, you would make a far better detective than me."

I snorted, crossing my arms over my chest. "Why's that?"

"Because you like to know things," Emma said simply. "And you're wickedly observant."

I pursed my lips. She had me there. I was a truth seeker by nature. Really, all songwriters and musicians were. We took in the world around us and tried to put words to all of life's moments—the big things, the little ones, and everything in between. I was in the business of capturing feelings, emotions, and sensations with both nuance and relatability. There was nothing quite as satisfying as landing on the exact turn of phrase that a listener could sing along to and say, "That. *That* is exactly how I feel." It took keen observation and meticulous attention to detail to take something indescribable and make it relatable.

But still. I wasn't sure that would translate into detective work.

"I don't know, Emma. What will the actual detectives say if they find us snooping around? Won't that make you seem even more suspicious?"

"Nope. Because I've already figured out our angle." Emma shot me a triumphant look.

I raised a brow. "We have an angle?"

Emma snapped her fingers. "You better believe we do, and here it is. There are two mysteries to solve, and we can use that to our advantage."

"Cal's death and—" I frowned. "What's the second mystery?"

"Why Cal told Red Vector you weren't a good fit for the job."

I cringed. "I don't want to make a big deal out of that."

Emma waved a hand in front of me. "It's already a big deal. I know you, Leigh. You aren't going to be able to let it go unless you figure out why, out of the blue, Cal decided that not only did he think you shouldn't take the job, but he took you out of the running."

Well, shoot. For as well as I knew Emma, she knew me better. As if sensing she had me waffling, she pressed onward. "If anyone asks what we're doing and why we're asking questions, we can say *that* is the mystery we're trying to solve."

I chewed on my lip. I didn't like it, but Emma was right.

"Admit it. You think this is a good idea." Emma reached forward and gave my shoulder a playful shove.

I took a dramatic step back. "Alright, fine. We'll do it."

Emma pumped her fist in the air. "You're the best!"

A firm knock sounded on the door, and Emma screamed. I jumped, and my pulse kicked hard, fight-or-flight response spiking.

"I'm sure it's the police," I said, recovering my wits.

I retraced my steps to the entryway, careful not to step on the glass shards from the broken vase. I peeked through the peephole to find two uniformed officers.

I exhaled and opened the door to let them into the condo.

Halfway through giving our statements, another knock sounded on the door.

One of the cops went to open it, and Detective Yance appeared in the living room where we were seated.

"Detective." Emma stood, tucking her blonde hair behind her ear. "Is everything okay?" Her voice came out pitched and breathy.

Interesting.

"I came to ask the same thing." Detective Yance took in the room before his gaze landed on Emma's bandaged hand, and a muscle in his jaw ticked. "What happened?"

I wasn't too thrilled about going over everything again, but I couldn't fault the guy for being here. Someone had broken into Cal's condo... two days after he was killed. What were they after? Why were they here?

Emma gave Detective Yance the rundown, and he circled the condo while the uniformed officer finished talking to us.

"I'll interview the neighbors and lobby staff, and we'll pull the security footage," he told us.

I didn't have much hope they'd figure out who was here. I couldn't even tell if it was a man or a woman who had knocked into me. Whoever it was wore gloves, so they didn't leave fingerprints. Figuring out their identity and motives felt like a lost cause.

Detective Yance stuck around and helped us clean up the shattered glass. When we were finished, he handed Emma his card and told her to call him if she remembered anything else. He directed one of the officers to wait outside until we were done. I breathed a little easier knowing we weren't being left here alone.

"Be in touch if you need me," Detective Yance said to us as he followed the officer into the hall.

"I will," Emma said, and after he closed the door to Cal's place behind himself, she stared for a beat before glancing around the condo. "Let's find the stuff my parents want. I'm ready to get out of here."

She handed me her phone, and I looked over the list she had typed up. Most of the items the Duttons wanted were sentimental.

"Why don't you grab the picture frames and the stuff at the top of the list. I'll get the music-related stuff."

Emma agreed, and we split up. She went to the bedroom, and I went to Cal's music room.

I gathered his favorite guitar, a framed piece of sheet music that had won an award back at music school, and some of the plaques that lined the window sill.

Getting everything stowed, I turned to the piano. A piece of sheet music rested on the lip above the keys. I walked over and sat down on the bench. My eyes drifted over the words scribbled below the bars. They were the incomplete lyrics to "Here to Catch You" that Cal and I had been working on at my apartment. He must've dropped them off after leaving the Village and before picking up Autumn on his way to the Banta Bowl. From the looks of the markings, Cal had started to fill in chords and notes.

I tapped out a few bars, singing the lyrics under my breath. It was good. Cal always had a knack for being innovative with his musicality.

"Leigh, you ready?" Emma's voice made me hit a wrong note, and I yanked my hand away from the piano as she popped into the room.

"Whatcha playing?"

I motioned to the paper. "The last song Cal and I worked on together."

"Can I hear it?" She came over and sat down next to me on the bench.

I shook my head. "It's not done."

"Oh. Well, take that with you then." She snatched the paper and handed it to me. "Someone ought to finish it."

I looked down at the sheet, reluctant to take it. My feelings toward Cal and our work together were complicated at the moment. Then again, as I scanned the page, I couldn't help but think it had the makings of what could be a hit.

We stood from the piano bench. I folded the sheet and tucked it into my back pocket before I hoisted the bag of Cal's awards with one hand and his guitar case with the other.

"Did you find everything?" I asked with a grunt.

"Everything except Grandpa's watch."

I frowned. "That's odd."

"I know. Cal was never without it, but Detective Yance said they didn't have it in evidence, and it wasn't with Cal's body when my parents went to claim his belongings at the morgue." Emma shivered. "Maybe they missed it."

Goosebumps prickled the back of my neck as an image of Cal in the Banta Bowl's dressing room streamed through my memory. I had a clear picture of his left arm flung across his body. It was bare.

"I don't think he was wearing it on Friday," I said.

Emma frowned. "Will you help me look for it?"

I followed her out to the kitchen and living room. I dropped the bags I'd collected and went with her to search Cal's room.

Twenty minutes later, we'd emptied every drawer, gone through his entire closet, and looked through the kitchen and living room.

"It's not here." Emma sat down on the overstuffed couch and leaned her head against the cushion. "My parents are going to be so mad. That was, like, the only thing they really wanted. It's an heirloom."

Cal had told me about the watch. His grandfather, who was a musician himself, had worn it his entire life. When he died, he passed it on to Cal, and Cal was rarely seen without it. In fact, in the photo that was posted with the PAP article, I could clearly see the gold band and oversized watch face on the hand Cal used to hold his microphone.

"It has to be somewhere. It didn't grow legs and walk away," I reasoned.

Emma waved around. "We've looked everywhere."

"It'll turn up. Come on. It's time to eat and figure out our next steps."

Emma brightened. "You're right. Operation Prove Emma's Innocence and Get Back Leigh's Mo-Jo begins now."

I rolled my eyes as we collected Cal's things, hoping against hope that we wouldn't regret this.

Here to Catch You by Cal Dutton and Leigh Notrap

I might say the wrong word,
Mix the wrong drink,
Get stuck inside my head
'Til you don't know what to think.
But darling, I've already fallen

Into true love's clear blue,
So don't doubt for one single second
That I won't be here
To catch you...

Catch you right in my arms,
Here in my heart,
No matter how far
Life pulls you out.
I'll follow behind, beside
Be wherever you need me
To be...

9

At ten o'clock the following morning, I stood outside the office building for Red Vector Publishing. Emma's idea was for me to go inside and inquire about the staff writer position. She figured if I went in person, I could talk to someone at the label and try to turn the conversation to Cal's last few days. Maybe they would be able to tell me who he was working with, what he was working on, and what might have triggered him to try to keep me away from his record company.

It was a shaky plan at best. Way too ambitious for a Monday morning, quite frankly, but I told Emma I would try, and I was nothing if not a woman of my word. For her part, she was off to work at the Banta Bowl. She was going to keep her head down while also attempting to figure out what Willie was up to. If there was an opening, she was going to ask around and see if any of the kitchen staff had noticed anything suspicious.

I brushed the wrinkles down on my graphic t-shirt and flicked a piece of lint from my wide-legged black pants. I'd ditched my scuffed cowgirl boots for my leopard-print flats in an attempt to make myself feel extra put-together.

I took one step toward the building—which I hoped held my future between its sleek silver-and-glass walls—but I froze when the door ahead of me swung open, and out walked Detective Ottom. He had his phone to his ear, and I immediately dropped my head and began rummaging through my bag, hoping he wouldn't identify me so I could listen in.

"What do you mean it doesn't line up? I thought you said you were ninety-five percent certain the tincture you found would be what killed him?" he said into the phone.

There was a pause as Detective Ottom listened to whoever he was talking to—Detective Yance, if I had to guess.

"Well, now. That's interesting. Let's look into it." Detective Ottom tugged at his belt. "Nah. Geffadab didn't give me much. He said he had his phone turned off all day yesterday, which is why he didn't come down to the station."

I pressed my lips together. The detectives wanted to interview the head of Red Vector Records? That was big. My mind immediately went to work trying to puzzle out why. I hadn't known Cal and Zac's relationship to be contentious, but that didn't mean there wasn't bad blood there.

"Nah." Detective Ottom continued talking into his phone. "He was cooperative. Told me all about Cal's contract. He mentioned that there had been a few disturbances with crazed fans that they were aware of."

Detective Ottom paused, and I held my breath, chancing a glance in his direction. He had stopped with his phone tucked between his shoulder and his ear. He shoved a hand into the pocket of his suit coat and retrieved a notebook, which he flipped open in one seamless motion.

"He actually mentioned Whitney Allerow. Isn't that the same person Ms. Dutton brought to our attention?" Detective Ottom flipped his notebook shut, turning toward me at the same time. I didn't have a chance to avert my gaze before his eyes landed on me.

Busted.

I smiled and waved, doing my best impression of someone who wasn't guilty of being caught eavesdropping on police business.

"Right," he said into the phone. "I'm going to go here, but yes, maybe we should. I'll see you back at the station, and we can go from there. Okay. Buh-bye." Detective Ottom clicked off the call and crossed the path toward me. "Ms. Notrap, isn't it?"

"That's me. Good morning, Detective Ottom." I had a lot of practice faking confidence when I didn't feel it, so I channeled past experience and kept my chin level, even though my mind was screaming at me to cower. "I didn't expect to see you here."

Detective Ottom tucked his thumbs through his belt loops. The motion made his slightly rounded belly protrude. "Just following up on a couple of things."

"Are you any closer to figuring out what happened to Cal?" I asked. May as well shoot my shot. What did I have to lose?

He shook his head. "I'm afraid I can't discuss an open investigation with a civilian."

"Understandable." I tilted my head to the side. "It's just that I saw the article in the PAP on Saturday. I'm sure you've seen it."

Detective Ottom's mouth thinned into a flat line. "That news outlet is worthless as gum on a boot heel."

I bit back a grin. "Most of the time, it's pretty harmless stuff, don't you think?"

The detective scoffed. "Harmless until whoever is running it starts putting their daggum nose where it doesn't belong."

I nodded. "Do you know how they got the information? You told us on Friday to keep our mouths shut about the case."

Detective Ottom frowned. "I have my suspicions."

I arched my eyebrows, but he didn't divulge his theories.

He stowed his notebook into his pocket before turning his sharp glare on me. "What brings you by Red Vector this morning, Ms. Notrap?" He kept his voice conversational, but his eyes were tracking my every movement, watching for telltale signs of nervousness. I felt like I was being wedged in a petri dish and put under a microscope.

I stood up a little straighter, deciding I may as well tell the truth. I didn't have anything to hide. "Actually, I'm inquiring about a job."

The detective's expression didn't change. "Songwriting, isn't that what you do?"

"It is," I said slowly, not sure what to make of his tone. It felt like he knew something I didn't.

"That's right. That's right. Well, don't let me keep you. I'm sure your work waits for no one."

"I could say the same for *your* work. We all appreciate what you're doing, making sure Cal gets justice." I offered him a sincere smile before pressing my luck. "Did I hear you say you were going to bring Whitney Allerow in for questioning?"

Detective Ottom frowned. "Again, that's not something I'm at liberty to discuss."

I held up my hands to signal that I meant no harm. "I get it. But in case you're wondering, I saw her at the Banta Bowl just before I went inside on Friday night. She looked uneasy, and she wasn't with her usual crew before the show. Her behavior was strange enough that it stood out to me."

Detective Ottom studied me for a second, his wide eyes narrowed to slits, before blinking and giving me a single nod. "I'll keep that in mind."

He paused, and I had the same feeling that he knew something I didn't, but when he didn't say anything else, I motioned toward the door. "I'll be going, then."

"You have a good day, Ms. Notrap. Tell your friend Emma we'll be speaking to her again soon." With that, Detective Ottom sauntered toward the parking lot.

The hairs on my arms stood up, and my morning coffee felt like it was burning the lining of my stomach. Was that a threat aimed at my best friend?

I watched him drive off, trying to bring my suddenly frantic heart rate back under control.

"What the actual heck is going on?" I muttered under my breath as I faced the Red Vector building. How was I supposed to try to professionally inquire about a job now when I had all of *that* on my mind?

I took a few deep breaths, blocking out my interaction with the detective. I'd revisit everything I learned from him later. For now, I needed to be on my game the second I walked through those doors, and in the words of Detective Ottom, *dagumit*, I would be.

10

Red Vector was an umbrella company that included a record label side of things and a publishing wing. Zac Geffadab had started the whole business and brought the differing lanes together under one company. In a way, it allowed him to secure more profit because not only did he get the money the label raked in, but he got to take a cut of the royalties from the publishing rights. It was in Red Vector's best interests to keep everything "in-house," so to speak, because they could double-dip on profits.

I pushed the door inward, and the air conditioning and the scent of cinnamon greeted me. A woman who looked to be about my age sat behind a half-circle-shaped desk straight ahead.

"Can I help you?" Her voice was perky, and her face held a look of innocence—like she hadn't been jaded by the industry or the town to this point.

I squared my shoulders and acted like I belonged there. "My name is Leigh Notrap. I was hoping to speak to Quentin Buffet in the A & R department. Is he in?"

Perky Face nodded. "Did you have an appointment?"

I shook my head. "No. Do I need one? I can always come back." A part of me would totally take this as an excuse to retreat and come at this again when I felt a little less ... frazzled.

Perky Face beamed a sugar-sweet smile at me. "Let me see what I can do." She clicked around on her computer. "I'll send him a quick message." Her acrylic nails made a *tap-tap-tap* sound, and then she paused, nibbling her lip.

A chime rang from the computer, and she smiled up at me.

"Mr. Buffet will see you. Go ahead and walk straight down this hallway, and then take your first right. The door to his office is the last one on the left."

"Thank you so much." I managed a smile and passed by her desk. Sure enough, when I made it to the end of the hallway, a door was cracked open. The placard outside of it read "Quentin Buffet, A & R."

I took a deep breath, steadying myself. A & R—Artists and Repertoire—personnel were notorious for being cutthroat. They were the ones who had to wheel and deal in the industry to get songs picked up and published. I got Quentin's name from Red Vector's website. As someone seeking a staff writing position, I figured he'd be a logical person to contact, and I hoped he'd have more intel on Cal than someone generic in HR. But I had no idea what to expect from this meeting.

I squeezed my hand into a tight fist, balling up all my nerves, and knocked on the door.

"Come in!"

I pushed the door open the rest of the way and stepped inside a nondescript office. "Mr. Buffet?"

"That's me." Quentin's eyes roamed over me. "Leigh Notrap."

He said my name with a silky-smooth voice. Once again, I resisted the urge to shrink back. "Yes. Thanks so much for making time to see me."

"Madison said you were here, in the flesh, so..."

Madison must have been Perky Face's name.

"What can I do for you on this fine day, Ms. Notrap?"

Here goes nothing.

"I caught wind of a staff writing position that's opening up, and I wanted to stop by to express my interest."

I don't know what I expected him to do or how I expected him to react, but when he just sat there in silence, staring at me, I broke out into a cold sweat. The kind that coats your back and makes your shirt stick to your skin in the worst sort of clammy perspiration.

"Uh—" I started and then stopped, trying to figure out what to say next. Quentin still hadn't offered me a seat, so I stood, towering over him from my position in front of his desk. Even though I had the physical upper hand, he clearly held all the cards.

Quentin blinked, and finally his expression changed into something that resembled a smile. "Why don't you sit down, Ms. Notrap."

"Thank you." I dropped into the chair across from him, clasping my hands in my lap.

I bit my lip when Quentin turned to his computer screen. I couldn't tell what he was doing, so I found myself focusing on the white of his scalp. It jumped out from beneath the layers of his black hair, slicked ever so perfectly to either side of his straight-line part. Quentin was probably in his early forties, but not a single gray hair threatened to make an appearance. He either had really good hair genes or a spectacular stylist. If I had to wager, I'd say it was the latter. His black hair looked more like it came from a bottle as opposed to being a gift from God.

I gave myself an internal shake. I should be less focused on his hair care routine and more focused on what he was thinking so I could try to anticipate questions he might have.

Finally, Quentin leaned back in his chair and crossed an ankle over his knee. He peered across the desk at me. "Tell me, Ms. Notrap ... where'd you hear about this job? We haven't made it public that we have an opening. Not that I'm disappointed to see someone like you interested."

I got an icky feeling in the base of my throat as he scanned me up and down and back up again, but I refused to cower. Instead, I shifted my gaze to catch his eye, making the split-second decision to keep my connection to Cal a secret.

"I heard rumblings." I pitched my voice to be purposefully breezy. "You know how word spreads in this town."

He snorted. "Fair point."

I jumped on his agreement and pressed the point. "I'm just trying to do my due diligence before I apply. Make sure it would be a good fit and that I'm not wasting anyone's time, you know?"

"My time is very valuable ... you've got that right," Quentin murmured. It felt like I was swimming with a shark. He watched my every move—like he was just waiting for the first hint of blood so he could pounce. "We only take on the best of the best here."

"Yeah, for sure," I said eagerly. "Red Vector is basically the dream." I checked my enthusiasm, remembering Emma and the whole reason I was there. "Though I'm sure the entire organization is shaken after what happened to Cal Dutton."

The blacks in Quentin's eyes glinted, but there was no warmth in them.

"Did you know him?" I probed.

"I knew Cal." Quentin laughed, but the sound was tinny and harsh.

"I'm sorry for your loss, then."

"Appreciate that." Quentin narrowed his eyes ever so slightly. "Though, it's no real loss to me. Between the two of us, Cal Dutton was a piece of work. Doing business with him was a nightmare, and I'm not the only one to think so. If you ask me, he got what he had coming."

My mouth fell open before I could snap it shut. I hadn't gotten a great vibe from Quentin from the second I stepped into his office, but I certainly wasn't expecting him to spew such *vitriol* where Cal was concerned.

"I tell ya what, Ms. Notrap. You're welcome to apply to join our team, and we would be glad to consider you. More than glad," he added with a wink that sent the contents of my stomach threatening to come back up. "But we don't deal well with folks who aren't all in. This role is very, very . . . *demanding*." The way he said the last word made my skin crawl. "If you can't promise to give us your all, then it'd be best if you moved on without bothering to apply."

"I always give my all," I said with all the confidence I didn't feel. It was true, but Quentin made warning alarms blare in my head, and I didn't want to stick around.

I stood, discreetly wiping my palms on my black pants before holding a hand out for him to shake. "Thank you for your time. I'll get to work on my application."

Quentin nodded, letting his gaze rove over my figure again before gripping my fingers in a bone-shattering hold. I resisted the urge to wince. I also resisted the urge to punch him in the face with my free hand.

Snap a picture, buddy ... it would last longer.

"You've got some chops coming in here. I respect that." Quentin smirked. "I'm looking forward to seeing what you got."

This man was a capital 'C' creep.

I could feel his eyes boring into my backside as I walked out the door. I offered him a tight smile as I closed the door. When it clicked, I closed my eyes and exhaled.

I slid to the side so that Quentin couldn't see my shadow and pressed my hand into the wall, centering myself and regaining my composure.

The thought of having Quentin as a boss made my skin crawl. Could he have been why Cal tried to steer me away from the position? Maybe Cal had sized Quentin up as a misogynistic pig and figured he'd save me the trouble of dealing with the creep.

But Cal *knew* me. He knew I could fend for myself. I've done that my whole life.

Sadly, guys like Quentin in country music were a dime a dozen. The culture was changing, thank heavens, compared to what pioneers like Shania Twain went through in the nineties, when all anyone would ask breakout female country stars about was their looks and who helped them get to where they were, but it still wasn't a level playing field. Women had to work twice as hard in this industry to make up half the ground.

Still, I refused to let Quentin bother me. Water off a duck's back and all that.

I made a mental note to talk to Emma about adding Quentin to a list of potential suspects. It didn't sound like Cal and Quentin got along. At all. Dislike didn't equate to murder, but I got a bad vibe from the guy.

He got what he had coming.

I shivered as his heartless voice rang in my ears. I hurried to the lobby and emerged into the open space just as a familiar figure entered from the opposite hall.

Our eyes connected, and I watched recognition flood his features.

11

"You." Zac Geffadab stalked toward me. "You're a friend of Cal's, aren't you? You were backstage at the Banta Bowl on Friday."

"Leigh Notrap." I held out my hand. It couldn't hurt to build up a relationship with the head of Red Vector. "It's—"

"Leigh. Right. Listen." Zac shook my hand quickly while talking over me. "We're putting together a tribute concert for Cal. It'll be held at the park down by the river tomorrow night."

"Oh. Wow. That's really nice, Mr. Geffadab." Honestly, I wasn't sure what to say to him. A tribute concert? Coming from Cal's record label, it seemed a little self-serving, if you asked me. Then again, songs had a way of bringing people together, and I knew firsthand the healing power of music.

He nodded. "We think it'll be a great way to honor Cal's life and his career. Autumn has agreed to perform, and Jace, too."

I nodded back, though a part of me wondered which Autumn would show up—the distraught, heartbroken girlfriend or the cool-as-a-cucumber superstar I'd spotted leaving the police station.

"You should come. We're not planning to do a lot of promotion, as we don't want things to get out of hand, but the event will be open to the public." Zac's phone buzzed, and he glanced down at the screen. "I've got to take this. Excuse me."

He stepped around me and headed down the hallway leading to Quentin's office.

I grabbed my phone out of my purse and pulled up my calendar. I entered the concert into the app.

I let out a grimace. My back ached from holding myself stiff under Quentin's scrutiny. I longed to get back to the Village and grab a quick bite to eat from Java Flo's. If I was lucky, Agnes would have her five-cheese grilled cheese sandwiches and homemade tomato soup on the menu.

Behind me, a throat cleared.

"You knew Cal, then?"

I spun around. Madison was looking at me, tears pooled in her eyes. I didn't know what to do, but I took a tentative step in her direction.

"I did," I said carefully, not wanting to further upset her. "We went to school together, and we co-wrote some songs in the past. His sister is my roommate. Are—were—you two close?"

Madison used the tips of her fake nails to wipe the tears away from her lashes. "I don't know if I'd say we were close, but I always looked up to Cal." Her voice cracked as she said his name. "He was so driven. He had a plan, and he executed it."

I couldn't argue with that. "All he ever wanted was to be a big star."

Madison's eyes widened as she nodded. "I know. I was sort of his unofficial personal assistant."

At my cocked brow, she continued. "I was here the day he signed with RVR. We hit it off, and I offered to help him out ... with whatever he needed." She blushed.

Oh boy.

She chuckled to herself. "I never knew what was going to come out of Cal's mouth. I adored that about him, how he kept everyone on their toes."

I was so busy thinking about how Cal often did that with his poor attitude and self-centered nature that I almost missed what she said next.

"A couple weeks ago, he asked me if I knew a good watch repairman. It was so random."

"Wait." I tried not to seem too eager. "Really? Do you? Have a watch repairman that you, um, frequent?" I asked, completely realizing how ridiculous I sounded.

Madison shook her head. "No, but I researched it for him. Found several in the area." She slapped a manicured hand over her mouth. "Oh my gosh, he told me not to tell anyone. I can't believe I just blabbed like that. Promise you won't say anything?"

"Don't worry about it. I won't say a word."

Except to Emma.

I tried to figure out how to play this, finally landing on my plan of attack.

"But actually." I held up my own wrist with a slim-banded watch secured around it. "Would you mind sharing your research? Ironically, this thing stopped working months ago, and I haven't had a chance to get it fixed. It was my grandmother's."

That was a lie. I got this out of a bin at the local thrift store last year, and it worked perfectly fine, but I needed an angle, and Madison looked like she was going to give me one.

She shuffled through a stack of papers on her desk. "I didn't want to leave an e-trail since Cal said it was important that the watch repairman thing was kept a secret, so I wrote it down. Let me see if I can find it." She grabbed a paper from the bottom of a stack to the right of her computer. She held it out for me to see. "Here it is."

"Super helpful. Do you mind if I take it with me?"

Madison pulled back, lines of hesitation creasing her forehead.

"Or I could take a photo of it so you could keep the original," I amended. If there was some sort of sentimental value to that paper for her, who was I to snatch it away?

"Sure. You can take a picture. That's what Cal did." She shrugged. "I guess I would like to keep this. Sort of like my last memento of him."

I retrieved my phone again, snapping a quick photo and making sure I got all the names and phone numbers listed in the frame. “Thank you so much. You don’t happen to know which watchmaker Cal went with, do you?”

She shook her head. “I don’t, sorry. He just thanked me and said he was going to call around.”

“Right. That makes sense. Just thought I’d ask. If a guy is good enough for Cal, then he’d be good enough for me.” I offered Madison a smile.

She managed one in return. “Definitely.”

“Will I see you at the tribute concert?” I asked, switching gears.

Madison shrugged. “Mr. Geffadab made it a mandatory event for all Red Vector employees. So yeah, I’ll be there.” She lowered her voice. “Besides, what woman in their right mind would turn down a chance to see Jace James perform ... for *free*?” She fanned herself.

I chuckled to myself. Madison didn’t just have a thing for Cal, she had a thing for *all* male musicians in the greater Nashburg area.

“Maybe I’ll see you there, then.” I held up my phone and waved it back and forth. “Thanks again for your help with this.”

“No prob. Nice to meet you.”

“You, too.”

I drove as quickly as I could back to the Village, knowing that Emma wouldn’t get off of work for another couple of hours. I wanted to touch base with Agnes, grab a bite to eat, and I needed to get some other work done.

When I arrived at Java Flo’s, the place was packed with the lunchtime rush. I chatted with a couple of Agnes’s regulars as I waited to place my order. I noticed the nerdy guy from a few nights ago. He was at a different table today, on the right side of the counter. I had to cover my grin with my hand when I saw the t-shirt he was sporting. It read: *Visit Pemberley, they said. He won’t be there, they said.*

Whoever this guy was, he had an eclectic taste and managed to pull off both science and literary humor. I should really introduce myself. He seemed like a person I'd want to know.

When it was my turn, I opened my mouth to order, but Agnes waved me off. "I put in for some tom and cheese for you when I saw you walk in."

"Bit presumptuous of you, wasn't it?"

"Oh, hush." Agnes tapped the keys on the register, and the drawer dinged as it opened. "How did it go this morning?"

I shot a look to my left and right before tipping my head closer to Agnes. "Quentin Buffet is a sleaze bag."

Agnes frowned. "I don't like to hear that. What'd he do?"

I leaned back and rolled my eyes. "Nothing I haven't seen before, but it's still annoying as heck. Zac Geffadab invited me to a tribute concert for Cal, though. The label is putting it on over at the park. Should be a nice event."

"Hmm. Anything else noteworthy?"

I smacked my forehead. "I almost forgot. I ran into Detective Ottom. Sounds like the police are going to be talking to Whitney Allerow, that over-the-top groupie of Cal's." Agnes nodded her recognition of the name. "Apparently, she's made enough of a fuss that the label has her on their radar."

"That's good for Emma, I suppose." Agnes cocked her head to the side to peek around me. "Let me take this next order real quick."

I moved out of the way for a mom with two young kids. When they were through ordering, the mom shooed her kids along, and I stepped back up to the register.

"They're cute," I said.

"That's Cindi with her kids Rocco and Reba. They live just up a few blocks. I'm surprised you haven't seen them before. Introduce yourself some time," Agnes went on. "She's great. But first, tell me what else happened this morning. Did you actually talk to the detective?"

"I did. He pretty much told me to mind my own business." I gave her a flat look to show her what I thought about that.

Agnes snorted. "That's what I told y'all, too, but it seems to have gone in one ear and out the other."

I smiled, my brain hitching on one other thing I caught from Detective Ottom's phone call. "Actually, I think the police may have run into a snafu with the poison they thought killed Cal."

"Wasn't that young detective pretty certain he knew what did it?"

"He seemed that way, but based on Detective Ottom's half of the phone conversation, there's some question about it. I don't know. Hopefully they'll hold a press conference or something so we can figure out what's going on."

"Maybe you should check the PAP. They seem to be up to date on Cal's case. Somehow." Agnes shrugged.

I nodded. It wasn't a bad idea.

The door to the kitchen swung open, and one of the servers bustled out. "Loaded grilled cheese and tomato soup to go, Leigh?"

"Thank you!" I grabbed my bag of food, careful not to tip it and spill the scalding soup. I said goodbye to Agnes and left the café.

Walking around the side of the building, I heard the door to the café open and shut behind me. I glanced over my shoulder, but whoever left after me must've headed in the opposite direction, because no one passed by me.

I walked up to my apartment. It was pushing one o'clock, and Emma would get done at two. Based on traffic, she probably wouldn't make it back home till closer to three, which meant I had a few hours to eat and try to get some writing done.

I dug into my food as I grabbed a sheet of paper, letting my thoughts wander to the kids I'd seen at the café. Their cuteness made the uglier parts of my day fade to the back of my mind.

Before I knew it, I had slurped up all my soup, and only crumbs remained on the wrapping of my sandwich. The makings for a song were penciled out on paper, and I walked over to the cozy chair I had tucked next to my piano. With a window that looked out over the road on the nearest wall, it was my favorite place to sit and watch the happenings on Crowbar Road below.

I tried out a couple more phrases as I stared down at folks scurrying around, and then I set the page aside and went to the piano. I sat down and plunked out the chords from the song I'd taken from Cal's apartment, humming the melody along with it. I did really love the "Here to Catch You" lyrics we'd worked out, and Cal had seemed extra committed to this song for some reason.

I turned the sheet over to jot down a couple more lyric ideas, but Cal had already used the back of the sheet music.

I stared at the lines in front of me. They were the start of another song.

"You'll pay for what you've done / the gag orders issued / the dismissed tears / you stole our best years / so watch your back now / here's your notice / you won't see me coming / and I won't stand for this."

Yikes. Sounded like Cal was working on a break-up anthem. The lyrics stood in stark contrast to the love song on the other side.

I plunked out the notes Cal had written in, trying out the words with the music.

G-E-F

Wait a minute.

I leaned closer to the page and double-checked what I was seeing.

G-E-F-F-A-D-A-B

The song was built around notes that spelled out *Geffadab*, as in Zac Geffadab.

I refused to believe that was some sort of weird coincidence. I was raised in the era of music where singers and songwriters gave their fans all sorts of hidden clues within their discography. This had to be intentional. Right?

Cal must've scribbled these lines either while he was still here on Friday afternoon before I kicked him out or when he stopped back at his place before heading to the Banta Bowl. Either way, they were the last words he'd ever write.

Unwelcome emotion gathered in the back of my throat like an oversized lump of dough.

My phone vibrated, and I jumped. Swallowing hard, I glanced at my screen and found a message from Emma.

Emma: We're short-staffed. I'm helping out behind the bar. Working till nine now. Hope you had a good morning! Can't wait to catch up when I get home.

I shook off my disappointment and typed back a quick response.

Leigh: All good. My morning was mostly productive. Hope all is going well there. Be safe. Xoxo.

A new message popped up almost immediately.

Emma: Nothing much to report on this end. Willie has kept to himself. Frustrating! But I'm not giving up.

I frowned. I didn't want Emma to do anything rash. Knowing her, she might. With Detective Ottom's warning ringing in my ears, I responded.

Leigh: Just don't push it!

Emma: Me? Push it!? ;)

Leigh: I'm serious! Be careful.

I waited for a response, but none came.

Emma must've gone back to work.

I stood and paced my apartment. I didn't know what to make of finding Zac Geffadab's last name written out in the music notes of a scathing break-up anthem. I did a quick internet search on my phone to see if anything stood out about the label president, but it was mostly old news, and nothing negative populated on the first two pages of results. I saw lots of words like *ambitious* and *cutting edge* and *forward-thinking*. I decided to table that line of reasoning for a moment, at least until I could pick Emma's brain.

With the day now freed up, I needed to be productive. Since I wasn't a full-time lyricist yet, I supplemented my income by working at Java Flo's, cleaning at the high school, and writing jingles for local and non-local businesses. In the same way that writers freelanced, I did, too ... just musically.

Rhyming "Floss" with "Boss" in a pithy play on words for a local dental practice's radio spot wasn't exactly what I envisioned when I made up my mind to be a songwriter, but it paid the bills, and beggars can't be choosers.

I poured some fish food into the bowl for Phelps. He mouthed his thanks, and I watched him swim in circles before getting to work.

After I banged out an ad slogan and song for an all-you-can-eat buffet two towns over and another one for a foot doctor in North Carolina, I decided to give my brain a rest.

I settled back into my vintage chair and pulled up the PAP, as Agnes had suggested I do. The article about Cal was still front and center on the homepage. A couple smaller articles had appeared with fan reactions to his death. There was a spotlight on Autumn and her career, but it was more of a "getting to know her" piece than anything incriminating. No mention was made of Emma from what I could see, and for that, I was grateful.

I closed out of the app and typed "Belladonna Tincture" into my search engine. I read through the pages that came up, trying to remember what chemical Detective Yance referenced backstage at the Banta Bowl.

"There it is." I grabbed my notebook and jotted down the name. "Atropine."

I read on.

Can cause sweating, skin redness, pupil dilation, and delirium.

Might have been the poison that killed Shakespeare's Juliet.

One of Agatha Christie's poisons of choice in her fictional murder mysteries.

Has been used in real-life murders.

Interesting. Whoever killed Cal knew what they were doing. When I considered who would have known he had the tincture containing atropine with him, all signs pointed to Autumn and Emma. Then again, I wouldn't put it past Whitney Allerow to somehow have figured it out, too. She knew enough about Cal's life to have knowledge of his medications and supplements ... somehow.

Sufficiently creeped out and in over my head with names of the chiral chemical compounds that make up atropine (l-hyoscyamine and d-hyoscyamine, for the record), the rest of the afternoon and evening passed much less morosely. I made myself a quick dinner and curled up in my chair with a cup of tea to watch reruns of *Full House* while I waited for Emma.

I must've drifted off, because the next thing I knew, my body slipped off the edge of the seat and slammed to the floor, and the sound of a scream pierced the darkness of our apartment.

12

I scrambled up off the floor in a flash, disoriented but keenly aware of the fact that I wasn't alone. If only I had a dog instead of Phelps. Maybe I would have had a warning.

My breathing was ragged as I snatched the closest thing I could find to use to protect myself, clutching my laptop to my chest.

"Oh no. No, no, no!" The wail of a female voice came from the kitchen, positioned just off the entrance to the apartment.

"Emma? Is that you?" I rushed across the living room and squinted when I stepped into the lit kitchen.

Emma was standing at the sink, gripping her phone with one hand and swiping down at the screen with the other. "How is this happening?" She jabbed at the phone, and suddenly, a newswoman's professional and staccato voice filled the small cooking area.

"ABC News Nashburg has obtained this footage, first posted to the local news app, Printer's Alley Press, of slain country music superstar Cal Dutton and his estranged sister, Emma Dutton. As the video shows, the two appear to be at odds, and things get physical before Cal throws Emma out of his apartment. We've reached out to the Nashburg Homicide Department for a comment on Cal's case and whether or not they believe this evidence incriminates Cal's sister. We're waiting for a response.

"As we reported to you first on Wake Up, Nashburg, Cal Dutton was found dead, apparently poisoned in his dressing room ahead of a sold-out show at the Banta Bowl on Friday night. Police have yet to comment on suspects, but local news sources have named both Cal's sister, Emma, who works at the venue, and his long-time girlfriend and fellow country music star, Autumn Silver, as persons of interest. This is an ongoing case, and anyone with information is encouraged to contact the Nashburg Police Department."

The video expired, and Emma and I stood in silence. Emma crammed her eyes shut and pressed her thumb and pointer finger into her eyelids, as if she could apply enough pressure to erase the video footage from both her mind and the inter-webs.

"Emma," I said after a minute. "Why didn't you tell me you had a massive blowout with Cal?" I tried to stay calm, but inside, my defenses were flying up faster than you could say *liar*. It felt like physical bricks were being stacked in my chest, walling off my heart. This sort of thing wreaked havoc on my already flimsy threads of trust. Why would Emma have kept something like this from me? "When was this?"

She sighed, her hand dropping to her side. "It was just last week."

"What was it all about?"

Emma rolled her eyes, flipping open the cabinet to the right of the sink and grabbing a glass before filling it from the faucet. "What it's always about. Cal's fame. His complete lack of care and concern for me and for the friends he left behind when he went and got himself a one-way ticket to superstardom."

I chewed my lip. "So you weren't arguing about anything specific?"

Emma rounded on me, her eyes flashing. "Why do you sound skeptical, Leigh? I just told you, it was the same old, same old."

I held up my hands. The last thing I wanted to do was make Emma feel cagy, even though *my* hackles were definitely raised. But I wasn't stupid.

I took a deep breath. "Look, I'm on your side. I just feel like if you had a fight with Cal about his fame, you would have told me about it. The fact that you didn't makes me think that there's something that you're hiding. Come on, Em. I'm your best friend."

Emma slumped against the counter, and a twinge of guilt pricked my conscience. I'd tossed out the best friend card, which was my ace in the hole—a surefire way to get Emma to tell me what was going on. The woman was nothing if not loyal.

I kicked myself for questioning if I could trust her. Of course I could. This was Emma. Maybe I shouldn't have pushed. Then again, if playing to her sympathies got results, in this case, it was worth it. I couldn't help her unless she let me in.

"This is such a mess." She dropped her head into her hands, covering her face and rocking back and forth on her heels.

I slid my computer onto our two-person dining table in the corner and went to her. I slung my arm around her shoulders and squeezed. "Come on. I'll make some cocoa, we can sit, and you can tell me what's going on."

When I got Emma settled on the couch with a steaming mug, I sat back and waited for her to explain.

She stirred her cocoa with a spoon, staring into the liquid mixture. Finally, she met my eye and sighed. "This is not how I wanted to tell you this."

"Okay." I stretched out the syllables. "You're scaring me."

"It's nothing bad," she assured, but then she frowned. "Or it shouldn't be. It's exciting, actually. I got a lead on a property that hasn't hit the market yet. It's in a prime location, and it's the perfect place to launch my own bar and restaurant. There's space for small, intimate concerts and comedy specials. The thing is, this is sooner than I was planning to make the leap and go out on my own. But if I don't move on it now, I'm going to miss out."

I nodded. She'd been researching and planning to open her own site for a while now. She'd learned a lot from Willie and his success at the Banta Bowl, but Emma didn't want to work under him for longer than she had to, and I couldn't blame her for wanting to have full control of her next venture.

"Sounds like a great opportunity. I'm really happy for you, Em."

"Don't be happy for me yet." Her voice came out in a wry tone. "I went to Cal to see if he would float me a starter loan. I didn't need much ... at least, not much by his standards. Just enough to add to what I have saved up for a down payment and what I'm preapproved for at the bank. He flat-out rejected me."

I grimaced. "That's what you were fighting about?"

Emma nodded into her mug.

"Why not go to your parents?"

Emma's features darkened. "Contrary to what everyone thinks, I'd rather have my parents love me than just act as my piggy bank."

"Sorry. I wasn't trying to imply—"

Emma waved me off. "It's fine. I shouldn't be so touchy about it. I just thought if I could do this on my own. Or get a loan from Cal and then pay him back with interest like a real grown-up would, then maybe people would start taking me seriously. Heck, I'm Willie's second in command at the Banta Bowl, but no one gives me any credit. Least of all Willie himself. I don't know what I have to do to prove myself. I was so mad at Cal for not understanding that."

I set my drink down on the coffee table. "Did you tell the police about all this?"

Emma sank back into the couch. "I didn't want to bring it up. It wasn't relevant. Cal died. It's impossible for me to get any money from him now, anyway. I had no idea there was video evidence of our fight. How in the world?"

I shrugged. "Cal must have security cameras set up in his apartment. I didn't notice any when we were there, though. Did you?"

Emma shook her head and coughed out a dry laugh. "Why would he have security inside his place? It's not like he needed to spy on himself."

"Maybe someone was spying on him."

Emma froze, her eyes bugging out. "You mean someone was filming him without him knowing? That's disturbing."

I nodded. "I could be wrong. I'm just thinking out loud."

Emma sat with that for a minute before leaning forward. "Or maybe Cal was worried about something or someone, and he installed the video cameras to collect evidence."

I tipped my head to the side. "That could be."

I thought about what Quentin had said earlier. If Cal had enemies, maybe he was recording everyone who came into his condo so he had proof of anything that went down when he was or wasn't there.

I quickly filled Emma in on what I'd learned at Red Vector. I was pleased to see some color return to her cheeks when I told her about my lead on Cal's watch.

"I'll go from the top of the list and start visiting watchmakers," I said. "See if I can track it down for you."

"I'll come with you if I don't have to work." She took another sip of her cocoa. "So you think Cal was trying to protect you from Quentin?"

I shrugged, the thought grating on me. I could take care of myself, and if Cal had his issues with Quentin, he should have left me out of it or at least explained himself so that I could have made the call on my own about whether or not I still wanted to pursue the opportunity. "Maybe."

"Do you feel better knowing that?" Emma asked.

"I'm not sure. Quentin obviously had a bone to pick with Cal. I think I should keep tabs on him, which shouldn't be too hard considering I'm going to apply for the staff writer position."

Emma reached over and squeezed my hand. "I'm excited for you. No matter what Cal said about it."

I smiled, grateful to have her support even if my feelings about the position were complicated. "RVR is hosting a benefit concert for Cal," I said, switching gears. "That'll be another chance to be around Red Vector staff and employees."

Emma nodded. "I heard rumblings about the concert at work today. It sounds like they have a lot of big names performing."

"Everyone wants to show their support, I guess."

Emma scoffed. "That, or they want good publicity for themselves."

She wasn't wrong, but the two of us had had this conversation before. We had a love-hate relationship with the industry we were embedded in. Dwelling on it wouldn't change it, so I brought us back to more pressing matters.

"How did things go with Willie? Did anything happen tonight?"

Emma shook her head. "We were slammed. I didn't have time to sneak into the kitchen and ask around. I did check the schedule and took a photo of the list of people who were working back there on Friday, though." She clicked on her phone and pulled up her photos. "At least I know who to start asking."

"That's good." I paused, considering how to verbalize my next thought.

"What is it?" Emma motioned to my mouth. "You're doing that thing where you bite your cheek and look all pensive."

I tried to relax my features. "I don't know. It's just that I got a weird feeling when I was talking to Detective Ottom."

Emma rolled her eyes. "That guy is harmless. He's like a big, lumbering oaf. If you ask me, Detective Yance is the brains of the operation—and the beauty."

"I knew it." I pointed at her. "You're crushing on the man who is interrogating you for your brother's murder? Really, Em?"

"I didn't say that. I'm merely calling out an objective fact. Besides, if you were stuck in a windowless room with only him to stare at, I bet you'd find him attractive, too."

I couldn't help the laugh that spluttered out. "You're ridiculous."

Emma shot me a grin. "Back to Detective Ottom. I think you're being paranoid."

"Maybe." I sobered and shook my head. "But if he wasn't on to us before, he might be now." Emma cocked a brow, waiting for me to go on. "Since that the video of you and Cal came out, I'm wondering if we were filmed too. The detectives could have seen all the footage, and they'd know what we were up to."

The more I thought about it, the more it fit with the weird feeling I'd had when I was with Detective Ottom.

Emma squinted at me. "But there was no audio on the clip they showed on the news."

"I know, but that doesn't mean it doesn't exist." I grabbed Emma's phone and clicked over to the PAP app. I pulled up the video there. Mercifully, it, too, was without sound. I exhaled. "Generally speaking, this is a good sign, but..." I trailed off.

"But we're screwed when it comes to the police," Emma finished for me, picking up on my train of thought. "So what, we just give up?"

I took a sip of cocoa, thinking through our options. "I'm all for seeing what we can figure out," I told her slowly, "but you're in hot water enough as it is. Oh gosh..." My eyes widened as another thought struck me.

"What? What is it?" Emma sat up.

"Are you in Cal's will?"

Her brows came together. "I have no idea. I doubt it. Why? Oh." I watched her fit the pieces together. "The police are going to argue my motive for killing Cal"—she made air quotes around the word *killing*—"was a financial one."

I nodded grimly.

Emma sighed and dragged an agitated hand through her hair. "Thank goodness the video on the news didn't have any audio. No one knows what we were fighting about, just that we were arguing. Gosh, this could ruin me."

We lapsed into silence.

"It's going to be okay," I said after a beat, but I couldn't help but worry my bottom lip.

Because if the truth of what Emma and Cal were arguing about came out, and I had no doubt it would—as pretty as Detective Yance was, he was equally, if not more so smart—then Emma's motive for Cal's murder just skyrocketed.

"Biding My Time" by Leigh Notrap, Cal Dutton, and Autumn Silver

Verse:
The moon's shining through
My window tonight.
I'm a long way from you.
One blurred town, two.
I can't keep them all right.
All I know is you're not by my side,
So there's no reason to delight
In Luna's silver rays.
Because they're not shining on your face.

Chorus:
Oh baby, I know it makes no sense
why I'm going round and round again.
You can't fit a circle into a square,
and believe me when I say I want to be there.
You're a perfect sphere and
I'm just over here being edged out.
But I promise this much is true:
I'm just biding my time.
Biding every last minute.
Till I can get back to you.

Verse:

You say you get it,
I know that you do.
Because while this is my dream,
It's always been yours, too.
But that don't make it easy,
No, it makes me love you more.
So I'm staring out the glass
Up at the stars,
Wishing this old van would take me
Straight back to your door.

Chorus:
Oh baby, I know it makes no sense
why I'm going round and round again.
You can't fit a circle into a square,
and believe me when I say I want to be there.
You're a perfect sphere and
I'm just over here being edged out.
But I promise this much is true:
I'm just biding my time.
Biding every last minute.
Till I can get back to you

Bridge:
The night's no longer young
And maybe it's me getting older, too,
But I swear I'm ready to give up
Every chance at a concrete star,
Every glance from a faceless screamer
For the promise of one night
Spent tucked inside your arms
Staring out into the Milky Way
That sparkles just for two dreamers
You and me.

13

Emma was called back to police headquarters the next morning. She took her lawyer with her, and I considered it a positive sign that the detectives hadn't held her there beyond the interview, but I couldn't help but think she was still on a short leash.

"What did they talk to you about?" I asked when we were reunited.

"The video, obviously." Emma scrolled through her phone in the passenger seat of my truck. We were driving over to the park for the remembrance concert for Cal. Her knee was bouncing, and she was smacking her gum in an absentminded way that told me she was on edge. I didn't blame her.

"And?" I prodded when she didn't continue.

"And I let my attorney do the talking. He told them the truth, Leigh. That's all," she snapped before letting loose a sigh. "Sorry. My mind's in a million different places. I know you're just trying to get on the same page so you can help me, but I'm freaking out. The detectives didn't like that I didn't disclose my fight with Cal upfront, but since there was no concrete evidence that I'd harmed him, they let me go with a directive to stay available for further questioning. Honestly, I'm terrified."

I shot her a sidelong look. "At least they didn't keep you there."

Emma blanched, and her knee bouncing ramped up.

"I mean, it's good they don't have enough evidence to arrest you or something," I hurried to add.

Emma firmed her lips, and I mentally smacked myself on the forehead. "I'm making this worse." I reached over and squeezed her knee. "It's going to be fine. You didn't do anything wrong. The police will do their job and figure out what happened. I'm sure of it."

I was pleased with how confident I sounded, and I credited my clear-headedness to the fact that I got in my most decent swim of the week while Emma was at police headquarters. I swam for a mile, and the makings of a clever hook had come to me round about lap fifty.

I parked my truck in the nearby ramp, and Emma and I strolled together until concrete opened up into green space. The venue at the park was not unlike Red Rocks out west. I mean, nothing was quite like that, but in this case, the land sloped into a bowl shape, with the stage at the lowest point. The sun shone bright and clear in the Nashburg sky, and music fans dotted the hill, some standing, some seated on blankets, in anticipation of the afternoon's festivities.

Emma looped her arm through mine as we approached the crowd. "I have no idea how I'm supposed to act," she murmured. "I feel like everyone is going to recognize me, and people are going to judge, and that stupid video is going to be the end of my credibility."

"I guarantee no one is thinking about that video as much as you are."

Except for maybe the police.

I didn't add that last thought. No need to make Emma more uptight.

I bumped my hip with hers. "This is going to be fun. Let's just relax and enjoy it. For Cal."

She let out a long hiss of a breath between her teeth. "You're right. I'm sorry. I'm all over the place."

"It's okay. I'm used to it."

That earned me a shove to the side.

"Watch it," she said. "I have yet to interrogate you about showing up to Cal's dressing room with one Jace James, but don't think that means I've forgotten about it."

I hitched my shoulder in an attempt at casualness. "You're going to be disappointed. There's nothing to report."

"If that were true, then you wouldn't have reacted like you just did." She smirked and used her pointer finger to make a circular motion in the direction of my face, which flamed like the sun. "No wonder you're so excited about this concert. It's another chance to see Jace."

I shook my head, trying to shake off my embarrassment. "Absolutely nothing is going on between Jace and me except for a half-expired friendship left over from music school. I happened to run into him at the Banta Bowl on Friday, completely unintentionally."

My pulse skittered at the memory of his touch, but I kept my burning face as impassive as possible.

Emma studied me. "You two would make a handsome couple if you ask me. Don't rule it out, okay?"

I snorted. "Doubtful."

"Oh, Leigh." She clucked her tongue in reproach. "I know all about you and your disdain for love, but if the opportunity presents itself with Jace, I'm just saying you should take it." She squared her shoulders then, and changed the subject. "But first, I want bubble tea. I see the boba truck across the way."

I followed her through the crowd of cowboy-hat-clad fans. Everyone was wearing a neon yellow wristband. Staff in crimson-colored Red Vector-branded t-shirts were handing them out. Emma and I each took one, and I read the inscription out loud. "In loving memory of Cal Dutton, whose music lives on in our hearts."

Emma didn't say anything. She fiddled with the bracelet before slipping it around her wrist. "Tea, then?"

I nodded, determining it was best not to push. We got our drinks and were mingling at the top of the hill, taking in the scene, when I felt eyes on my back. I pivoted slowly, trying to figure out why I suddenly had goosebumps scurrying up and back down my arms.

I scanned my surroundings, but I didn't see anyone or anything out of the ordinary. In fact, no one seemed to be paying Emma and me any attention at all.

"So, is there anything we can accomplish here for our, er, investigation?" Emma caught my attention, saying the last word in an exaggerated whisper.

I shifted my focus to her and screwed my mouth to the side. "I'm going to keep an eye out for Quentin Buffet. See what he's up to. That's mostly for selfish reasons, though. I've got to get a read on the guy if I'm going to be interviewing with him." I already felt like I was behind the curve based on our initial exchange, plus Cal's lack of support. "Anything I find out may turn out to implicate him in Cal's death. You never know."

Even as I said it, I had a difficult time believing my own reasoning. Was I really suspecting a man of murder just because he seemed like a jerk? If that was the case, then half of the graduating class at the elite private high school I attended could have landed themselves in jail just by virtue of existing.

I shook my head and refocused my thoughts. "We could also try to chat with Autumn. I haven't talked with her since Friday. Have you?"

"Nope," Emma said. "What do you think she can tell us that we don't already know?"

"Not sure, but it's worth asking. She knew Cal best."

We slurped our tea and chatted about life, letting ourselves be swept up in the throngs of country music fans as we made our way closer to the stage.

"My parents are pulling themselves together. Barely," Emma said with a sigh. "Cal's funeral isn't scheduled until next Monday, and that will be an emotional day. You'll be there, right?"

"Of course." I got out my phone and entered the information into my calendar. "You should tell Agnes, too. She'll want to pay her respects."

"Good idea. Hey, I see Autumn." Emma pointed to the side of the stage.

Autumn had stepped out from one of the trailers on the far side. I was surprised to see her without any sort of posse. I glanced around, wondering if we were the only ones who had caught sight of her.

"Let's go. Maybe we can talk to her before she performs." I took off through the crowd, keeping my eye on Autumn.

As we got closer, she disappeared into the trailer. We had to stop when we got to the edge of the crowd. Access to the musicians' trailers was roped off, and there were security guards stationed at equal intervals along the rope.

"Which one do you think we should sweet talk?" Emma asked under her breath, bobbing her head at the security.

"I have no clue." I studied the men and women in charge of protecting the performers, each of varying degrees of girth. They all looked like they could snap us in half with the flick of their wrists.

The door to Autumn's trailer opened again, and she stepped outside. Now that we were closer, I could tell she was upset.

"Autumn!" I yelled.

Her head jerked up, and she searched the crowd.

I held up my hand and waved.

Recognition colored her features, mixed with what I'd like to believe was a hint of relief, when she saw Emma and me.

I stepped closer to the rope and the nearest security guard.

"Let them through, please." Autumn's melodic voice produced instant results.

The guard lifted the rope, and Emma and I scooted underneath, crossing the rest of the grassy area and making our way to the base of the steps leading up to Autumn's trailer.

"It's good to see a couple of familiar faces." Autumn turned to go inside. "Come on in."

Emma and I exchanged a look before we followed her. I really wished I had thought through exactly what I wanted to say and how I wanted to frame it before I landed myself on the small couch inside Autumn Silver's trailer. But alas. Here we were, and I couldn't let the opportunity pass me by without at least trying to learn a little bit more about Cal and his final days.

"How are you holding up, Autumn?" I asked.

Autumn sank down onto the bench opposite where Emma and I sat. "Not great."

Her voice hitched, and I looked at my lap. Emma shifted her weight next to me.

I glanced up after a second and watched as Autumn took a fortifying breath.

"How are you guys doing? Emma, I saw the video—" She cut off as if realizing that might be a touchy subject.

I eyed Emma, who was grimacing.

"Yeah," she said. "I was afraid of that. I'm sure everyone has seen it. It isn't what it looked like. Well, I guess it is. We did have that fight, but I didn't kill Cal."

Autumn shook her head promptly. "I never believed you did."

"Really?" Emma slumped in her seat next to me. "Thank you for saying that."

"Of course. You and Cal had your differences, but even in spite of that, I truly believe you both cared for each other."

"Any chance you could tell that to the police?" Emma's voice gave an uncharacteristic wobble.

Autumn's eyes softened even further. "They've been talking to you, too, huh?"

Emma nodded. "They called me in again this morning."

"If it helps, I can tell them that Cal told me about the fight. I actually told him he should lend you the seed money, but he said he wanted you to do it on your own. If he got involved, then it would turn into a whole big thing, and he didn't want that for you."

I looked at Emma's profile. Her mouth opened on a gasp. "Wow. I-I hadn't thought of it that way." She closed her mouth and swallowed. "I'd appreciate any good word you could put in for me with the detectives."

"Speaking of the detectives," I said, grateful for the segue. "Why are they questioning you?"

Autumn raised a delicate shoulder. "I'm sure it's protocol. I was the last person to see Cal alive, which I guess makes me suspicious. I was in the room when he drank the tea."

Emma swished her drink around with her straw. "So it was the tea that killed him? Or something in it?"

Autumn nodded. "That's what I gather."

"Did you know much about the belladonna tincture Cal was taking?" I asked.

"Some. I don't know if he took any that night. His asthma wasn't flaring, so I don't know why he would have."

I combed my memory for what else I could ask Autumn. "You said that he complained about the tea tasting bitter, right?"

Autumn nodded.

I turned to Emma. "Do you know if adding too much of the tincture would have caused that?"

Emma pursed her lips in thought. "I would have to ask Whitmore." She turned to Autumn. "My ex."

"I remember hearing about him," Autumn commented.

"He knows everything there is to know about alternative medicine."

"Gotcha." Autumn blinked, and her shoulders dipped. She looked like a woman who was carrying a giant weight on her back. "I don't think the usual dose had much of a taste. Cal would add it to whatever he was drinking. But if someone poured the whole bottle into the tea, then I guess it probably would have affected the flavor."

"Who knows how much of the tincture was left in the bottle, though," I mused aloud. "Detective Yance seemed to think it was pretty telling that it was empty when he found it in Cal's dressing room."

Autumn shook her head. "I told them about that. Cal had just placed an order for more, so I think it must've been nearly gone."

Interesting. This was new information. If there wasn't enough tincture left in the bottle to poison Cal, then whoever killed him would have had to do so in an alternative way.

"I wonder if the poison that killed him was even atropine after all."

"Atropine?" Autumn crinkled her nose. "What's that?"

"It's one of the chemicals in belladonna. The main one."

She arched her eyebrow at me.

Dang it.

I hadn't meant to let on to my research.

"I...uh... looked it up after Detective Yance mentioned it. I like to know things."

Autumn's mouth curved into a small smile. "Cal liked that about you, I think. And hey, you should go forward with the writing job with Red Vector. It would be cool to work together."

"But you're with Ducal, aren't you?" That was one of the downsides of becoming a staff writer. I'd no longer be able to freelance. I'd only write for Red Vector, and they'd pair my songs with their artists. I'd have less creative autonomy.

Autumn shook her head. "My contract is up. I'm in talks right now to sign with RVR. I hadn't considered Red Vector, but Zac has been lobbying my team pretty hard lately, and he's saying all the right things. So, we'll see. I didn't even tell Cal I was in talks to join his label. I wanted to surprise him."

Anguish darkened her features. She had to swallow a few times before speaking. "Anyway, I have no clue why Cal would have warned you away from applying at Red Vector. It's an amazing opportunity."

I dipped my head in acknowledgment. "I appreciate that. He didn't mention anything about me to you?"

She shook her head. "Sorry. No. But you're mega-talented. Any publisher would be lucky to have you. When we wrote together a few months back, I had so much fun, and it was so inspiring. I'm hoping to use that song on my upcoming album."

"'Biding My Time'?" I asked, perking up.

Cal, Autumn, and I had been messing around one afternoon, and we ended up coming up with a slow song that read in complete contrast to our slap-happy mood.

"That's the one." Autumn smiled, but then the corners of her lips dropped. "I thought it would be nice to pay tribute to Cal with it, too."

"I love that idea." Not gonna lie, I also loved the idea of the royalties that would come my way if it became a hit. A part of me felt like a cow for thinking about money at a time like this, but it wasn't like I could turn off the switch in my brain that was constantly calculating what I was spending versus what I was raking in. Starving artists are a stereotype for a reason.

The three of us sat in silence for a beat.

Autumn stared out the trailer window before exhaling a shaky breath. "I don't know how I'm going to get through the set today."

Emma and I nodded. It was a lot to ask of Autumn—to sing a complete set list less than a week after the man who inspired many of the love songs on that very list—and who had written or co-written many of the other ones—had died. She'd been there to witness his passing, no less. We were trained to grow thick skin in this industry, but this seemed extreme.

"No one would blame you if you had to step back," Emma said softly.

I watched Autumn carefully, so I caught the look of uncertainty that crossed her face before it was replaced with resolve. She tucked her hair behind her ears.

"It's alright. I'm sure I'll be fine. It's for Cal. I can do it."

She stood, and I took that as our cue to leave. "We'll let you get warmed up. Thanks for taking the time to talk to us."

"Yeah." Emma gave Autumn a hug. "If you need anything, don't hesitate to reach out."

"Thank you." Autumn leaned back. "Thank you both."

I hugged her, too, and then Emma and I exited the trailer.

Just as we reached the security rope, I caught sight of a familiar figure making his way toward the trailer. He kept his head down, but I still recognized him immediately.

"Come on, you two. Let's go." The security guard had the rope raised, and fans from the other side were jostling him, trying to push their way forward. The crowd had grown while we were talking to Autumn.

I ducked under the rope after Emma, but I glanced over my shoulder in time to see the man enter Autumn's trailer. Just before the door swung shut, I caught sight of him reaching up to cup Autumn's face in his hands—an embrace that looked a full ruler's length shy of platonic.

I turned to Emma after we were on the stage-side of the rope, and her eyes went wide. "Was that who I think it was?"

14

"Cal's manager, Phil McMann," I whispered. I was stunned.

Emma glanced around before dipping her head toward me. "Did they look, um, *involved* to you?"

I nodded, trying to reconcile the bereaved, in-love Autumn with the woman I just saw who, by all appearances, seemed ready to be swept off her feet by another man.

I felt the same sort of incongruous way I had when I saw Autumn leaving the police station—all business-like and unaffected. How was that the same person who had sobbed uncontrollably in Cal's dressing room?

"What in the world are we supposed to make of that?" The bewilderment in Emma's voice was evident.

"No idea, but I don't know if we can trust Autumn."

Emma hummed in agreement. "Come on, I think Jace James is up next." She winked at me, and I rolled my eyes.

I tuned my ears to the music, and it was only then that I realized who was currently on stage. I gritted my teeth. "What are they doing here? They aren't with Red Vector."

Pita Paige and Penn Stewart stood holding each other's hands and peering into each other's eyes as they sang about forever love.

I wanted to gag.

"I have no idea." Emma shot me a concerned look, knowing full well that my history with Pita and Penn was rocky, to say the least. That's what happened when artists stole other artists' work and used it for their own ends ... without giving credit where credit was due. When I thought about the royalties I should be receiving for their song—*my* song—it made my stomach sour.

"Are you okay?" Emma asked.

I nodded quickly. "I'm just going to wander for a bit. I don't want to make eye contact."

Emma frowned, glancing back and forth between me and the stage. "I can come with you if you want."

"No." I shook my head. "Why don't you stay here and hold our spots."

"You sure?"

"Positive." I mustered up a carefree smile and headed off before Emma could protest.

Truth be told, I felt like I was going to hyperventilate. It always happened to me when I ended up orbiting the same sphere as Pita and Penn. I hated myself for still being so affected, but I couldn't help it. It was so like them—to show up here at an event being held in Cal's honor. They didn't know him at all, but they were always trying to be the center of attention, no matter who they had to step on to get to the top. I'd know, considering they walked all over me.

I cut through the groups of people who were congregated on the hill and facing the stage, trying not to be annoyed at the couples whose hands were linked or who stood pressed against each other, singing every word of the sugary-sweet love song as if it were gospel.

I swung around and ducked into one of the porta potties. It was saying a lot about how I felt about Pita and Penn that I preferred being in here to their singing.

When I stepped back out and took a breath of fresh air, I surveyed my surroundings. There was a gap in the crowd between where I stood at the top of the hill, near the food and drink trucks, and where the fans had gathered to listen to the concert.

My gaze wandered to where the trailers were parked beyond the stage area. What was going on between Autumn and Phil? I replayed what I saw over and over again, glad to have something to focus on that wasn't the performers on stage. Was it possible I misinterpreted what was about to happen in Autumn's trailer? My eyes could have been playing a trick on me. Then again, Emma had seen it too.

My mind churned with a new possibility. If Autumn and Phil were romantically involved, and Cal somehow found out, maybe they teamed up to kill him to clear the path for their relationship.

I let my head fall back. It was a stretch. No matter who I came up with as a suspect and what their motives might be, I still couldn't imagine any sort of disagreement with Cal escalating to murder.

But still, I should touch base with Phil and pick his brain. Cal had connected us when I first moved to Nashburg, and he had used some of his contacts to get me some freelance gigs. I would consider myself an acquaintance of his, so it wouldn't be out of the ordinary for me to ask him to grab coffee. Hopefully he'd say yes.

I blinked and swung my head to the far side of the venue. I did a double take when I recognized a familiar duo lingering on the outskirts of the crowd.

As if he knew I was looking at him, Detective Yance glanced at me, and our gazes connected. *Shoot.* Should I acknowledge him? Look away? Pretend I didn't recognize him?

Before I could figure out a game plan, he tilted his head toward Detective Ottom and spoke into his ear. They turned and walked in my direction.

A whole-body tremor overtook me, from my feet to my forehead, but I gave myself a quick pep talk. I had done nothing wrong. Neither had Emma. I needed to relax. If I could get my thoughts in order, maybe I could learn something from the detectives.

I rearranged my features, trying to appear calm and pleasant. Easier said than done when my resting face was more pit bull than golden retriever.

"Detectives." I nodded at them as they came to a stop in front of me. "How are y'all tonight?"

"Just fine, Ms. Notrap. Yourself?" Detective Yance pinned me with an unreadable look before scanning everyone around me. I couldn't help but wonder if he was looking for Emma. Whether it was of personal interest or professional, I couldn't tell.

"All good." I motioned toward the crowd. "It's a nice event Red Vector put together."

"Indeed." Detective Ottom studied me, and I waited for him to say something more. They had approached me, after all. Surely, they had something to say beyond just *hello* and *how are you.*

When the silence stretched on for an awkward thirty seconds, I cleared my throat. "What brings you out here tonight? Looking for someone in particular?"

Both detectives snapped their gazes to my face. Detective Yance's eyebrows lifted, but it was Detective Ottom who spoke first, a small smirk gracing his lips. "Who do you think we might be wanting to see?"

I swallowed, steadying myself as I worked to remain nonchalant. "I don't know. I figured since you're together, you must be here in a work capacity. Not for pleasure. Then again, maybe you two hang out in your free time?"

Detective Yance's lips twitched, and I gave myself a mental pat on the back for cracking his stoic outer shell.

Emboldened, I continued. "Is there anyone I can help you find?"

"We're just here to observe." Detective Ottom shot me a hard look. "Might I add, Ms. Notrap, that you'd do well to remember that *we* are the detectives and *you* are a songwriter. Let's keep the duties of our jobs separate, shall we?"

My eyes widened of their own accord, but I forced them back to their normal size. "I'm curious why you think I'm trying to infringe on your job, Detective. What gave you that impression?"

Detective Ottom harrumphed. "We have you admitting to undertaking an amateur investigation on video, so you best hear me when I say back off, Ms. Notrap. That friend of yours is in hot water. I'm sure you understand why."

My face flamed, and my skin felt hot and sticky. So there *was* audio connected to whatever device had recorded Emma and Cal's fight. It had also recorded Emma and me while we cleaned out Cal's place. It was creepy as all get out to know we'd not only been watched but listened to.

"Do you have anything to say for your friend?" Detective Yance spoke up, his tone cool and even.

I straightened. "Only that Emma's innocent. You heard her say so yourself. She would never have hurt Cal. And"—I pinned him with my best steely glare—"I'd appreciate it if you did your jobs and found the actual murderer. She has a reputation to maintain."

I didn't break eye contact with Detective Yance. He stared me down as if trying to see through me.

Detective Ottom scoffed, drawing my attention. "Ms. Dutton's reputation is the least of my concerns. Interesting how she brought her attorney with her this morning. People who are guilty are usually the ones who lawyer up."

I couldn't stop an eye roll at that. "Don't patronize me, Detective. In this day and age, where police TV shows and true crime podcasts are a dime-a-dozen, everyone knows the importance of legal representation. It's a basic right."

Detective Ottom's mouth dropped open a hair before he snapped it shut.

"And," I said, pushing my advantage, "if you're making that sort of blanket statement, then I have to assume you think both Autumn Silver and Willie Davis have something to hide since they had lawyers with them when they were questioned." I crossed my arms. "By the way, I assume you've asked Willie about *his* fight with Cal. The one they had less than an hour before Cal turned up dead."

When the detectives didn't respond, I continued. "Because Willie is nervous about it, for some reason. You might want to press him on that if you haven't already. As for Autumn, there's something she's not being completely honest about."

I stopped short of sharing what Emma and I had witnessed in the trailer. A lingering respect for Autumn that I wasn't quite ready to discard held me back. Maybe she could explain herself.

Detective Yance's face remained impassive, but Detective Ottom's eyes flashed, and he pointed a finger at me. "You better watch yourself, missy. You leave our jobs to us and stay out of this investigation before someone else gets hurt."

I shrugged, forcing myself to remain composed even though my heart was beating wildly. I guess my years of etiquette training were good for something. "I'm only trying to help."

"I'm sure you are." Detective Ottom rolled his eyes. "Let's go." He turned away from me.

Detective Yance looked in my direction for another beat before nodding and following his partner.

"Hey," I called out before they were beyond earshot.

Both detectives looked over their shoulders. Detective Ottom's expression was one of exasperation. Detective Yance's face was blank.

"We want the same thing, you know."

Detective Ottom frowned. "What's that?"

"The truth."

15

The truth.

My own words rattled around in my brain, and I had to work to silence the tinny voice that taunted me, calling me a hypocrite for saying I wanted the truth when my whole life, my whole identity for the past ten years, had been an attempt to hide the truth.

I rubbed my hands up and down my arms, physically trying to pull myself together as I walked away from the detectives.

By the time I made it back down the hill to where Emma was holding our seats, I had my racing pulse under control. Going toe-to-toe with the detectives was unsettling, to say the least, and as much as I liked to think of myself as a self-made woman—and I *was*—authority figures still intimidated me.

Emma had finally relaxed and was enjoying the concert. I didn't want to send her spiraling again by mentioning my encounter with the police. No use having both of us worried about it tonight.

Mercifully, Pita Paige and Penn Stewart had exited the stage, and much to my delight—though I refused to let on—Jace James had taken their place.

He sounded good, and if it was possible, he looked even better.

I let the low rumble of his country-twang voice wash over me. Emma and I raised our cell phone flashlights with the rest of the crowd on the hill, and we sang every word to his hit song, "Nobody For Me But You."

When Jace got close to the end of his set, he looked out over the crowd. His gaze latched onto mine. If I didn't know better, I'd say his eyes lit up. Then again, that was probably just a trick of the setting sun and the stage lights.

"Alright, folks. Thanks so much for coming out to see us tonight. I've got one more song for y'all before I turn the stage over to the lovely Ms. Autumn Silver." Jace paused when the fans clapped and cheered their appreciation for Autumn.

When the noise simmered down, Jace pulled the microphone close to his mouth again. "This last piece is a new song I've been working on. It's about friends, lost and found, and the hope that maybe, someday, we could be more than friends."

The crowd's screams grew deafening.

Jace kept his eyes laser-focused on me. "It's called 'Now You Know.' I hope you like it." He glanced down at his guitar and plucked out the opening chords. He didn't look at me again as he started singing the lyrics to a song about best friends. By the time he sang the bridge, I knew exactly where the lyrics were going. My traitorous heart had leaped into my throat at his opening to the song, and it was currently wedged there.

Emma elbowed me in the side. "Are you hearing this?" she squealed.

I shook my head, too stunned to speak. Had Jace James really just hinted that he wrote this song with me in mind? It seemed preposterous, and yet a part of me wanted to believe it.

The song was beautiful. The lyrics dripped with meaning and heart. It was the kind of song that, once polished, would be an overnight sensation. Every bride and groom for the next decade would dance to it at their wedding.

My mind flitted to Cal and the folded-up sheet of lyrics we'd been working on together. That had been Cal's goal, hadn't it? To pen a timeless classic. He hadn't lived long enough to make it happen. I'd tucked the seedling of that song away, but I made a decision right then and there to get it out and work on it myself to honor Cal's memory.

I returned my focus to the stage as Jace crooned the last lyric.

"All these years spent living so close but still apart have torn me up inside / Because I've held you close to my heart in secret, waiting for a chance to show / You love, my true love, and now you know."

The crowd erupted in applause. Emma whooped next to me, sticking her fingers in her mouth and whistling.

I swallowed around the rapid pulse in my throat and clapped my hands together. My movements were stilted, as if the shock of the moment had slipped under my skin and limited my mobility.

Jace didn't look at me again. He lifted both hands in the air and waved to the crowd on the hill before taking a bow and jogging off the stage.

"Are you kidding me right now?" Emma shrieked with glee.

When I turned to face her, her eyes were wide, and she sported a huge grin.

"What?" I stuck my hands in my back pockets, my fingers knocking into where I had wedged my phone.

"You know what! That was so romantic."

I shrugged, trying to play it off as no big deal, even though it felt like the biggest deal of my life. "I guess."

"You *guess*? That's all you're going to say? You know Jace meant that for you!"

I leveled Emma with a look. "Not necessarily."

Before Friday night, Jace and I hadn't talked in over a year. It was all ridiculous. My own heart was ridiculous for speeding up at the notion. My own mind was ridiculous for *having* the thought.

Emma crossed her arms. "Did you even listen to the lyrics? That's your thing, Leigh, and those words were about *you*."

I shook my head and faced the stage as a familiar voice boomed through the speakers.

“Ladies and gentlemen, if you’d allow me a moment of your time, I’d like to say a few words.” Zac Geffadab stood in front of the mic. “On behalf of the entire team at Red Vector, thank you for coming out to show your love for Cal Dutton.” Zac dropped his head and paused, as if collecting himself. When he looked up, he wiped a stray tear from below his eye. “Cal was one in a million. One of a kind, some may say. We had huge plans for him at Red Vector, and we’re so saddened by his tragic death. His loss is felt by the music community as a whole and, in a special way, by all of us who worked with him at Red Vector.” Zac motioned to his employees, who were lined up in their red t-shirts.

I spotted Quentin standing near the side of the stage. Based on the scowl marring his features, he’d rather be doing anything else than paying tribute to Cal.

Zac finished his spiel, announcing Autumn, but I kept my eyes trained on Quentin. As Zac walked off the stage past him, the two exchanged words. Quentin’s eyes blazed bright enough for me to notice, even from my position on the hill.

Autumn walked onto the stage, waving to the cheering crowd, and my attention shifted to her, only to be ripped away by a disturbance near the stairs.

“What’s going on?” I raised up on my tip-toes in time to see a flash of long blonde hair. A woman broke free and charged toward the microphone.

“My name is Whitney Allerow, and I lead Cal’s fan group, Cal’s Crew. We wanted to thank Mr. Geffadab and the entire Red Vector organization for putting this together.” Whitney’s words came out in a breathy rush, echoing throughout the grounds.

“Do you think this was planned?” I asked Emma.

“No clue.” She craned her neck next to me, trying to get a better look.

“But.” Whitney’s eyes narrowed, and she leaned toward the mic. “I think we’re all fooling ourselves if we don’t call out the culprit in Cal’s death. She’s here tonight.”

16

An anxious purr rolled through the crowd at Whitney's declaration.

"So definitely not planned, then," Emma said, rocking back on her heels and taking the last slurp of her bubble tea.

"What is she doing?" I mumbled.

The crowd quieted, and Whitney swung her gaze directly to where I was standing, settling her glare on Emma. Before I knew what was happening, she was pointing a finger at us.

"Cal's sister, Emma, should answer for what she's done!"

My jaw dropped as I digested her words and took in the crazed look in Whitney's eyes.

Her voice rose another octave. "She has some nerve showing up tonight! She stole Cal from us at the dawn of his career. We want justice for him!" She pumped her fist in the air. "Emma must pay! Emma must pay! Emma must pay!"

Emma's face paled, and she shrunk into herself, her cup slipping from her hand and dropping to the ground.

I looped my arm around her shoulders and pressed her head into my neck, shielding her from the prying eyes of the thousands of people who had filled the park.

On stage, Autumn tugged on Whitney's arm, trying to get her to step away from the microphone as her cronies off to the side of the stage took up the chant.

"Emma must pay! Emma must pay!"

Whoever was working the camera at the park found us, and now I saw Emma and me splashed up on the oversized projection screen.

I spun around and shoved my way through the crowd as the chants continued. I kept Emma pressed tightly to my side. She stumbled, but I held her upright, steering us out into the open green space at the back of the hill.

Before we made it there, a male voice came over the speakers. "Okay. Okay. That's enough of that, folks. The police haven't made any arrests in regard to Cal's death. We need to let them do their job."

I glanced over my shoulder to see Phil, Cal's manager, at the mic. Autumn stood a step to his left. Her mouth was hanging open an inch in shock. Behind them, Detective Ottom and Detective Yance were trying to corral a flailing Whitney.

Even through the din of the concert-goers, I could make out Whitney's shrieks. She'd always been passionate where Cal was concerned, but tonight, she'd come unhinged.

The next thing I heard was Autumn's voice. She went right into a song, which was probably the most merciful thing she could have done for Emma since she drew the attention of the fans and the cameraman, who no longer had his lens trained on us.

We plowed our way through the rest of the crowd and popped out on the back half of the hill.

"Let's go," I said. "The truck's this way."

"What am I going to do?" Emma shook like a leaf where she was still tucked under my arm.

"You're not going to do anything right now. You're going to call your lawyer and have him talk to the police about Whitney's completely inappropriate behavior."

Emma filled her lungs with oxygen, making her entire body expand at my side. "This is a nightmare," she whispered, her voice feeble and hopeless.

I squeezed her. "Hey, look at me." I waited for Emma to meet my eye before continuing. Her expression broke my heart and steeled my resolve. "You haven't done anything wrong," I told her firmly. "I'm sorry this is happening, but the detectives will figure out what really happened." I paused, shifting my jaw, now more determined than ever. "And if they don't, then we will."

Emma nodded, though she didn't look so sure. I hated seeing her like this—so not herself.

I released my grip on her back and clapped my hands once. "That's it. We're going dancing."

Emma let out a bark of laughter. "What? What are you talking about?"

"Dancing. You. Me. At a dive bar. You need to do something to take your mind off of Cal and what just went down here. Don't tell me you don't want to." I raised my eyebrows and waited to see if Emma would contradict me.

She wouldn't. She never said no to dancing.

Emma pressed her lips together, and a slow grin spread across her face. "Let's do it. You're the best, Leigh. Thank you." She gave me a side hug as we walked the rest of the way to my car.

I toyed with the idea of going back to the Village and hitting up one of the local establishments on Crowbar Road, but instinct told me Emma needed to be anonymous tonight—to let loose and dance without a second thought of who was watching her.

I drove us to a bar in Midtown known for its party atmosphere. Hot Diggity was its name, and like everywhere in Nashburg, it had live music every night of the week. What Hot Diggity could also boast was a giant dance floor that was constantly packed.

Twenty minutes later, we each had a drink in our hand, and our eyes had adjusted to the neon light of the bar. The music was so loud I couldn't hear myself think, but it was worth it as I watched the stress lines on Emma's face turn to laugh lines as she let some guy in a black cowboy hat pull her out onto the dance floor to join in a line dance.

I hung back and smiled into my seltzer water as the cowboy-hat-clad gentleman swung Emma around. She tossed her head back in laughter, squealing when she rounded a turn and faced me.

I waved, and then she was flying in the other direction as the dancers moved around the floor.

The lead singer of the band was good, and while I didn't recognize the song, I assumed it was an original. I closed my eyes and let the lyrics wrap themselves around me. It was a feel-good melody with words to match, and I absently wondered what the writers' process was.

For me, writing songs was as much a part of my life as breathing. I'd always been a lyricist, before I even knew it was a thing. Growing up, I thought in lyrics—first from other people's songs and later, my own. It took me until midway through middle school to realize that not everyone else was coming up with lines upon lines of poetry each day and matching them to tunes they'd developed. That was just me.

Which was probably also the case for the guy behind the mic tonight. If I had to bet, I'd say he'd composed this song. He embodied the energy of it. The words rolled off his tongue with an ease that only came when you had bled lyrics and rhythms into a song of your own creation.

There was a sign behind the stage that read 'The Campbells.' I palmed my phone to look up the band, but the music changed, and Emma was at my side, pulling me out onto the dance floor.

"Hey!" I yelled as I slid my phone back into my pocket and hurried to keep up with her.

"You said *we* were going to dance. That's *we*, plural."

I started to protest, but before I knew it, I was giggling and cozied up to a mountain of a man who was surprisingly fleet of foot.

An hour later, we were sweaty and happy as we slumped our tired bodies into the chairs positioned around a small table off to the side of the stage. The lead singer told the packed bar that he was taking a twenty-minute break.

"Perfect timing." Emma stretched out her legs, knocking them into mine. "I'm parched."

"I'll go get you something." I wedged my way out of the booth.

"You're the best, Leigh. I owe you for this." Emma smiled a loopy smile, and I wasn't sure if she was buzzed on her gin and tonic or on the energy in the room. I figured I better grab us some waters, just in case.

I patted her arm. "That's what friends are for. Stay put. I'll be right back."

I made my way over to the bar and nestled into the only open spot. I caught the bartender's eye, and when he strolled over to hand a drink to the guy next to me, I asked for two ice waters.

"Takin' 'er easy tonight, are we?"

I turned to the man who had retrieved his drink, only to find the lead singer grinning at me. I cocked my head and shot him a smile. "I'm the designated driver, and my friend has *not* taken it easy to this point, so it's time to rein her back in."

The singer's eyes danced with mirth. "Fair enough."

"Y'all have been excellent." I tipped my head to the stage. "I can tell it's not your first rodeo. I'm Leigh, by the way." I held out my hand.

He shook it. "Jon. Jon Campbell. Nice to meet ya, ma'am."

"You too." I wanted to confirm my hunch, so I asked, "You write your own stuff?"

Jon nodded. "My brother, David, and I write together." He motioned to the guy who I recognized as the band's drummer.

I flipped my gaze between the pair. "Twins?"

"My mama says so." Jon laughed. "I'm older by three minutes, and I don't let him forget it."

I reached over and grabbed the waters from the bartender, thanking him before turning back to Jon. His smile, and the warmth in his tone, led me to believe that these were two siblings who genuinely cared about each other. It was refreshing to see.

"You two are close, huh?"

He grinned. "We want to be the next Brothers Osborne."

I raised my eyebrows. "Lofty goal." I thought over the music they played and the atmosphere they'd created in the bar, and I could see it. These guys had the talent. "Judging from the way you had the crowd eating out of the palm of your hand tonight, I'd say you're well on your way."

He blinked away the compliment with an attractive dose of humility. "Thanks."

When Jon met my gaze again, though, a look of frustration snaked its way across his face. "Thought we might be getting close, but now I'm not so sure."

I winced on his behalf. I could relate. "Sorry to hear that."

He scuffed a worn cowboy boot over the sticky floor. "Me too. That's the business we're in, isn't it? I guess I don't know what business you're in," he added with a chuckle.

"The same one as you, actually." I smiled. "I'm a songwriter."

Jon's eyes widened. "Takes one to know one, I guess." He nudged my shoulder in a friendly way before sobering. "I can't believe the news out of the Banta Bowl, can you? Did you know Cal Dutton?"

I choked on the sip of water I had just taken. I coughed a couple of times, clearing my windpipe. Those were the last words I expected to come out of Jon's mouth. "I do know Cal, actually. Or I did. How did *you* know him?"

Jon leaned in. "He reached out to David and me and said he wanted to talk about our career aspirations. We figured we caught the eye of someone at Red Vector Records at the Jaybird Café."

"Who was it?" I asked, shooting a glance over to where Emma was still seated. It looked like one of the guys she'd been dancing with joined her at the table. I didn't want to leave her hanging. "Can you walk with me for a second?" I hooked my thumb in the direction of our table.

"Sure." We eased away from the bar, and Jon picked the conversation up. "I don't know who the guy was. I saw him talking in the back of the Jaybird to Zac Geffadab, who runs things over at RVR. Then Cal reached out. I figured it wasn't a coincidence. We hoped he would seal the deal. We were supposed to meet on Friday, but he texted and said he had to cancel."

"Did he say anything else?" I asked. If I could just piece together more of Cal's last days, maybe I would have a better idea of what he'd gotten himself into ... what had gotten him killed.

Jon shook his head. "He was apologetic, but said he needed to prep for his concert that night and that we'd have to schedule another time to meet." He frowned. "It was a little confusing, honestly."

"What was?" I shot Emma a look. She was shooing the guy away on her own, so I turned back to Jon.

"We thought he would prime the pump for us with Red Vector. Sorta mentor us, ya know?" I nodded, motioning for him to go on. "Then, in his last text, he said he had something major in the works, and he wanted to bring us in on the ground floor. That doesn't really line up with welcoming us into the existing fold at RVR, does it?"

I pressed my lips together. "Weird."

Jon took off his cowboy hat and combed his fingers through his sweat-damp hair. "I can't believe he's dead."

"You and me both," I murmured, mulling over what he'd just shared with me. I wasn't the only one Cal had left in the lurch.

Jon pointed to where the band was slipping into their positions at the instruments. "I should get back up there."

I nodded. "Do you have a card or something? I'd love to stay in touch, and if I hear anything about RVR, I'd be happy to pass it along." I hesitated, unsure whether I wanted to share more. I'd only just met Jon Campbell, but he screamed *trustworthy*, so I went for it. "I'm applying to be a staff writer at Red Vector, so I'll keep an ear out for you."

A huge smile brightened Jon's face, like a kid going to Disney World for the first time. "Really? That'd be incredible." He reached into his back pocket and retrieved his wallet. He slipped out a worn business card and handed it over to me. "All of my contact information is there."

I glanced down at it before looking up at him. "I'll text you my number. We should write together sometime, if you're interested."

If I got the job with Red Vector, my work would be done on staff, and the songs I helped pen would be used at their discretion. Again, a tiny twinge of something that felt like hesitation tickled the hair on my neck, but I ignored it. The stability of a staff writing position far outweighed the thrill of stumbling upon a writing partner or a breakout star who there was a small chance of making lyrical magic with.

That didn't mean I wasn't going to take every opportunity to bottle up some of that magic right now, though.

Jon nodded heartily. "I'd like that."

I grinned back. "I'll be in touch, and hey, if you think of anything else Cal told you before he died, can you let me know?"

"Sure thing."

"Thanks. Keep killin' it up there." I winked, cocking my head to the stage.

He grinned, dipping his cowboy hat. "Count on that. Pleasure to meet ya."

With a long stride, he leaped onto the stage and took his position behind the microphone.

When I made it back to our table, Emma wagged her brows at me. "Making a move on the lead singer, huh?"

I rolled my eyes. "I don't know what you're talking about. Here, drink your water."

"I know what I saw!" She got her lips around her straw and took a long sip.

We chatted for a while at our table, and then Emma said she was tired, so we left. Before I even made it out of Midtown, she was quietly passed out and snoring in the passenger seat.

I sighed, letting my head fall back against the headrest. The city lights streaked past my window like comets in the night sky as I merged onto the interstate and drove the rest of the way to the Village. My brain engaged in a tug-of-war with each of the day's major events.

Details of the conversation we'd had with Autumn blurred with images of her with Phil. The pleasant glow of Jace's new song was mired with the sounds of Pita and Penn. The detectives' warnings overlapped with the sound of the chants Whitney had started.

Then there was Jon Campbell. A nice guy. One of the good ones whom I'd like to see make it in this town. What had Cal been up to that he wanted to bring Jon and his brother in on? If I could figure that out, maybe that would lead me to the reason why someone wanted him dead.

I glanced in the rearview mirror as headlights lit up my car. The vehicle behind me was following too close for comfort. In the black of night, I couldn't see who was driving, but the feeling of being watched—of being followed—which I had let go of at Hot Diggity, returned now, sending a cold shiver trailing down my spine.

I gripped the steering wheel, focusing on the road ahead, even as the car behind me tailed me so close that I could no longer see its headlights. I had a mile to go until our exit, and my blood pressure was through the roof.

I went back and forth over whether to wake Emma as I white-knuckled it home. I didn't exhale until I was halfway down the exit ramp and the car sped onward down the highway.

I rolled my shoulders, my anxiety transforming into anger—first at the road rager, then at myself for being so rattled. I needed to get my head in the game. No one was following us. No one was out to get me. I was a competent, independent woman, and I had been for some time now.

The sooner I stopped jumping at shadows, the better.

I pulled into a parking spot a half block from Java Flo's and our apartment. I switched off the ignition. Emma was still zonked, and I sat for a second in the quiet car, letting the air conditioning fade away and giving my pulse a chance to settle down.

My phone buzzed, rattling around in the cup holder. I snatched it just as Emma bolted upright, swiveling her head from side to side. "Who is it? Who's there?"

"It's okay." I clicked open my phone. I had a message from Pita Paige that must've come in when we were dancing at the bar. I quickly deleted it. I should really just block her number, and Penn's, too, but for some reason, I couldn't bring myself to do that. Maybe I was a sucker for punishment.

My mood shifted from annoyance to a weird sort of giddiness, though, when I saw the name of the sender of the most recent message.

Jace James.

Jace: Leigh, I know it's been a while, and I'm not sure if you still have the same number as you did at school ... thought I'd try anyway. This is Jace James. Saw you at the concert tonight and saw what happened with Emma. Hope you guys are okay. Would love to grab coffee and catch up. Let me know if you're up for it.

"Why are you smiling like that?" Emma's voice amplified itself in the silent car.

I blinked and side-eyed her. "Like what?"

"Like you're in on a really good secret. Who's the message from?"

I clicked my phone off and tucked it into my purse. I'd respond later, when Emma wasn't analyzing my every move. "No one. Come on. Let's get inside and get to bed."

Emma harrumphed. "You *are* keeping secrets."

I kept my mouth shut as we walked across the street, around the back of Java Flo's, and up the stairs to our apartment. When I said goodnight to Emma and tucked myself in bed, I allowed myself a silent squeal of excitement.

Of all the things that happened today, Jace James wanting to have coffee with me—*me*—is what I decided to fall asleep thinking about.

17

Emma had off on Wednesday morning, so we decided to go visit the watchmakers on the list Madison at Red Vector had given me.

"First stop, coffee," Emma declared, slinging her bag over her shoulder as I locked the door to our apartment.

At the mention of "coffee," my heart gave a silly little lurch. I'd texted Jace back this morning, and we'd set a time to meet at a local café. I was trying to be cool about it, but to say I was looking forward to seeing him would have been an understatement.

Rationally, a relationship with Jace James would not be a good idea. I didn't even *want* a relationship. Really. But attention from him was nice, I had to admit. I would also like to get to the bottom of that song he played. Could it really have been for me?

These were the thoughts that tied up my brain as we traipsed down the stairs and snuck into Java Flo's through the kitchen entrance.

Dot was behind the stove. "You two look like you're up to no good," she said over the sound of sizzling bacon. I was glad to see she was wearing the soft knee brace I'd left on the counter for her the other day.

"You know us," I deadpanned, but then I cast a look around. "Maybe be careful not to say that too loudly, though."

I was only half kidding. Emma hadn't heard from Detective Yance or Detective Ottom since the concert, but it was only a matter of time. She was meeting with her lawyer later this afternoon to go over their game plan.

We said goodbye to Dot, pushing through the swinging door behind the counter.

Agnes was tending to her morning regulars as we assumed our spot in line. I recognized the mom with two kids I had seen earlier in the week. The older child was reading a book, and the younger one was coloring at a table in the corner while the mom typed on her cell phone. I spotted a few other people I knew, and the guy with the funny t-shirts was back again. Today, his tee said, "Who could ever learn to love a beast?" with a picture of a single rose lying horizontal beneath the words.

I smiled to myself at the reference, nudging Emma and nodding toward his table. "Do you know who that guy is?"

She turned and glanced in his direction before facing me again. "Never seen him before. Why?"

"No reason. He's been in here a couple of times. We should introduce ourselves at some point."

Emma arched her brow. "Are you *interested* in him?"

"What? No. Of course not. I'm trying to be neighborly."

Emma *tsked*, arching her sculpted eyebrows. "I don't know, Leigh. First Jace, then the lead singer at the bar last night, and now this guy. I sense a change coming over you. I'm here for it."

I rolled my eyes. I'd casually mentioned my plans to get coffee with Jace to Emma, which was a huge mistake. She wouldn't sleep until she'd analyzed the prospect of our meeting *ad nauseam*, and I knew that after our coffee date—if you could even call it a date—was over, she'd want a full report, every exchanged word and glance included.

I loved my best friend—I did. But she was a romantic, and I was not. I was also still trying to get used to people genuinely wanting what was good for me. My parents had not given me an example of that, but Emma always had my back. She wanted me to open my heart because she loved me and wanted me to be happy. I wasn't sure exactly how that would look yet.

"Whatever." I shoved her forward as Agnes stepped up to the register. "I'm just here for the coffee. Let's go."

"Morning, ladies. What can I make up for you?"

"Lavender latte for me with skim milk, please," Emma requested.

"I'm going to do the blueberry vanilla latte, iced," I added.

"You got it." Agnes punched in our order and then set to work making it. "Where are you two off to?"

"We're hunting down Cal's watch. He was having it fixed before he died, and my parents are desperate to get their hands on it ahead of his funeral." Emma started to roll her eyes but stopped herself, shaking her head instead. "I don't know if they plan to bury him with it, or what. Seems like a waste of a perfectly good heirloom if you ask me."

"Fair," I replied as Agnes nodded in agreement. "But as I've been thinking about it, I realized that this watchmaker, whoever he or she is, would have seen Cal in his final days. Maybe we can learn something that'll help us figure out what Cal was up to."

Agnes slid our drinks toward us, one at a time.

Emma raised her to-go cup to me. "Here's to hoping."

"Be careful, you two. I don't want to see you caught up in any funny business."

"Only serious business on tap for us, Agnes." Emma crossed her heart. "I promise."

Agnes rolled her eyes. "What am I going to do with you?"

I smirked. "We love you too!"

We thanked her and said goodbye just as a large group entered the coffee shop.

"Business is booming." Emma looked behind us as we crossed the street toward our car. "I hope I can be as successful as her someday."

"You will be."

Emma shot me a grateful look.

"Any more plans to move on that property?" I asked as I situated myself behind the wheel.

Emma opened the passenger door and slid inside. "My plans aren't the problem. I have lots of plans—big, grand plans. I need the money for a down payment, and I'm short. I've got to come up with an investor. Every day that passes is another day I'm afraid someone else is going to scoop up the building ahead of me."

I racked my brain for anyone I might know who would have the money to support Emma. Pita and Penn came to mind, but I swore long ago that I wouldn't trust them with anything like this. Not after they burned me. Besides, Cal didn't want his name overshadowing Emma's business venture, and he was onto something. Knowing Pita and Penn and their habit of making things all about them, Emma should steer clear.

Our conversation shifted to other topics as I drove us to the first watchmaker on our list. It turned out to be a wasted trip. He had never worked with Cal. We got the same response at our next two stops.

"This feels like a wild goose chase," Emma said with a sigh as we climbed back into my truck.

My jaw stiffened as I tried to tamp down my frustration. We only had one place left to check. If Cal didn't end up using any of the watchmakers on Madison's list, then what were we going to do?

Emma's knee bounced as I drove us to the final stop. About Time was housed in a quaint-looking building on the outskirts of the Village.

"Cal used to live down here, right? Maybe he picked this place because he felt like he could trust the locals," I suggested.

"We can only hope," Emma said dryly, slamming the truck door shut.

A brass bell rang as we entered the shop. The interior was dim, and the walls were lined with an assortment of different timepieces. There was a gentle ticking as each of the clocks kept time. The room smelled of wood polish. From a small workshop in the back half of the shop, a voice called out to us. "I'll be right with you. Just give me one moment."

"Thank you!" Emma called back. "This place is awesome," she said to me.

I agreed. I wandered over to a large grandfather clock that stood along the nearest wall. It was two feet taller than I was, with a majestic pendulum and Roman numerals on the clock face.

"Look at these!" Emma's squeal from across the room drew my attention. "Pocket watches."

I crossed over to her and studied them. "They look straight out of a storybook, don't they?"

"Is it weird that I want to date a guy who is dignified enough to carry a pocket watch? Wiltmore Bentley could *never*." Emma nudged me. "What do you think, could Jace pull it off?"

She was goading me, and I let her, mostly because this was the Emma I knew and loved—playful, fun-loving, and carefree. It was good to catch a glimpse of her old self again.

I shook my head, and before I could respond, a man with white, wispy hair, wearing magnifying spectacles, appeared from the workshop.

"So sorry to keep you two waiting." He lifted the glasses, pushing them onto his head. "I'm Lyle Sinclair, owner and operator of About Time. What can I help you with today?"

Emma stepped forward, a soft smile on her face. "My name is Emma Dutton."

I saw a light of recognition in the watchmaker's eyes when Emma said her last name. My hope soared, but I held my breath as she continued.

"I'm trying to track down a watch that belonged to my brother, Cal Dutton."

Here, Emma paused, but Lyle didn't say anything.

Emma glanced at me, and I gave her a slight nod.

"We were informed he brought his watch somewhere for repair," she continued. "We're not sure if he came here, but it would mean a lot to my parents if they could have the watch back." She clasped her hands together.

Lyle considered Emma carefully for an extended moment. "Well, now." He scratched his stubbly chin. "Are you hoping to wear the watch in question yourself, Ms. Dutton?"

Emma shook her head. "I don't want it to wear, sir. It's just that it's important to our family's history. It would have been passed down to Cal's son if he'd had one." Emma bit her lip and looked away.

I stepped forward, picking up the conversation. "Does this mean you have the watch?"

The watchmaker swung his gaze to me, pale blue eyes searching my face. "And you are?"

"Leigh Notrap. I'm a friend of Emma and Cal's. Here for moral support."

"I see. Well, you're in luck. At least, partially in luck. Come on back. Let me show you what I mean." Lyle turned and hobbled away.

Emma shot me a look with one eyebrow raised. I shrugged, but offered her a thumbs-up.

"Right over here." Lyle pointed to the far wall, where a long workbench was mounted. It was strewn with every gizmo and gadget imaginable—springs and chimes and watch faces.

He walked to one side of the workspace and stopped, motioning for Emma and me to join him.

"That's it!" Emma cried. "That's the family watch. Oh, thank you so much! I'm so glad you have it!" She reached for the timepiece, but the watchmaker shot out his hand, stopping her.

"Careful there," he cautioned. "I don't have this guy put back together quite yet."

"Oh." Emma frowned. "Was it badly damaged?"

Lyle tipped his head. "Not damaged, no. In fact, it was the strangest thing."

"What was?" I peered over Emma's shoulder to get a better look at the timepiece. It was lying face up with the band spread up and down like the north and south lines on a compass.

"Mr. Dutton didn't want me to fix his watch. He wanted me to ruin it."

Emma jerked back. "Ruin it? What do you mean?"

Lyle reached out and, with delicate care, turned the watch over.

I sucked in a breath. While the watch looked normal from the top looking down, the second he flipped it, I saw what he meant.

"Where are all the"—Emma searched for the right word—"innards?"

"Cal asked me to take them out."

"What?" I asked, bewildered. "Why?"

Lyle set the watch back down with a gentleness usually reserved for newborn babies before holding his arms out in an expression of utter confusion. "I have no idea. I tried asking him."

Emma was staring at the watch, but she turned to the watchmaker. "What did he say?"

"Just that he had something special he needed to put in there. You see, he wanted me to build him a secret compartment where the mechanisms of the watch once were. It would be like a tiny storage spot."

My breathing sped up. "Did he say what he wanted that for?"

Lyle shook his head. "Sorry. No. He didn't. I was supposed to have it done for him by early next week. I've been out of town and a bit off the grid, so I didn't catch wind of the news of Cal's death until yesterday." He looked between the two of us. "I should have said this already, but I'm so sorry for your loss. Both of you."

"Thank you," Emma murmured, though she sounded a thousand miles away. She shook her head. "Sorry. You'll have to forgive me. I am just so stunned that Cal would intentionally ruin a family heirloom. What was his endgame?"

I wasn't sure how to answer Emma's question, but this felt significant. Turning to the watchmaker, I forced a smile. "Can you tell us how Cal acted when he was here? Did he seem anxious or excited or anything out of the ordinary?"

"Well, now, I don't know what Cal's 'ordinary' behavior was like." The watchmaker looked up to the ceiling as if trying to conjure up the memory of Cal's time in the shop. "He was on his phone with someone when he arrived."

"When exactly was that?"

"It would have been early last week. I could check my books for you if the exact date matters that much."

"No. Thank you, though." I smiled. "We're just trying to get a full picture of Cal's last few days." I side-eyed Emma, and then I lied. "To give us a little closure."

Lyle seemed to buy that, and I was grateful he was willing to answer our questions.

"Yes, of course. Let me see. I don't know who he was talking to, but I remember he said, 'You let me deal with them. They won't even see me coming.' Then he hung up, and we got right down to business. I don't make it a point of prying into the lives of my customers, especially not the famous ones. Best to leave them to their messes, I always say." He gave a soft chuckle, but then, as if sensing that was maybe not so tactful, he cleared his throat. "Anyway. Cal told me what he wanted. I tried to talk him out of destroying such a stunning timepiece, but he was adamant. He said what he was going to put in here would change the course of the rest of his life."

"Cal said that?" Emma's eyes widened, and she looked at me.

Lyle nodded. "I'm quite sure. I don't think I would have been able to come up with something that dramatic if it were up to me."

I chewed on the watchmaker's words. Something big was going down in Cal's life leading up to his death. What that was, at this point, was anyone's guess, but there was a solid chance it played a role in his poisoning.

"Mr. Sinclair, you said you just got back into town. I don't know if you know, but Cal's death is being investigated as a homicide. I think it would be wise if you told the detectives assigned to his case this information. It might help them in some way."

It was the watchmaker's turn to look surprised. "You think his watch had something to do with his death."

"Not necessarily, but you saw him in the last week of his life, and what you just told us might shed some light on his final affairs."

Lyle mulled that over. "I suppose you're right. What should I do, just call them up and say I have information for them?"

Emma smiled kindly. "I have the detectives' contact information. I'll write down their number for you." She glanced at the watch. "Do you think you'll have it put back together in time for Cal's funeral?"

Lyla nodded. "Now that I don't have to build out a compartment, it shouldn't take me too long at all. I was going to make it thicker to match the specifications Cal had given me. The watch's head would have sat a few centimeters off the wrist—not at all how it should have fit." The watchmaker frowned. "But Cal insisted, and now, I suppose, it doesn't matter. I'll get it reassembled for you."

"Thank you." Emma breathed a sigh of relief before adding, "Of course, we'll pay you for your work."

They worked out a time for pick up, and we said our goodbyes, exchanging the dim light of the watchmaker's shop for the bright midday sun.

As we made our way back to my car, I turned to Emma. "Are you thinking what I'm thinking?"

Emma nodded. “What was so important for Cal to hide that he was willing to destroy our grandfather’s watch to keep it on his person at all times?”

18

After an uneventful Wednesday afternoon, I got up on Thursday and booked it downtown. I was meeting a couple songwriters I'd met at a writer's night for a songwriting session. Fortunately, I was able to put the questions about Cal's motives out of my mind long enough to have a productive few hours. We strung together a complete song that had me grinning as I made the drive back home. It didn't hurt that the radio was blaring a song by an up-and-coming star. I had written a song with her that I prayed had the potential to make her debut album and maybe even make it to the radio.

The air in my truck hung heavy with potential. Deciding to keep my creative juices flowing, I bypassed the exit to the Village and went one farther, steering toward Hooks High. I had my swim bag in the back, and doing some laps sounded like exactly what I needed. Besides, after tamping thoughts of Cal down for the better part of the afternoon, my brain was now full to the brim, and I needed to try to blow off some steam so I could piece things out.

I made quick work of changing into my suit and dropped into one end of the pool. I kicked off the wall and found my stroke, slowing my breath to match it and willing my mind to quiet itself enough that I could sort through what I knew and what I needed to figure out.

I had so many questions. Not a bad thing. Quite the contrary. Questions made me a good songwriter. I asked questions and answered them with lyrics that resonated with listeners. No, I wasn't bothered by questions—but I also liked having answers, and right now, I had no idea what headspace Cal was in the week he died.

What was he working on? What was he hiding? Who had he made his enemy?

I chronicled the suspects.

Quentin at Red Vector. He was shady, and the epitome of a red flag.

Whitney, the super fan. She was all too quick to point the finger at Emma, and I'd seen her sneaking around the Banta Bowl the night of Cal's death.

Autumn, too, seemed to be hiding something ... or at least not showing all her cards.

I kicked off the wall on the far side of the pool and popped back up to the surface. I still had no idea what Willie Davis was fighting with Cal about just before he took that fateful sip of tea.

Speaking of the tea, if the belladonna tincture in Cal's possession wasn't used to poison him, then what was?

I hoisted myself out of the pool thirty minutes later, sending a trickle of water cascading off my body and tinkling to the tile pool surround, no closer to an answer for any of the questions plaguing me. Taking a deep breath of the heavy, chlorine-soaked air, I concluded that I needed more information.

Quentin—though the thought pained me—was low-hanging fruit. Something was up at Red Vector. My conversation with Jon Campbell solidified it, and if I could use the guise of my job hunt to gain some intel, then that's what I would do.

I'd sent in my application and had received a canned email thanking me for applying and inviting me to a Red Vector mixer ahead of the Country Music Festival. Going to the mixer was the very last thing I wanted to do. But I needed to be a gamer. A joiner.

If I was going to prove that I truly wanted this job and had what it took to make it in the industry, I had to show my face.

Network.

Mingle.

As much as I hated it, it came with the territory.

Maybe it could also shed some light on the case.

I took a quick shower and slipped into a cotton sundress before flipping my head upside down under the electric hand dryer and letting it do a number on my short hair. My mother would die if she saw me styling my hair like this. So uncouth. So grimy! That thought—coupled with the knowledge that I had a game plan to find out more about who wanted Cal dead—put a spring in my step as I tidied up the locker room and headed out to the high school parking lot.

Summer nights were one of my very favorite times of year. The school sat silent, smelling faintly of cleaning solution and used-up pencil lead. Soon, these halls would be full again, but for now, they were just a shell, holding memories from the past and hopes for the future.

There was a song there.

I jogged across the parking lot, whipping out my cell phone and pulling up my notes app. I frantically typed away the lyrics that seemed to pour out of me, just as the water had poured off my body. Effortless—with nowhere else to go but on the page.

Untitled by Leigh Notrap

If these halls could talk
They'd tell a story
Of days gone by
And hometown glory
Of a letter jacket-wearing

Homecoming queen
And the boy she loved at
Seventeen.
But that boy was fleeting
And her dreams were true
So she left town
Said goodbye to everyone she knew
Set out on her own
To Nashburg, Tennessee
And now she sings 'bout the days
Of her and me.
In high school
Yeah, in high school

They tell you when you're in it
It goes too fast
So soak it all up
Try to make them feelings last
'Cause one day when it's over
And she's long gone
All that's left'll be you
And the words of a song
About high school
Yeah, high school.

It's hard to believe
My best days are behind
Me, and my girl
Is no longer mine
'Cuz this ain't high school
Ain't high school.

19

I sat back in the driver's seat of my truck after a frantic fifteen minutes of typing and read through the lyrics. I couldn't have stopped the smile that spread across my face if I wanted to. This song was good. It had legs—and I couldn't wait to see where it would run.

I blinked a couple of times, bringing my senses into sharper focus. When I was songwriting, especially when I was at it alone, everything around me faded to a muted haze. Now, I realized I'd left the truck door open, and my window was still rolled down.

I peered around the parking lot. It was empty but for my truck and a beat-up blue car parked off to one side. With the way the sun hit the windshield, I couldn't tell if the other vehicle was occupied or not.

I reached out and yanked the truck door shut, putting my key in the ignition. I'd lingered long enough. I cranked up the music on the radio and headed for home. It wasn't until I merged onto the highway in the direction of the Village that I spotted it. The same blue car from the high school parking lot was behind me.

I peered in my rearview mirror, trying to make certain I wasn't imagining things. I changed lanes, and two seconds later, so did the blue car. I set my cruise control for five miles per hour slower, waiting to see if whoever was driving would go past, but they didn't.

I bit my cheek. Who would want to follow me? And why? More importantly, what in the world was I supposed to do? I didn't want to lead them directly back to the Village and my apartment, even though every fiber in my body cried out to get to my home turf and the safety it provided.

I wrestled those emotions into check and forced myself to think.

I changed lanes again, this time speeding up. The blue car followed right on my heels.

I made up my mind, then, and drove directly to police headquarters. I'd seen that once in a TV show, or read it in a book, or something. I figured whoever was tailing me wouldn't want to be noticed by the swarm of law enforcement present at the nearest precinct.

Sure enough, when I put my turn signal on to enter the parking lot at the facility where Detectives Ottom and Yance had interviewed Emma, the blue car blew by me. I couldn't make out much about the driver. They had a baseball cap on and the brim pulled low over their face, and they were intentionally angling their body away from me.

"Take that, whoever you are," I said out loud to my lit-up dashboard.

I parked in the back of the police lot and blew out a breath, debating whether to go inside and report what had just happened. But what would I say? It hardly seemed significant enough to warrant a report.

Instead, I texted Emma.

Leigh: You at home?

Her response came immediately.

Emma: Downstairs with Agnes. Where are you?

Leigh: At police headquarters. I was being followed. Long story. I'm fine and heading your way now.

Emma: ??? Need anything? Are you safe?

Leigh: Just watch for me. Be there in fifteen.

I stowed my phone, checked my surroundings to ensure the blue car hadn't circled back, and then headed for the Village.

Of course, by the time I got there, Crowbar Road was packed with parked cars and pedestrians. Not for the first time did I wish Java Flo's had a parking lot so we weren't at the mercy of street parking. Still, the tension that made my back ache eased. I was among friends. Even if I had to walk a couple blocks home, it wasn't like I would be alone.

I snagged a spot near one of the bars on the corner and locked my truck. Tucking my purse into the crook of my arm, I strolled toward Java Flo's. Laughter and music chorused around me, but the skin on the back of my neck prickled.

Someone was watching me. I dug out my phone to call Emma, but first went into my camera app. I flipped the screen so it was facing me and discreetly held it up. I saw him a half block back. A lanky man in a baseball hat. That was my guy.

Well, not *my* guy, but the guy I'm pretty sure had been driving the blue car.

I swallowed down a surge of panic at his knowing where I'd be and picked up my pace. I dodged around a couple of groups out on the town, all but forgetting about my idea to call Emma. I kept my phone out and camera open so I could keep an eye on the man.

He was keeping pace with me, but he made no move to overtake or approach me. It was like he was just watching me.

All at once, my fear turned to anger. How *dare* this person make me feel unsafe, especially here in the Village. If he thought I would cower, he picked the wrong girl. I didn't make it on my own for the past however many years by being scared. No, now I was determined to figure out who he was and what he was doing.

I darted into Java Flo's at almost a complete sprint.

"Leigh. Thank goodness." Emma stood from where she sat at a table near the door, but I didn't bother to stop. I blew by her and headed for the kitchen.

"Hi, Dot!" I held up my hand in a wave as I jogged toward the rear entrance. Pushing open the back door, I slowed my pace enough to hide my panting as I crept around the side of the building. Sure enough, the man had stopped in front of Java Flo's and was peering in the large plate glass windows.

I stepped back out onto the sidewalk, my sidewalk, and put my hands on my hips.

"What do you think you're doing?" The man faced me, and my eyes nearly popped out of their sockets. "*You!*"

20

I hadn't expected to recognize the person tailing me, but if the round glasses peeking out from under the baseball hat hadn't given him away, then the *Alexander Hamilton for President* phrase on the t-shirt under his jacket sold him out.

I narrowed my gaze at the t-shirt-clad man I'd seen at Java Flo's the past week or so. "Who are you? Why are you following me?"

Emma burst through the front door of the coffee shop, her cell phone in hand. "Leigh, what's going on? Are you alright? Should I call the police?"

She looked between me and the t-shirt man.

"No! Not the police." He held up his hands and took a step back. "I mean no harm."

"Then don't you dare bolt on me." I snaked out an arm and grabbed his wrist.

"Look, I come in peace. I can explain." He used the hand I didn't have a death grip on to shove his glasses up his nose before removing his baseball hat. "Please. Can we talk?"

I glanced over at Emma. She shrugged. "Your call."

I stared down the mysterious man before jutting my chin toward Java Flo's. "In here."

Emma went inside first, and I shoved the t-shirt guy in front of me, letting go of his wrist so he could walk ahead but pulling in a firm grip of cotton at the small of his back. No way was I taking a chance on him darting off.

The dining room at Java Flo's was almost completely full with the dinner rush. The man I was clinging to stiffened, his muscles bunching up beneath his shirt enough that I could feel them shift under my knuckles.

He craned his neck. "Can we go someplace more private?" he murmured over his shoulder.

While I appreciated the strength in numbers that the regulars at Java Flo's provided, I nodded and pointed him in the direction of the kitchen.

Catching Agnes's wide eyes behind the counter, I shot her a grim smile. "Can we use your table back there?"

Emma caught my drift and didn't wait for a response from Agnes before pushing open the swinging door and entering the kitchen work space. The man and I followed close behind.

"What's your name?" I asked as soon as the door flung shut on Agnes's pinched brows. I was tired of thinking of him as *the t-shirt man*.

"If I tell you, I'll have to kill you."

I tightened my grip on his shirt, and Emma reached for the utensil block, retrieving a large butcher's knife. She held it out in front of her like a lightsaber. "Try me."

Gosh, I loved her and her dramatics. The guy who was following me shot me a look that said, *Is she for real?* I just arched a brow. Let him wonder.

"That was a joke." He flicked his gaze between Emma and me. "Like I said, I ... I come in peace. The three of us could be mutually beneficial to each other, that's all."

"Still haven't heard your name." I tapped my foot.

The guy glanced around the kitchen. Dot was peering at us from behind the cooktop. I caught her quizzical glance and gave her a slight shake of my head. She went back to preparing food with a roll of her shoulders.

"Look, can we sit down?" Whoever this guy was, he seemed to be in it for the long haul.

I kicked out a chair, and he readily dropped into it. I felt a little better about letting him out of my clutches since he obviously wasn't trying to flee.

Emma took the chair opposite his, and I pulled up the stool Agnes had used the other day.

"Talk," I said.

He looked at me for the first time—head on. It was only then that I realized his thick-rimmed glasses hid the most piercing blue eyes I'd ever seen. Turquoise, if I had to be more specific. Those were the kind of eyes a girl could write a song about.

Not the time to wax poetic, Leigh.

The man sighed and slumped in his seat. "First of all, I'm sorry if I scared you."

I crossed my arms, but stayed silent. The last thing I wanted to do was show weakness or fear.

"It's just that you're my best intelligence source," he added.

Emma snorted, and I let out a slight gasp despite myself. "What's that supposed to mean?"

"In regard to Cal Dutton's murder. The action surrounding the case seems to follow you. Both of you." He glanced between Emma and me. "Intel is very important to a guy like me."

"What kind of guy are you?" I asked at the same time Emma threw her hands up and said, "What are you talking about?"

The man blew out a breath. "I'm about to tell you who I am and what I do, but I need to swear you to secrecy. If my identity got out, I—" He rubbed the back of his neck. "Let's just say, it wouldn't be good."

A pang of sympathy arced from the center of my chest. I could relate.

"I can keep a secret," I said, and Emma nodded.

The guy pinned me in place with his blue eyes. "My name is Bobby Cruz. I'm the guy behind the Printer's Alley Press."

If there were sound effects in real life, this would be the place for a record scratch.

Emma's jaw came unhinged. Mine did the same, but I quickly snapped it shut. Had we just stumbled upon the truth behind the biggest secret in Nashburg? Had the biggest secret in Nashburg been *stalking* me?

"Prove it," I said, not willing to be played a fool.

Bobby seemed to be expecting my demand. He pulled out his phone, tapped around, and spun the screen to face me. "Here's the back-end app interphase." He scrolled. "This is the draft of an article I'm working on about the menu change at Luke Bryan's restaurant."

Emma leaned in, taking a good look at the screen. She shot me a sidelong glance. "Seems legit." She rounded on Bobby, a renewed fire in her gaze. "Which means I have you to blame for ruining my reputation when you posted that video of my fight with Cal."

Bobby had the self-awareness to look repentant. "Guilty as charged."

Emma shoved her chair back from the table and stood as if she was going to lay into him, but instead, she started pacing, working out her pent-up energy. "I should wring your neck, you know that? I could be completely discredited, and all because of you! You ... you ... *blowhard*." She spun around and pointed at him. "Where'd you get the video?"

"I'd like to know that too," I piped up. "Do you have a source within the police department feeding you tips? Or is it the other way around? Are you the one providing information to the detectives?"

"I shared the video with the police. Or I should say, videos. I'm on the cusp of figuring out where they originated from." Bobby checked himself, and his blue eyes hardened. He leaned back in his chair, looking like a man who knew he had our attention. "Before I tell you anything else, I want to make a deal."

Bobby Cruz knew how to pique a girl's interest, that was for sure, but I was instantly on guard. My distrust for people I didn't know—heck, even people I *did* know—ran deep.

"What sort of deal?" I didn't bother hiding my skepticism.

"We share our information. All our information. We want the same thing here. You want justice for Cal and to clear your name," he added, looking to Emma. She nodded. "I want that, too. I also want to prove myself as a legitimate journalist."

I mulled over his proposition. Next to me, Emma opened her mouth as if ready to give a response, but I cut her off. "Can you give us a moment?" I asked Bobby.

"Sure." He shrugged. "I've got nowhere else to be."

"Good. Don't move. Dot"—I stood and pivoted to face the chef—"if he tries anything, throw the spatula at him, will ya?"

"You got it!" Dot waved her utensil of choice in the air.

Bobby chuckled as I pulled Emma back through the swinging doors and into the cramped space behind the register. Agnes was still taking orders, but I could tell she was craning her ear to try to hear our hushed conversation.

"What are you thinking?" I asked Emma.

Emma laced her fingers behind her head. "I mean, if he is who he says he is, I'm floored. Still don't think we should work with him, though."

"What's your reasoning?"

"Leigh, come on! You honestly think we should join forces with the modern-day equivalent of Lady Whistledown?" She hissed her last words as if embarrassed to say the name of the mysterious reporter from the *Bridgerton* romance novels.

"Hey, I love Lady Whistledown. Girl's got chops."

"Focus, Leigh. This guy sold me out. He was following you! How can I—how can *we*—know for sure he's not using us for our information only to paint us in a bad light and get more clicks on his little app?"

I shifted my jaw. We couldn't know that. Not with any degree of certainty, anyway. But I had a gut instinct about Bobby.

"It might be our only chance to get to the bottom of Cal's murder," I argued. "I didn't tell you at the memorial concert because

I didn't want to freak you out, but I ran into the detectives. They were asking about you."

Emma's skin went a shade shy of gray, and she grabbed my arm as if she needed to anchor herself. "Are you serious?"

"I wouldn't joke about something like that, Em."

"I know. I know you wouldn't. Gosh! I hate this." Emma's voice rose to a near shriek, drawing attention. The locals in the Village knew her and had her back, but there was still no use making a scene.

Agnes shot me a you-need-to-handle-this look.

"Em, listen to me." I tried to steer her away from the register, but she was flailing her limbs, and I didn't want to get caught in the crossfire. "It's gonna be okay."

"That guy has built his livelihood on keeping his real self a secret. How are we supposed to trust him?"

"How do you trust me?" I countered, my voice quiet.

Emma stilled, and her stern expression softened. "That's completely different."

"Is it? I can't explain it, but I feel like Bobby deserves the benefit of the doubt. I know how it feels to try to prove yourself. I think you do too."

Emma was quiet for a beat. She tugged her bottom lip between her teeth. "Fine," she said, letting out a huff. "If this goes sideways, it's on you."

I nodded. "I can live with that."

We ducked back into the kitchen. Dot gave us a quick wave, and I let out a breath when Bobby still sat with his back to the door, right where we left him.

"I knew you had a thing for the guy," Emma muttered into my ear. "It was the Pemberley t-shirt, wasn't it?"

"Not. Funny." I shoved her in his direction, willing the flush creeping into my cheeks to recede.

We had a journalist to interrogate and a murder to solve.

21

"Dot, can we get three platters of pancakes?" I sank into the chair across from Bobby and shrugged at his raised eyebrow. "It's a comfort food. We all could use that right now, don't you think?"

Bobby sized me up as Dot called out, "Coming right up!"

"So, we're doing this?" he asked.

I opened my mouth to respond in the affirmative, but Emma cut me off. "On one condition."

Bobby narrowed his gaze. "What's that?"

"You agree not to post anything else that'll incriminate me." Emma stared him down, and Bobby stared right back, neither of them blinking.

"How can I be sure you didn't do it?"

I scoffed at that. "You wouldn't be sitting here trying to make this deal if you thought Emma had anything to do with Cal's death. You think it's something bigger. Something more newsworthy than a sibling squabble."

Bobby swung his gaze to me. "You've got me there."

"Good. Then we have a deal." I sat back as Emma leaned forward.

She clasped her hands on the table and cut right to the chase. "What do you know?"

Bobby glanced over his shoulder before leaning in. "I got a tip about a music industry shake-up, and I have reason to believe it came from Cal."

I rested my elbows on the table. "What sort of shake-up?"

Bobby shook his head. "Don't know for sure. The tip came from someone claiming to be a big name. This person wanted to meet with me to give me information on"—he pulled up his phone and read straight from the screen—"corruption and shoddy business practices at one of country music's biggest labels."

"What makes you think it was Cal?" I asked. My mind buzzed over the possibility. It fit with the other bits and pieces of information I had at my disposal. If Cal uncovered something going on at Red Vector, of course he'd steer me away from them.

"The person who sent me the tip wanted to meet here, in the Village, at Java Flo's, for one thing. That's why I've been hanging around here more often."

"So we've noticed," Emma said dryly. "Some of us more than others," she added under her breath.

I shot her a *behave* look before turning my attention back to Bobby.

"How'd you make the jump, though?" I asked. "It's not like Cal is the only artist with ties to the Village."

Bobby tipped his head. "That's true, but I did my homework. When I found out that his sister and one of his co-writers lived above this fine establishment, it seemed like too much of a coincidence. When he turned up dead the day before I was supposed to meet with my anonymous source, my suspicions only grew."

Agnes bustled into the kitchen, her beaded necklace and the crucifix dangling from her neck banging against her chest in a familiar and comforting sound, like the cubes that swirl around when you mix iced coffee. She stared us down, nose scrunched up. "Do I even want to know what y'all are up to? Bobby, are these girls behaving?"

My jaw may as well have taken up permanent residence on the floor for all the time it was spending down there. "Agnes, you *know* him?"

"'Course I do. I know everyone around here. Now, I'm not even going to ask. If y'all need anything, you know where to find me."

She disappeared into the café before any of us could respond. Dot sauntered over with three platters of pancakes stacked up her arm. She deposited them on the table, and we all tucked in. I let the soothing taste of buttermilk soak my tongue and calm my frazzled nerves.

"Well, then," Emma said after we ate in silence for several minutes. "Where were we?"

"I think Cal was going to tell me about something shady happening within Red Vector. Now that he's gone, I'm hoping you two can help me bring it to light. My hypothesis is that whatever he had to say—whatever story he wanted me to break—it got him killed."

Emma and I exchanged a glance, and when neither of us responded right away, Bobby set his fork down with a clatter. "This is a two-way street. Your turn. Tell me what you know. I'm mostly curious about why you were on a tour of watch shops.

Emma explained our mission, and Bobby let out an impressed whistle when she finished.

"You don't have any idea what he might have wanted to hide in the watch?" he asked.

"If I had to guess, it was some type of incriminating evidence that he'd collected on Red Vector. Everything points to that, doesn't it?" I said.

Bobby nodded. "But what exactly *is* it that's going on there?"

"I wish I knew." I dragged my last bite of pancake around in pure maple syrup before popping it in my mouth. "I don't get a great vibe from my A&R contact, but Zac Geffadab, the RVR president, has been all chummy with me, so I don't really know. I'm planning to attend a mixer there tomorrow."

"We could go together."

Bobby said it so casually, I had to replay his statement. When I did, I scrambled to find a kind way to let him down. He didn't strike me as the type to invite himself on a date, but then again,

I'd only known him for an hour, and the first half of that, he'd been following me like a creepy stalker man, so...

"Sorry. My invite didn't come with a plus one."

"Oh no, that's not what I meant." His cheeks flushed pink. "It's just, I was invited, too."

"You? How? Why?" Emma abandoned all Southern manners.

Bobby shifted his position in his chair. "They've bought a couple of my songs."

There went my jaw again. "*You* write music?"

"I dabble."

"Unbelievable," Emma scoffed, crossing her arms and leaning back in her chair. "I swear, *everyone* in this town writes music."

I waved her off. "You say that like it's a bad thing." Turning my focus back to Bobby, I added, "Anything I've heard of?"

Bobby rattled off three titles, and I was impressed. "Those are great."

He dipped his chin. "Thanks. I write under a pen name. Bo Finlay. Best to keep my multiple personalities separate, I've found."

"Some people call that a disorder," Emma chimed in.

"Em!" I scolded.

"What! I'm just sayin'."

I shook my head. "Excuse her. We're a little on edge."

"Don't blame you, but I make no apologies. My songwriting royalties helped get the PAP off the ground before ad income took over." Bobby shrugged and turned to me. "I think we could do some reconnaissance at Red Vector. What do you say?" His face held such a boyish expression of enthusiasm that I found myself smiling without really thinking about it. I would feel better going into the Red Vector event with an ally too.

"I say let's do it."

Bobby and I exchanged contact information, and he stood to leave. "I can pick you up here at, say, eight-ish?"

I checked my watch. "That'll work. We can tell everyone we met at a writer's night in town."

"Good plan. I'll see ya later."

He waved to Dot and disappeared through the kitchen door and back into the café proper.

Feeling Emma's stare heavy on the side of my face, I gulped down a drink of water before turning to her. "That was something, wasn't it?"

"You like him." She smirked.

I let my head fall back. "Emma. Why? *Why* do you think I'm carrying a torch for every man I encounter?"

"I do not. I didn't see any sparks between you and Lyle."

An image of the ancient watchmaker with his wispy white hair flashed before my eyes, and I laughed. "Good one. For real, though, give me a break. I have no feelings one way or another for Bobby Cruz other than relief in knowing he isn't some hired hit man sent to take me out."

"Fine." Emma held up her hands. "I'm glad about that, too. Promise you guys won't ditch me?"

"What do you mean?"

"You two are going to be out there doing all the leg work, and I'll be back here, wallowing and wondering if and when my entire life and career is going to be flushed the rest of the way down the toilet."

"Nothing like that's going to happen," I said firmly, sending up a silent prayer at the same time. "We won't let it. It's a good thing we have Bobby on our team now, right? The more information we can gather, the better."

Emma nodded. "I guess he showed his loyalty by not releasing the audio to the argument video. He obviously sent it to the police if they know about us investigating. But the public doesn't know, and for that I'm grateful."

I'd been thinking the same thing. "Bobby's actions weren't malicious. We can hardly blame him for following the story."

"True. Can you believe we now know the man behind the PAP?" Emma's face took on an expression of wonder. "I feel like I've peaked."

"I know," I said, letting the shock of the revelation tinge my voice with awe. "He's not at all what I expected. Much more down to earth."

"If by down to earth you mean nerdy, then yes."

I didn't respond. Bobby did look a little—okay, a *lot*—nerdy. I was slightly anxious about what sort of impression he'd make around the Red Vector bigwigs and all the talent that was bound to be in the room tonight.

Apprehension crawled over my skin like a racing centipede. The last thing I wanted was for him to embarrass me, even if by association.

Stop it, Leigh.

I shoved that idea away and mentally stomped on the centipede with my shoe. Those were the pretentious thoughts of my upbringing rearing their ugly heads. There was no place for them, here or now. I wasn't that person, and Bobby didn't deserve my snap judgments. After all, he'd sold stuff to Red Vector and other labels—good stuff. He deserved to be in the room as much, or more than, anyone. As much as me.

Beyond that, the man had built up a media empire. He was obviously good at his job. I'd made the decision to trust him, and there was no backing out now.

What remained to be seen was how well we worked together.

22

The dining room at Java Flo's was half full when I came downstairs at ten minutes to eight Friday night. Emma was at work, so I briefed Agnes on the game plan for the evening: learn as much as I could about Red Vector by observing those in charge and mingling with the underlings.

"You look fab, darlin'. Just be safe. I'm glad you'll be with Bobby." She wished me a hurried good luck, turning to wait on her next customer, and I took a seat at a table by the door to wait.

I studied my reflection in the plate glass window. I'd opted for my favorite little black dress. I only broke it out for the most special of occasions, and tonight qualified. It fit me perfectly, hugging my curves enough to make me feel confident, but not enough that I couldn't breathe. It was sleeveless and hit at mid-thigh, but the skin I revealed was countered by a high neckline that wrapped around and fell in two panels down my back. I paired it with platform heels that made my legs look great. My pink rose-colored lipstick wasn't as bold as a classic red, but it did the job.

Bobby arrived right on time, and if I hadn't been expecting him, I might not have known it was him. It was like he was Taylor Swift at the end of the "You Belong With Me" music video. Gone was the geeky guy with the t-shirts. Walking toward me was a suave and put-together man. He had slicked back his unruly hair into a fashionable mess and ditched his glasses. He wore a fitted button-down, rolled at the elbow to reveal tanned forearms. His dark wash jeans were a breath away from being too tight, and a broken-in pair of cowboy boots completed his look.

"You look—" I was at a loss. Because Bobby looked good ... handsome, even. But I found myself missing his more relaxed style in an odd sort of way.

He smiled at me, motioning to my attire. "Right back atcha."

I ducked my chin in appreciation, praying my cheeks didn't match my lipstick.

Bobby hooked his thumb toward the door, breaking what could have become an awkward stretch of silence. "You ready?"

"Let's do this."

I waved to Agnes and stepped into the warm night air, pausing on the sidewalk so Bobby could lead the way to his car. He expertly navigated the Village parking situation and the crowds forming on Crowbar Road, making me wonder if he'd been around these parts for longer than he let on.

"I never asked you where you lived," I began, watching the quaint Village streets pass by as Bobby angled toward the interstate.

"Germantown," he supplied, but then, as if understanding what I left unsaid, he added, "I spent a lot of time in the Village as a kid."

"I love this area."

"Small-town vibes with all the perks of the big city."

"Exactly."

He drove on. My mind whirred, and my stomach was filled with what felt like one part excitement and two parts dread. Events like this were part of the job. I'd been attending them since arriving in Nashburg in order to get my name out and prove my worth and credibility as a songwriter. I couldn't help but wonder when I'd stop worrying about someone figuring out who I really was.

"So you're gunning to be a staff writer for Red Vector, huh?" Bobby glanced at me out of his peripheral.

I nodded, grateful to have something to think about that wasn't my past life. "That's the plan. Though Cal told them I wasn't right for the job before he died." I explained the final exchange I'd had with Cal, remorse making my throat feel tight.

Bobby worked his jaw. "It tracks with what we know. Or at least what we think."

"I know."

"You're still going to apply?" he asked.

I shrugged. "At this point, I'm just using it as a chance to gather information. But also, it'd be a really good gig. Being able to ditch my day job. Day jobs," I amended, "and focus on doing what I love? I'd be stupid not to go for it."

"I get it." Bobby shot me a look. "Job security in a town that doesn't owe you anything is a big deal."

"That's exactly how I feel."

"Let's figure out what's really going on before you sign your life away, though."

I blew out a breath. "Right. That. They haven't even scheduled an interview, so it's not a given." My stomach tumbled with unease. I changed the subject. "You said you're close to figuring out who was leaking the footage from Cal's apartment."

"Yeah. I'm working on a couple of angles. I have a hunch, but I don't want to throw anyone under the bus until I'm sure."

I frowned. "What happened to telling each other everything?"

Bobby's face was all shadows. "I *will* tell you ... when I have something concrete."

"How are you going about that?"

"I have a skill set that comes in handy when I need to uncover incriminating information in a technological setting."

I stared at him. "Bobby Cruz, are you telling me you're a hacker?" I couldn't mask a hint of amusement in my voice.

He shifted, gripping the wheel and then releasing it. "I wouldn't go so far as to say ... well, yeah. I guess in this case, yes."

It shouldn't have surprised me. He had the skills to build up the entire PAP app. Of course he could figure out the backend channels of who was sending him contraband videos.

"I don't want you to get the wrong idea," he said. "I respect the privacy of all those who reach out to the PAP through my anonymous tip line, but this was a case of extenuating circumstances."

I nodded. "If you can figure out who's throwing shade at Emma, maybe it'll lead to the actual killer."

"That was my line of thinking. My hands aren't tied with as many rules and regulations as the police, so I figured I'd make a go of it."

"Do the police know you're looking into it?"

"Not exactly."

I pictured Detective Ottom and Detective Yance. There was no way they'd be happy about Bobby's involvement.

"The police don't know who I am. Remember? Nobody knows I'm behind the app." Bobby's voice came out pleading.

"I know. I know." I glanced at him. He was messing with his hair, nerves on full display. "Your secret is safe with me, I promise."

His shoulders relaxed, and he dropped his hand. "I'll let them know if I figure anything out. I'm sure they're working on it, too, but I have the source material they don't have."

"And no red tape to cut through."

Bobby inclined his head.

"Wait, but if you can work backward and figure out who sent you the video, can't you do the same thing and figure out if it was Cal who sent you the message about the music city shake-up?"

He snorted. "Give me a little credit."

"Let me guess. You tried and failed? Some hacker," I teased.

He flattened his mouth and rolled his eyes. "I traced the message back to an IP address at the Nashburg Public Library."

I sighed. "So a dead end."

"If we get desperate, we could go to the police and see if they could get a warrant for video footage on the day I got the tip, but there's no way any judge would go for that on such shaky grounds."

I nodded. "For now, we'll do some digging on our own. How are we going to play this?"

Bobby took the exit and headed toward The Lounge, the swanky bar and restaurant where the Red Vector mixer was set to take place.

"We listen. Observe. Act natural. And ask questions that won't raise any suspicion."

I let out a nervous laugh. "It's like you've done this before."

He shot me an unreadable look as he hunted for a parking spot.

Right. He was an undercover journalist. He probably *had* done this before.

Journalist. Songwriter. Hacker for hire. What couldn't he do? More importantly, *who* was he, really?

"What am I supposed to call you, by the way? Bobby? Bo?"

"I'm Bo to these people, so we should stick with that." He executed an impressive parallel park job, and all too soon, we were walking toward The Lounge.

"Here goes nothing." Bobby held the door open for me to go in ahead of him.

The air of uncertainty swirling around Red Vector and the fallout of Cal's death had me on edge, but I shot him a strained smile before schooling my features. I had been trained to look this part, and as much as I hated it, I could still seamlessly blend in with the Nashburg elite.

A quick scan of The Lounge proved that things tonight were going to run exactly as I expected. Red Vector had spared no expense. The venue was swathed in rich red fabrics. Everything from the walls to the tables was covered in it. Shiny faux albums were hanging in shadow boxes on one wall, and hopeful singers and songwriters alike flitted all around. The room reeked of men's cologne and money.

Bobby came to stand next to me. "Something to drink?"

"Definitely."

We shifted toward one of the servers who was circling with a platter full of champagne flutes.

"What are we celebrating?" I murmured under my breath before taking a slightly oversized swig. I expected expensive booze, but what I tasted was anything but. I nearly choked on it, but managed to force it down.

"See anyone you know?" Bobby dangled his own flute from his fingers, his blue eyes surveying the crowd.

Following his gaze, I spotted several up-and-coming artists. Zac Geffadab was holding court in one corner, a large group hanging on his every word. As I was staring, the whole circle he chatted up erupted in laughter.

Shifting, I noticed Jace James standing near one of the framed albums. He seemed to be almost pinned to the wall by a couple of overeager newbies. I caught his eye, and he shot me a pleading look. Without thinking, I took another sip of champagne and then nearly gagged.

"Ugh. This stuff is the worst."

Bobby chuckled. "Seems more for show than anything, doesn't it?"

I nodded. "Will you excuse me? I see someone in need of rescuing."

Bobby followed my line of sight and audibly inhaled. "Could have mentioned that you know Jace James."

My cheeks burned, but maybe no one would notice in the dim light of The Lounge. "We went to school together. I'll be right back."

I strode across the room toward Jace. If anyone knew what was going on at Red Vector, it was probably the label's golden boy. Maybe he could help me.

I dropped my champagne flute back on a tray and made it to his side in time to hear one of the hopefuls say, "I'd love to come backstage sometime to really get a feel for how you do your thing. Here's my contact info."

Jace visibly squirmed when the eager dude held out a card.

I felt a pang of sympathy for both parties. Networking was ruthless, and it was probably as uncomfortable for him to be putting himself out there as it was for Jace to try to field his interest.

Jace—because he's a decent guy—reached out and took the business card. I could make out the hopeful man's sweaty fingerprints on the shiny finish.

"I'll have my manager get in touch if we can make something happen," Jace said with a forced smile. "If you don't mind, there's someone I've been waiting to talk to."

I stepped forward and Jace grabbed for my hand, bringing it to his lips. Butterflies dive-bombed in my stomach, but I tried to ignore them.

"Quite the hello," I teased.

Instead of letting go of my hand, Jace squeezed it and tucked it into the crook of his arm. "You're an actual lifesaver, you know that? I was hoping you'd be here."

"Oh? Why's that?" I barely recognized the flirty lit of my voice. *What* had gotten into me?

"Because with you, an event like this becomes bearable. Enjoyable, even."

"High praise. I'll try not to let you down."

"You could never." Jace winked, and I felt it behind my knees.

Still, my brain latched on to what he wasn't saying. "Are these events not usually much fun? This is my first RVR outing. I'm getting a feel for it because I'm applying for the songwriting position on staff. I'm gonna need someone to show me the ropes."

"I'm your man, then." He held my gaze for an extra beat, and I was sure my blush was painfully evident.

With a small smirk, Jace broke eye contact and surveyed the room. "Let me explain to you how these things go down. Over there"—he motioned with the arm that wasn't holding mine—"Zac will do his best to wow the crowd for most of the evening."

"Who are all those people? I only recognize Autumn."

She was standing off to the side, smiling at Zac, who was telling a story with a lot of hand motions. Everyone else in the group was foreign to me.

"Autumn is a saint," Jace said with reverence. "Zac's been lobbying her people hard to get her to make the jump to RVR, and it sounds like they signed paperwork today. She's taking one for the team tonight, since Zac usually corrals one of us more well-known artists to be his pseudo-arm candy at these things. He likes to parade us around as proof of how successful these less experienced artists can be if they give it their all." He gave his head a rueful shake. "As if there's some magic formula beyond a lot of hard work and a hefty dose of luck."

"Luck doesn't mean much unless you're prepared to grab it."

"Is that a proverb or something?" Jace asked with a laugh.

I nudged his shoulder with mine, relishing the solid feel of his bicep. "That came from the wise mind of Leigh Notrap, thank you very much."

"A wise mind, indeed. To go along with your beautiful face. Listen, Leigh—"

"Jace!"

I turned to see Quentin Buffet flagging Jace over, even as his eyes lasered in on me.

"A word," Quentin said.

Jace's shoulders slumped. "The bigwigs beckon."

I chuckled, pleased that I was able to make my laugh sound something like it normally did. Jace James had called me beautiful. Jace freaking James.

"You go ahead. I'll see you for coffee, if nothing else, right?"

"Yeah." He nodded. "And I'll circle back. I promise. Save a dance for me?" His eyes locked on mine, and he squeezed my fingers where they still rested in the crook of his elbow.

The rest of the room blurred, my gaze focused only on him. “Sure.”

He winked and then he was off, sauntering across The Lounge toward Quentin like he owned the room.

To be fair, he did.

And he'd been flirting with *me*.

I gave my head a slight shake. I'd failed miserably in learning anything about Red Vector that would help Bobby, Emma, and me, but the night was young.

I swiveled around, looking for someone else I could talk to.

Two hours later, my feet ached, and I thought my face might crack where I'd plastered on a permanent smile. After my conversation with Jace, I'd barely seen him. Quentin must've whisked him off somewhere. I'd found Bobby, who was talking to several people I didn't recognize. Bobby introduced me, and we chatted for a bit. When our conversation broke up, he and I split up and made the rounds, striking up conversations with anyone we could.

I introduced myself as a prospective Red Vector staff writer, and that seemed to earn me a different response from different people, and I was beginning to see a pattern.

On one hand, I piqued the interest of a lot of the recently signed singers. I championed my work and experience as much as I could without seeming too boastful, and the newer talent ate it up. All I had to do was name-drop Cal and Autumn, and they were falling all over themselves with excitement.

“I'd love to write with you!”

“Keep me in mind if you're writing anything.”

“So excited we might end up on the same recording team!”

It was good for my ego.

On the other hand, the more seasoned musicians were less bubbly. In fact, their response to me was not unlike the cheap champagne I'd been subjected to when we'd arrived.

When I asked how they liked working with Red Vector, almost to a person, the response was something along the lines of, "I'm honored to be represented by such an impressive label. There's nowhere else I'd rather be." Very few of them met my gaze head-on. Several actually shook their heads as they said the words, so I had a hard time believing them, and by the time the sixth mid-level artist said the same thing back at me, I dragged Bobby over to a private corner.

"This is weird," I told him, leaning against the wall to give my feet a break.

"What is?" He pulled a chair over from a high-top table nearby and gestured for me to sit.

I shot him a grateful look and had to hold back a moan of relief when I sat and relieved the pressure from the balls of my feet. "These artists are saying they're happy to work with Red Vector, but their eyes and body language say something completely different."

Bobby reached up to press his glasses into place, only to realize he wasn't wearing them.

I stifled a giggle but then turned serious. "What do you think it means? Have you learned anything?"

Bobby glanced around. "We shouldn't talk about this here. Are you about ready to go?"

The soles of my feet screamed a resounding *yes*, but I was holding out hope that I'd catch Jace again. "I—"

My cell phone buzzed from where I stashed it in my purse, cutting off my train of thought.

I fished it out, and all the blood drained from my face.

23

The message was from Emma's phone number, but the first line of the text revealed it was actually her mother who sent it.

Emma: Leigh, this is Sandra Dutton. I have Emma's phone because she was taken in by the police tonight. No formal arrest has been made, but they've threatened as much. They're holding her at police headquarters. She wanted me to let you know.

"Are you okay?" Bobby's question snapped me out of the fog of panic I had fallen into.

I shook my head. "No. I'm not. Can we leave? Now?"

"Definitely." Bobby grabbed my hand and pulled me toward the door. Somewhere in the back of my head, I registered the poor form it was to leave without bidding any of the higher-ups goodbye. I couldn't care less at the moment.

Bobby and I stepped outside, and the pulse of the street somehow soothed my nerves. The cacophony of music was like a warm blanket on a winter night.

I typed a quick message back to Emma's mom asking if there was anything I could do while Bobby and I walked back to his car. Her response was less than encouraging.

I explained everything I knew to Bobby as he pulled out of his parking spot. "Emma's in police custody. Her mom said the detectives showed up at the Banta Bowl while she was working tonight and searched her office."

"On what grounds?" Bobby sounded as incredulous as I felt, and I was grateful to not be alone.

"Don't know. She didn't say. I'm guessing Em gave her permission. Then they found something in her desk, apparently."

"What was it?"

"A prescription of some sort."

Bobby remained silent.

"Sandra—that's Emma's mom—is at the station waiting for more information, but she said they're keeping Emma overnight while they run further tests." I caught sight of Bobby's grim expression in the neon lights of West End Avenue. "What are you thinking?"

He shot me a look before returning his focus to the road. "That they're going to test the medication or whatever was in those prescription bottles against the drug they think killed Cal. They have grounds to detain her as long as they're actively investigating."

"But Emma didn't do it!"

"I'm not saying she did." Bobby remained calm in spite of my outburst. "I'm telling you what I'd guess is going on."

I blew out a shaky breath. "Sorry. I know. I'm just anxious. What can I do for her?" I added after a second.

Bobby motioned toward his cell phone. "Hold that up for me, will ya?"

I did what he asked. He unlocked his screen with facial recognition. "Okay. Go to the PAP app."

In spite of myself, I snorted. "Did you plan that rhyme when you named your brainchild?"

Bobby shot me a wry grin. "It's an earworm. Don't hate."

"Not hating. I know good marketing when I see it." I found the app and clicked on it. It was prefigured to be logged in to Bobby's master account. "I can't believe you're trusting me with this," I mumbled, mostly to myself.

"Consider it repayment for freaking you out by following you this week. I've been thinking about what a bonehead idea that was, and I'm really sorry."

I waved him off. “Over and done with. Now what do I do?”

“Check the anonymous tip line. We might learn something.”

Bobby walked me through how to access his tips. The sight before my eyes made me gasp. There were over a hundred unread messages.

“How do you keep track of this all?”

Bobby eyed the phone. “That’s what I get for not checking in for an entire evening.” He flicked his gaze to me and shrugged. “You get used to it—the full inbox. Or I do, at least. It becomes pretty easy to weed out the garbage from the gems. Look for keywords like Cal Dutton and murder, and Emma’s name, of course.”

“Of course,” I parroted, already up to my eyeballs sifting through the information on the app. “I can’t believe people text you about all this. You have a message letting you know that a man was walking around in nothing but a thong and a football jersey on Boardwalk Way. That came in at nine fifteen.”

“Par for the course,” Bobby said, unfazed.

I couldn’t argue with him there. You did see some characters in Nashburg at night.

“Bingo.” My eyes landed on a message with the subject line “Cal Dutton’s Sister is Hiding Something.” “Should I click on this?”

“May as well see what this person knows. Or thinks they know. Go ahead.”

My fingers jabbed the screen.

“What does it say?” Bobby prompted.

I was skimming the message as fast as I could. “Not much that we don’t already know. Whoever this is was at the Banta Bowl tonight. Oh gosh, there’s a video attached. Is it okay to open?”

At Bobby’s nod, I clicked on the play button. A video of a pale-faced Emma being walked out of the Banta Bowl between Detective Ottom and Detective Yance appeared in front of me.

“You can’t post this.” I hated the tremor in my voice and willed my composure to remain intact.

"Hey. I won't. I promised not to. I'm a man of my word." Bobby sounded slightly hurt that I'd even think he would do such a thing. Maybe I should feel guilty for not trusting him, but in this town, where people could be ruthless to get a leg up and our relationship with him was still new, I hadn't been sure what would happen when the rubber met the road.

I shot him a relieved—albeit wobbly—smile. "Thank you. Sorry."

"Don't mention it. Check some other news sites. See if they're running this story yet or if it's still under the radar."

I clicked out of the PAP app and pulled up a local news app Bobby had loaded on his phone.

"There isn't any new news being circulated about Cal's case. At least not here." I scrolled down and kept an eye out for keywords, but the latest bit of information was about the remembrance concert Red Vector had thrown in the late musician's honor.

"That's good. I can't imagine the police would drag Emma in front of the cameras or anything like that."

I chewed my lip and clicked back into the PAP app to pull up the video again. I studied Emma's ashen complexion. Detective Ottom's chest was puffed out, and his face held an all-business expression, but on closer inspection, it almost looked like Detective Yance was positioning himself to try to shield Emma from unwanted scrutiny.

The video had obviously been taken from some distance, so the police likely had no idea the moment was captured on film.

"Do you think I should check the backend data and see if I can figure out who sent this tip?" Bobby asked. "I know I said I don't do that often, and I don't. But..." he trailed off with a shrug.

I squinted my eyes closer to Bobby's phone, and a tingle ran down my spine. "I don't think you need to. I know who took this video."

24

"What? How?" Bobby pulled to the side of the road outside Java Flo's and swung his gaze toward me.

"Look at the table in the foreground." I held out the phone for him to examine. "Do you see the purse?"

He took the device and held it up to his nose. "It looks like the same type of crossbody bag every woman under fifty is carrying around these days."

"Look closer. There's a pin on the strap."

Bobby frowned as he zoomed in. "Does that say 'Cal's Crew'?"

"It sure does. See the number in the middle?"

"Number one."

"Do you know who wears that pin and considers herself the number one fan of Cal Dutton?"

"Whitney Allerow."

We said the name together and then stared at each other for a prolonged second.

"What do you want to do?" Bobby asked, cutting into my thoughts.

"We need to go and have a conversation with Whitney. Can you drive me to the Banta Bowl?"

"Sure." Bobby put the car in drive and checked his blind spot before pulling out. "What makes you think she'll still be there, though? I wonder how she was there in the first place?" he added, more to himself than me.

I had the same thought. I pulled out my phone as Bobby navigated out of the Village and onto the interstate toward the Banta Bowl.

"I'm guessing"—I clicked around and pulled up a schedule of events—"that Whitney got lucky. She was probably at the Banta Bowl listening to the Gremlin Gang, who were set to start performing at nine. It wouldn't surprise me if she's been haunting the halls of the Banta Bowl since Cal's death because it makes her feel closer to him."

Bobby made a gagging expression. "Was she obsessed with him or something?"

"Pretty much." I rearranged my dress and stared out the window. "All the members of Cal's Crew were pretty over the top ... Whitney, especially. Cal didn't seem to mind. It drove Emma crazy that he put up with their antics, but he just brushed it off as part of the job."

"Interesting. Did Whitney know that Emma didn't think highly of her and her fan group?"

I shrugged, and the memory of seeing Whitney the night of Cal's death popped into my head. I filled Bobby in on that little tidbit. "I'm not sure how much direct interaction the two women have had, honestly, but if she's been around the Banta Bowl, then I'm guessing they've crossed paths."

"Do you think Whitney is dangerous?"

"No." I leaned forward to adjust the strap of my high-heeled shoe that was digging into my ankle. "Besides, if she's still at the Banta Bowl, then we'll be surrounded by people. What's she going to do?"

My cell phone buzzed. I glanced at the screen to find a message from Jace.

Jace: I missed saying goodbye. Looking forward to coffee tomorrow.

My pulse skittered, and I typed back a quick message. I shouldn't be excited about a breakfast date with Jace when Emma was in jail. What kind of friend was I? Still, the chance to pick his brain would be useful.

Just before I was about to stow my phone again, the screen lit up with an incoming call. I couldn't hide my grunt of disgust when I saw the caller ID read "Pita Paige."

"Woah, you know Pita Paige?" Bobby stared at the screen.

I silenced the vibrations and ignored the call. "She's the bane of my existence."

Bobby coughed out a laugh.

I quirked a brow. "What?"

"Nothing. That's just not what I'd expect most people to say about the queen of country music."

I shook my head. "Let's just say our history isn't great."

I really should block her number. That way I wouldn't be caught off guard when she randomly decided to contact me. But a part of me—way down deep in the bottom chamber of my heart—clung to the hope of what could have been. The longing to have a pair of seasoned professionals in the industry take me under their wing and actually help me instead of taking advantage of my skill.

I knew my hope was futile. People like Pita and Penn never changed. And people like me always got burned.

"Should I ask?" Bobby glanced at me out of the corner of his eye.

"I'd rather you didn't."

He nodded and redirected his attention to the road.

Ten minutes later, we walked into the dimly lit Banta Bowl.

"There." Bobby motioned with his chin to the far end of the long bar at the same moment I spotted Whitney.

"Yep. It's go time." I maneuvered through the crowd, around the highball tables, and toward where Whitney was sitting with a dirty martini in front of her. Bobby kept pace behind me.

"Should we have a game plan?" he whispered before we got within earshot of Cal's biggest fan.

"Follow my lead. I'm just going to wing it."

"You sure know how to inspire confidence."

A nervous giggle bubbled up in my chest, but I swallowed it. This woman had it out for my best friend, and I was about to figure out why.

"Hello, Whitney." I stopped and dropped into the open chair next to her.

She lowered the martini glass from her lips and raised a perfectly sculpted eyebrow in my direction. "I'm sorry. Should I know you?"

I didn't appreciate her snooty tone, especially since *yes*, she knew me. Cal had introduced us on several occasions.

Bobby came to a stop and stood between our two chairs. He was a smart cookie to block her exit. I'd have to remember to compliment him later. For now, I fixed on a sugary sweet smile that would have made my mother weep tears of gladness. It was the Southern kind of smile that was the equivalent of saying "bless your heart." I was feeling the exact opposite of sweet, and Whitney knew it.

Her eyes flashed with confusion when I reached over and patted her arm. "You remember me, don't you? Leigh Notrap. I wrote a lot of music with Cal. This is my friend, Bo, a fellow songwriter. We just have a few questions for you."

"What sort of questions?" Whitney shot Bobby an appraising look, and while she was ogling him, I put a game plan together.

"First, let me just say, I am so sorry for your loss. I know you and Cal had a special bond."

Whitney immediately relaxed. Her posture turned to that of a woman who felt self-important, but there was also some real emotion in her eyes when she swung her gaze back to me. "Thank you for saying that. No one believed me when I told them what Cal and I shared, but it was real. I *know* it was real." Whitney's eyes flashed with stubborn determination.

I made a cooing noise. "This must be so hard for you. When's the last time you saw Cal?"

Whitney sniffed and paused before answering. "At a meet-and-greet about a week before he died. He was so full of life then. Like he always is, chatting up the room. I was so happy to be there with him."

Blergh. She made it sound like she was on his arm or something. I was beginning to get a very clear sense of how far Whitney's delusions went.

I opened my mouth to ask another question, but she plowed ahead.

"But then that wench showed up." Whitney took a giant sip of her martini.

Bobby and I exchanged a glance. Was she talking about Emma?

"Who's that?" Bobby asked.

"Autumn Silver," Whitney spat. "She always put Cal in a sour mood."

I leaned an elbow against the bar, blocking Whitney from the rest of the happenings at the Banta Bowl. I wanted her full attention for as long as possible. If she was in a chatty mood, we might learn something. "How so?"

She scoffed. "She tried to steal his spotlight, riding his coattails to stardom. It was repugnant if you ask me. She turned every conversation toward *her* and *her* music and *her* career. Cal was too much of a gentleman to complain, but I knew it annoyed him whenever she got on a roll about how she was making a huge name for herself."

"Didn't she sign a record deal before he did, though?" Bobby asked casually.

Whitney glared at him, and if looks could kill… "Yes, but for your information, that was only because Cal was building up a strong foundation."

I made some sort of grunt that Whitney obviously took for agreement because she prattled on.

"It doesn't matter, though. Because Cal was going to end things with Autumn."

This was news to me. “How do you know that?”

“Because she wasn’t being honest with him.”

Bobby leaned in. “About what?”

“She didn’t love him like she swore she did.”

I shot Bobby a look out of the corner of my eye, unsure how to proceed. I opened my mouth, not quite sure what words I was formulating to come out, but as it happened, Whitney cut me off.

“All the women in Cal’s life were traitors,” she spat. “Except for his mother. I’m sure she was lovely. Had to be to raise such an impressive man.”

“Er, what do you mean by ‘all the women’ in Cal’s life?” Bobby questioned.

“Autumn, obviously. And his sniveling sister, Emma.” Whitney said Emma’s name with a sneer. “She’s about to get hers, though, so I guess that’s something.”

My blood pressure skyrocketed, and I clenched my fist on the bar. Bobby placed a hand on the small of my back and applied subtle pressure. I stilled and blew out a breath. Thank goodness he was here or I might have made good on my desire to land a solid jab to Whitney’s too-perfect face. How dare she insinuate that Emma had anything to do with Cal’s death.

“What do you have against Emma?” Bobby’s even voice stood in stark contrast to my boiling blood, but if letting him run with this would get us the most information, then I was content to bite my tongue.

Whitney scoffed again. “What don’t I have against Emma? Like Autumn, she was only interested in Cal for his connections and his money.”

My spine snapped straighter. “Hey—”

“How do you know that?” Bobby cut me off, shooting me a half-apologetic, half-pleading look.

“They say a picture’s worth a thousand words, right?” Whitney smirked. “Well, I got the video. The one the PAP posted of Cal and Emma’s huge fight when he wouldn’t lend her money.”

"Ah." Bobby nodded to show her he had seen the video. Little did she know he'd posted it. "But there was no sound when the PAP published that story. How do you know what they were fighting about?"

Whitney blinked and looked like a deer caught in headlights. "Uh—I . . . well—"

"Did you take the video, Whitney?" I did my best to act impressed.

Whitney recovered and waved me off. "I might have obtained the footage and shared it with a few select sources. But that fight is the least of Emma Dutton's concerns now. She was escorted out of here not two hours ago. Have you heard? I'm guessing the PAP will break that story in no time." She pulled up her phone, clicked around, frowned, and set it back down. "Nothing yet, but I saw Emma led out of here with my own two eyes."

Bobby and I exchanged a knowing look. When we were all done with this, I was going to write him the most heartfelt thank-you card for being a man of his word. Heck, maybe I'd write him a song. Maybe we could write one together.

Focus, Leigh.

I blew out a breath. Something about what Whitney said earlier wasn't adding up. "Let me get this straight. You think that Emma was trying to get Cal to give her money?"

"She wanted to start another business. Like this one." Whitney downed the rest of her martini. I had to wonder how many of those she'd had. She was partially slurring her words and appeared close to tipping off her barstool. "Cal told her no. As he should have," she added, looking proud. "She needs to make her own way. Not rely on her brother for everything." Whitney's gaze hardened. "But I'm sure the little weasel didn't like it when Cal stood up to her. That's probably why she was helping Autumn carry out her deceit."

I threw up my hands. "*What* deceit?"

Whitney narrowed her glassy eyes at me. "Her affair."

I sat back. “Autumn was having an affair?”

A single tear ran down Whitney’s cheek. “With Cal’s agent. Phil McMann.”

25

Whitney burst into body-racking sobs. Apparently she'd reached the weepy phase of being drunk. She dramatically flung her arms onto the bar and buried her face in the crook of her elbow.

I shifted on my barstool when Whitney let out a particularly guttural wail. It wasn't that big emotions made me uncomfortable. Heck, big emotions sold music lyrics. I catered to big emotions all the time. But my defense mechanism was to keep a stiff upper lip. This sort of outburst unnerved me, and a twinge of annoyance pricked at the base of my spine. If Whitney would pull herself together, then we could make sense of all the information she was handing out like free candy.

As if reading my mind, she shot me a watery look. "Sorry, I'm a mess. It's just"—*hiccup*—"he didn't deserve that, you know?"—*sniffle*—"Cal loved Autumn, but his love was misplaced. That's what I kept trying to tell him."

I cocked my head, a puzzle piece sliding into place. I'd circle back to that. I intentionally softened my voice. "Whitney, I want to help you. I want justice for Cal just like you do, but I need you to explain some of what you've said to me. Do you think you can do that?"

Bobby held out a tissue. She took it and blew her nose, looking between the two of us and finally nodding.

I leaned back. "Okay. First, I'm going to be honest with you. Emma is my best friend, and I don't like what you've insinuated about her, but I'll give you a chance to say your piece and then

I'll say mine." I waited for Whitney to nod. Her movements were slow, but her crying spell seemed to sober her up enough that I could tell she understood. "Why do you think Emma had anything to do with Autumn, or was somehow hiding Autumn's affair?"

"Because I saw Autumn and Phil together the day of Cal's death." Whitney's voice wobbled, but she swallowed and squared her shoulders. "They were together backstage, here"—she pointed to the floor of the Banta Bowl—"sneaking around, using Emma's office as a rendezvous for their affair."

I frowned. It was a massive jump—like Grand Canyon level—to assume that because Whitney saw Autumn and Phil sneaking around Emma's office that Emma was somehow in on their affair. The whole point of an affair was that no one was in on it. My father knew that well.

I shook my head. "I think you're mistaken."

Whitney flinched. "I am not. I know what I saw."

Her posture said she was ready to do battle.

Sensing that the two of us were gridlocked, Bobby stepped forward. "You saw Autumn and Phil together the night Cal was killed? So you were backstage?"

Whitney got the deer-in-the-headlights look again.

Bobby pressed his advantage. "Do the police know you were here?"

Whitney sniffed, not making eye contact. "It's irrelevant."

"Hardly," I huffed. "Whitney, that's a huge omission. You may have seen something that could help with the case." What I didn't say but was thinking was, *You may have killed Cal yourself!*

But the more I thought of it, the more it didn't line up. Whitney was obsessed with Cal. I could see that clear as the blue sky on a Nashburg summer day. She wouldn't have wanted to kill him. Not in a premeditative way that poisoning suggests. I wouldn't put a crime of passion past her, but that was not what we were dealing with.

"I *told* you. I *did* see something. I saw Autumn and Phil. In Emma's office." She enunciated as if I were a child and she was trying to get a simple message through to me.

"Wait. Wait. Wait." I held up my hands. "You said you told Cal about Autumn and Phil, right? Did you speak to him that night? The night he died? Here? Is that why you were late to meet up with the rest of the Crew?"

Whitney's lip started quivering. I braced myself for a renewed round of tears, but she kept the waterworks off. "Yes," she croaked out in a whisper, swallowing hard. "I've been wracked with guilt ever since. I can't help but think that if I had just kept him with me or convinced him not to go to his dressing room—something, *anything*—then he'd still be here today."

Whitney buried her head in her hands.

Bobby caught my attention and widened his eyes.

I nodded and mouthed, "What do we do now?"

He shrugged.

I faced Whitney again. She was weeping into her hands, and I tried to think quickly about what I still hoped to learn from her. When she took a breath, I took the opening. "Whitney, can you tell me everything you remember about Cal that night? What was he doing? How was he acting?"

Whitney sniffed. "I'll remember that night forever. *Forever.*"

Bobby and I exchanged another look. Her dramatics were grating to say the least, but she was the key to some important information that, as far as I knew, no one else had, so I needed to buck up and deal with her.

"I knew that Cal was anxious about his show that night. I could tell from the tone of his social media posts, so I thought I'd go backstage and try to calm his nerves."

"Go on," Bobby said.

"Well, when I got backstage"—she had the wherewithal to look a little sheepish—"I still know the passcode from when I bartended here a year or so back."

I nodded encouragingly. Whitney's trespassing was the least of my worries at the moment.

"When I got here, I heard yelling coming from Willie's office. It's right near Emma's, you know? Anyway, I recognized Cal's voice immediately. He was in a huge fight."

"Did you hear what the fight was about?"

Whitney nibbled her lip. "Cal said something to the effect of 'I'm done and there's nothing you can do to stop me.'"

"Sounds serious," Bobby mused.

"That's what I thought, too," Whitney concurred. "I hung back, which is when I saw Autumn sneak through Emma's open office door with Phil. They'd obviously used that room before, because they had no qualms about heading right inside and making themselves comfortable." Whitney stuck up her nose in disgust. "Makes me sick just thinking about it."

I pressed my lips together. We'd definitely need to revisit that, or at least have the police look into the affair. Hopefully we could convince Whitney to be honest with them. For now, I really wanted to hear about Cal.

"When did you actually talk to Cal?" I asked.

"When he stormed out of Willie's office. I followed him toward his dressing room and called out to him. He was surprised to see me, I think. But not unhappy," she added with wistfulness.

"What did you two talk about?" Bobby pressed, and I could have hugged him for keeping Whitney focused. This woman was draining me.

"I asked him if he was okay. I told him that he could talk to me, and that I was here for him. It was then I made a mistake and brought up Autumn."

"Why was it a mistake?"

"Because he turned stormy. I tried to tell him that he could catch Autumn and Phil in the act, right then, but he scowled and said I was wrong. He and Autumn loved each other, that's what he told me. I don't see how he could be in love with *her* when he was supposed to be in love with *me*."

"What did he do then?" I asked before she could devolve into hysterics about Cal's misplaced affection.

"He said he needed some air and stepped outside the building through the staff entrance. I followed him out, but I didn't linger. I know when it's best to give a relationship some space to breathe."

I fought an eye roll.

"I cut around to the front of the building to meet up with my posse, figuring I'd catch Cal some other time," Whitney explained. "Little did I know..."

She trailed off, but I got the point. She blamed herself. Whitney thought Cal loved her, and her motivations for going after Emma were misguided, not malicious. She was trying to fix the blame on someone because it was helping her cope with Cal's loss. No matter what the actual relationship between her and Cal was, she was grieving for him as if they'd been close. Because in her mind, they had been.

"So Cal was fighting with Willie on the night of his death. When you got here, you saw Autumn and Phil together in Emma's office. You talked to Cal, and he maintained his love for Autumn, in spite of you telling him about the affair." This piece was key. If Cal knew about Autumn and Phil, and they knew that he knew, maybe they'd wanted him out of the picture.

I frowned. It all seemed so rash. Why kill a man when you could just break up with him?

"That's right," Whitney spoke up, drawing me out of my thoughts. "Except Cal wasn't arguing with Willie."

Bobby rolled his head next to me, as if trying to work out a kink in his neck. I couldn't blame him.

"You said they were fighting in Willie's office," Bobby reminded her.

Whitney shook her head. "No, I said Cal was fighting in Willie's office, but it wasn't Willie's voice I heard."

I crossed my arms, the goosebumps that appeared suddenly on my skin a sign that a new piece of the puzzle was going to drop from the sky. This always happened to me when I was on the brink of writing the perfect bridge to complete a song. It was like my body was preparing for something that my mind needed to catch up to. In this case, "Then whose voice was it?"

"Zac Geffadab."

I blinked, and Bobby let out a low whistle.

Now *that* was something. Something that once again pointed to Zac and Cal being at odds.

We wrapped up our conversation with Whitney, and after encouraging her to go to the police and please, for the love of all that is good, stop accusing Emma, Bobby drove me back toward the Village.

"What a night," I breathed to the darkness of the car. It was late. My feet ached, and my mind was overrun with endless thoughts.

"What are you going to do next?"

I nibbled on my lip. "I'll check in with Emma's parents first thing in the morning to see if there's anything she needs or anything I can do. Then, I'm going to get coffee with Jace and see if I can ask him about Red Vector."

Bobby nodded. "The way I see it, there are two angles to Cal's death. The Red Vector angle, and the love affair angle."

"One of us should try to talk to Phil McMann or Autumn again, but I don't know how we do that without showing our hand. And if they're dangerous—"

"Yeah. We don't want to put ourselves in harm's way. Which is why you should be careful when you deal with RVR for this job application stuff, too."

"I can't imagine anything would happen surrounded by the human resources team, but yeah, I'll keep my eyes and ears open."

"There are a lot of loose ends." He pulled up outside of Java Flo's. The chairs were stacked on the tables, and the café was quiet, all customers long gone for the evening. "Why don't we touch base tomorrow after your coffee date?"

"It's not really a date," I countered.

"Semantics." Bobby shrugged with a small smile. "Let's just connect and decide what to do then. Sound good?"

"Sounds good." I sat still in my seat, fiddling with the hem of my dress. Bobby and I had been through a lot tonight. I felt like I should hug him, but I wasn't really a hugger. "Thanks for being here with me tonight. And thank you for not posting the video Whitney sent of Emma."

Bobby deflected. "No need to thank me. That's not the type of news I'm after. No one likes a smear campaign. But everyone likes to see justice, so let's make sure Cal gets that."

"Deal." Without thinking too much about it, I reached across the console and gave Bobby a quick peck on the cheek. He blushed and looked adorably awkward. "Talk to you tomorrow."

"'Night, Leigh."

I hopped out of the car and jogged across the street. I dreaded going into my apartment knowing that Emma was spending the night in jail. I slogged my way up the stairs, unlocked the door, and flipped on the light. Phelps was swimming laps in his fish bowl. At least I had him.

I crossed the room and dropped some food into his bowl. I might have been projecting, but he looked like he missed Emma too. His eyes were all watery and forlorn.

"Don't worry, buddy. I'll figure out how to get her home." I made a fish face with my lips as I kicked off my shoes and plopped down on the couch. I leaned my head back against the cushion and closed my eyes. I knew sleep wouldn't come. Not when my brain was working a mile a minute.

I scooched forward again and grabbed for the leather-bound notepad I had sitting on the coffee table, strategically placed for those bouts of inspiration that struck when I least expected them to—when I was doing something like folding socks.

Uncapping my pen and turning to a new page, I let my thoughts loose. Everything I knew about Cal and his death, everything I felt about it all, poured out onto the page. All my hunches, all the question marks, my prayers for Emma, my annoyance with Pita Paige, my excitement over my non-date with Jace. Everything went down into the journal.

Writing was therapy for me. If I couldn't make sense of my thoughts, at least I could gain some control over them by writing them down—even if that control only came in naming them.

26

I woke the next morning to my alarm blaring. Jolting upright, I had to unstick the crusted pages of my notebook from where I'd fallen asleep pressed against the open pad.

"Lovely." I scrubbed my hands over my face a couple of times and cringed when I recalled I was still in full make-up and my dress from the Red Vector mixer. I hopped off the couch and headed straight for the shower. I needed to get cleaned up and ready for the day, and then I needed a steaming mug of Java Flo's coffee.

Less than an hour later, Agnes slid a mug of coffee toward me where I sat at one of the barstools near the pastry case. "Here ya go, Leigh. Just what the doctor ordered."

"Thank you." I breathed in the heavenly aroma and took a cautious sip.

"So, where are you meeting Jace?" Agnes propped one hand on her hip. Were the circumstances different and Emma here with us, Agnes would have been teasing me incessantly about this meetup. The two of them were always up in my business when it came to my love life ... or lack thereof.

My heart twisted at the thought of Emma. How had she survived the night?

I tugged my phone out of my crossbody bag and typed a quick message to Emma's mom, asking for an update. So far, it had been radio silence. I wasn't sure what to make of that.

Stowing away the phone again, I answered Agnes. "We're meeting at a diner near Millennial Park. We may walk and talk."

She angled her head, and because she just couldn't help herself, added, "Sounds romantic."

I rolled my eyes. "I'm more interested in what he can tell me about Red Vector."

"Hopefully something useful. The longer this goes on, the more concerned I am. Have you officially applied?" Agnes worried her bottom lip.

I nodded. "Interview is scheduled for next week. Cal's case should all be sorted out before then."

Agnes kissed her fingers, touched them to her heart, and pointed to the sky. "From your lips to God's ears, child."

I held up my mug in agreement. Agnes left me to my coffee as the café quickly filled to near capacity. I scanned the crowded dining room for any signs of Bobby, but I didn't see him. He was probably sleeping off the night before like any normal person would.

I downed the rest of my coffee, ordered a quick espresso shot for the road, and set off. By the time I got to the address of the coffee shop Jace had texted me, he was waiting outside. He held open his arms, and I gladly stepped into a hug.

He smelled like evergreen breath mints.

"Shall we?" he asked, motioning to the breakfast spot when I pulled back.

I nodded and let him guide me inside.

"Sorry I didn't get a chance to say goodbye last night. I got caught up with some people," he said.

I shook my head. "Not your fault. I left sooner than I expected to." I filled him in on Emma, appreciating the solidarity when his eyes widened in horror.

"You're kidding."

"I wish. It's bad, but it's got to work itself out, right? The police can't arrest her. She didn't do it."

Jace nodded, but his body language told me he knew as well as I did that the police sometimes *did* arrest the wrong person.

We got seated and, when the server came around, we placed our breakfast orders. I opted for a veggie omelet, a side of buttermilk pancakes, and orange juice. I'd reached my coffee quota for at least a couple hours.

Jace opted for a platter of over-easy eggs, bacon, and toast. He leaned across the table when our server left to put in our order. "I like this place because they don't make a big deal about me being, well, me."

"I imagine it's hard to find somewhere like that." I glanced around. The diner was crowded, but not too crowded, and no one seemed to be paying us any attention.

Just the way I liked it.

Jace rested back against his side of the booth and shot a lazy smile in my direction. Before he got too comfortable, I decided I should ask what I came here to ask. "Hey, is it alright if I ask you a couple questions about Red Vector? I've got an interview coming up."

He grinned. "You're going to crush it. I'm happy to answer any questions you have. Not sure how much help I can be, but shoot."

I blew out a breath. He was being so nice. "I hope I don't come across sounding crazy or paranoid." I let out a nervous chuckle before diving into my concerns and observations. I chose my words carefully since I had to leave out all the information I had from Bobby. I couldn't admit that part of my assumptions about Red Vector were due to an anonymous tip to the PAP, because that would raise Jace's perfectly sculpted eyebrows to new levels.

Instead, I focused on what I'd learned on my own: Cal steering me away from the job. What Jon Campbell told me about Cal trying to dissuade him and his brother from a Red Vector deal. The vibe I got from the more seasoned artists at the label last night.

"I don't know, it's all so weird," I concluded. "Maybe I'm reading into something that isn't really happening, but I thought if anyone would be able to shed some light on what was going on at RVR, it was you."

"Glad to know you think so highly of me." He winked, and the tension in my body melted away.

A giggle bubbled up before I could stop it. "Kind of hard not to with you being a megastar and all," I said, lifting my shoulder as if it was no big deal.

Jace laughed outright at that before sobering. "I truly don't know what to tell you. I'm supremely happy with everyone I know at Red Vector. They've done a world of good for my career. Shot me into the stratosphere of megastardom, if you will."

I smiled at that. "Megastardom couldn't have happened to a nicer guy." I paused. "How's Quentin?"

"In A&R?" Jace asked, and I nodded. "Why? Was he giving you trouble?"

"He just said some stuff that came across as really misogynistic. I wondered if he was who Cal was trying to warn me away from."

"Might have been, though Cal should know you could handle yourself where Quentin is concerned."

I sat a little taller at that, grateful that Jace recognized I wasn't a helpless damsel in distress.

"Quentin is all smoke and no fire," he went on. "Zac has talked to him about his tone and style, so I know everyone is aware of some of his more inappropriate behavior. But the guy gets results."

Jace was saying all the right things, and I had a strong urge to go sink into the seat next to him on his side of the booth and wrap my arms around him in a hug.

The server returned with our food, and Jace and I tucked in. After a couple of bites, I set my fork to rest on my plate and grabbed for my orange juice. "One more thing, and then I promise we can talk about something that doesn't have to do with Cal for the rest of breakfast."

"Hit me," Jace said, crunching on a piece of bacon.

I swallowed. "Do you know if there was bad blood between Zac and Cal? Someone overheard the two of them fighting the night Cal was killed."

Jace's eyes widened. "Really? Yikes. I hadn't heard about that." He cocked his head to the side. "You know how Cal is—was. He had a strong personality, and he liked things the way he liked them. Maybe he and Zac were clashing. Since Cal signed with RVR, he would have to do things the way they wanted him to do. I mean, you get some leeway, but mostly you've got to play the game, and RVR knows how to win."

I nodded, mulling this over. "Cal did like control. My eyewitness—" I cut myself off on Jace's boyish grin. "What?"

"You sound so official. 'My eyewitness.' It's like you're a real-life detective yourself. You going to moonlight as an informant for the Nashburg PD, Secret Agent Leigh Notrap?"

"Hardly," I snickered. "Mostly I just like knowing things, and this is driving me crazy."

"Understandable." Jace inclined his head. "Sorry, go on. What were you saying about your eyewitness?"

I shot him a pretend scowl when he wiggled his eyebrows, but my lips quirked. "They said they overheard Cal talking about how he had information that he was going public with, and there was nothing Zac could do about it. Any idea what that would be in reference to?"

Jace tossed his napkin on his plate. A crease formed on the center of his forehead. "I can't think of anything."

I sighed. A dead end. Cringing at the accuracy of *that* too-close-to-home analogy, I finished the last few bites of my omelet. Someone would have to try to figure it out from Zac himself, but I was going to leave that to the real professionals. A trip to the Nashburg Police Headquarters was in my future. Maybe this information would somehow help to clear Emma's name.

"The only thing I'd heard," Jace spoke again, cutting into my thoughts, "in relation to Cal and his career in the lead up to his death was that he was contemplating firing his manager."

I sucked in a breath. "Phil? Why?"

Jace shook his head. "He didn't say, but that was the last thing we talked about. He said he felt like they were on two different pages, and he was considering going in a different direction." Jace pointed at me from across the table. "Why are you looking like that?"

I forced my face to look less puckered, and I leaned in. "This could be nothing, but I've also heard that Phil was having an affair with Autumn."

If Phil had found out that Cal was going to fire him, that would have been a huge professional black mark. Was it a dark enough one to spur him to murder, though?

Jace's forehead creased. "Now *that* I hadn't heard, but," he shrugged, "I find it kinda hard to believe."

"I know. And it's just gossip and hearsay." I groaned. "What a mess. All of it." Jace nodded, looking thoughtful. I went on. "I don't mean to beat a dead horse, but doesn't it seem like Cal was privy to some sort of information about the music group? Something that he was holding over Zac? Or something that was making him warn others off?"

Jace nodded again. "Based on what you told me, yeah, it does. Do the police know all this?"

I raised my hands, palms up. "I don't know. They didn't love that I was asking questions and poking my nose into Cal's affairs." I picked up my fork and wedged off a bite. "If only I could find something concrete. I'm just surprised there's no paper trail."

My mind flashed to Cal's watch. He was carving out a secret compartment in the least likely of places—a family heirloom. It must have been for something important. Something he didn't want to risk falling into the wrong hands. The niche Lyle had fashioned beneath the watch face would have been tiny, but they made flash drives even tinier these days. Was it possible Cal had saved incriminating information about Zac or Red Vector onto a fingernail-sized flash drive, with the intention to keep it on his person as soon as the watch was ready?

If Bobby was correct and Cal had contacted him about a music industry shake-up, then it followed that Cal would have information to prove himself. So where was it now? Bobby had said the tip came from an IP address at the Nashburg Public Library. Might Cal have done most of his computer work on a public device? He'd still have to have saved it somewhere, so maybe there was a flash drive hidden in his apartment.

But why the secrecy? Why not use his personal devices?

My mind worked through the possibilities. Paranoia? Whitney *was* videoing him, and he likely didn't know it. Maybe he sensed he was being watched. Maybe he was afraid that someone could access his personal computer. Who would have access to it that he was worried about?

Autumn. Was *she* in on the Red Vector schemes? They'd just signed her to their label, after all. The timing of that was suspect.

I rubbed my temples. My head felt like it was going to explode. None of this was concrete information, and I'd be the first to admit it.

When I looked up, I found Jace studying me with an expression that bordered on amused.

"Are you sure your real name isn't Nancy Drew?"

I stiffened at the mention of a *real name*, but shook it off. "Ha. Hardly. I'm a complete failure at this, obviously."

"If it helps, I'll try to poke around a bit. If Zac, Autumn, or anyone else for that matter, is acting suspicious, I'll let you know. Though I'm admittedly going back out on the road in the not-so-distant future." His shoulders lifted in an apologetic shrug.

"Thanks, Jace." I dusted off my hands and smiled. "Enough about me and my amateur detecting."

I turned the conversation to him and his music.

While taking care of the bill and wandering through Millennial Park, we talked about the next single from his current album, his favorite part of being on the road, and our mutual school friends and what they were up to nowadays. It all felt remarkably normal, despite the fact that this was Jace James.

"Hey." He touched my elbow when we'd circled back to where I had parked. "What do you say about doing some studio time together? I have this hook I haven't been able to get out of my head."

"Yeah?" A flutter of excitement tickled my ribcage. Getting the chance to write with Jace was a huge opportunity. Something I could tout in a job interview with Red Vector, too. Since he was under their umbrella, and I would potentially be too, this could be an ongoing partnership. Professionally.

And maybe personally, too.

"Yeah. I've got some time set aside on Wednesday at ten o'clock to use the studio at RVR. Join me?"

I mentally flipped through my schedule, even though there was no real need to—I'd cancel anything else to make this happen. "Okay, yeah, sure, that should work."

"Great. I'll meet you there." Jace leaned in and kissed me on the cheek.

"Great," I echoed with a smile, catching a whiff of bacon mixed with evergreen. I slid into the front seat of my truck and watched as Jace disappeared around the corner. I used the voice activation in my car to dial Bobby's number. "Want to meet me at the police station?" I asked when he picked up.

"I can meet you there in, say, an hour?"

I agreed, hung up the phone, and glanced at the clock on my dashboard. I had just enough time to make a quick pit stop.

27

I parked outside of the Banta Bowl and scanned the cars in the parking lot. I had no idea what sort of vehicle Willie drove, but my hope was to catch him in his office. If he were any type of businessman, he'd be on the premises overseeing things himself since his site manager was currently in police custody. But I didn't trust Willie as far as I could throw him.

When Whitney told us it wasn't Willie who was fighting with Cal the night of his death but Zac, it got me thinking. What had Willie been so worried about the morning after the murder, when I'd seen him and his lawyer at police headquarters?

I started toward the main entrance, but then a thought struck me. I quickly changed course and casually walked around the side of the building. I skirted the building, checking over my shoulder as I walked down the alley. At least since Bobby and I had joined forces, I no longer felt like there was someone watching me, but today, the little hairs on the back of my neck stood up for a different reason. One I couldn't quite put my finger on. Maybe it was the fact that Cal had been alive here not one week ago, and now he wasn't. Maybe it was because I knew Willie was hiding something. Maybe it was because my best friend was in jail, and I was nowhere close to having any concrete answers about what really happened.

I tabled those thoughts as I circled the building. The baseball field off to my left was quiet, with just a few grounds crew workers stenciling fresh lines on the infield. There was a set of stairs that led down to a back entrance to the Banta Bowl, and I figured this was where Cal had probably stepped out to get some air.

I descended the steps and tried the door. I bit my lip when I found it unlocked. I wasn't the breaking-and-entering type, but this would get me into the backend offices quicker than trying to finagle my way in from the bar. Decision made, I snuck inside. I took a minute to catch my breath, which was suddenly coming in shallow wheezes. I forced myself to stand up straight. I wasn't doing anything wrong per say. I just wanted to talk to Willie.

I tuned my senses to my surroundings. A quiet hum of business replaced the noise and activity of the Nashburg streets I'd left outside. Faintly, I could hear the shouts of the maintenance workers getting the venue ready for tonight's festivities.

Ahead of me was a long corridor. Striding forward, I tried to keep my tread light. Better to catch them when they didn't see me coming.

All of the doors along this hallway were closed and appeared to be used for storage. When I came to an intersecting hallway, I poked my head out and looked left and then right. Near the end of one hallway, I spotted police tape.

Cal's dressing room.

Fighting against a wave of renewed nausea, I turned in the opposite direction, toward the staff offices. Emma's office was this way; I'd visited her here a few times. I assumed Willie's was nearby.

I slowed my stride, as several doors in this wing were opened. A masculine voice wafted out from one that had the name placard "Willie Davis, Owner" just outside of it.

Spotting a tiny alcove off to one side of the hallway that dead-ended, I ducked into it just as I heard Willie bid someone goodbye. I backed myself into a corner, hoping whoever left Willie's office wouldn't notice me.

Relief flooded me when a woman in chef whites strode down the hallway without glancing in my direction. I blew out a breath and stepped forward, realizing all at once that this must've been where Whitney hid when she overheard Cal and Zac's fight.

I slowed my breathing and focused on how I was going to approach Willie. My plan was to make sure he knew about Emma's predicament and then casually prod for more information about the night of Cal's death. I was mentally running through talking points when Willie's voice reached me, and it sounded more hostile than it had before.

"What do you want, Zac?" he growled.

I held my breath, waiting to see if I could hear what happened next. Willie was obviously on the phone, most likely with Zac Geffadab. Sure, there were other Zacs in Nashburg, but I didn't believe in coincidences.

"I can't imagine you'd possibly need anything else." Willie's voice grew louder. He must have stood and approached the door.

A second later, I heard it close with an angry click.

"Dang it," I whispered.

How had Whitney heard so much of Cal and Zac's fight? Had they really been careless enough to leave the door open?

I leaned my ear up against the wall the alcove shared with Willie's office, and my eyes bugged out. I could hear Willie's conversation with crystal clarity.

"I don't appreciate your tone," Willie hissed from his end of the phone call.

A pause.

"No, you listen to me. I will have you brought up on charges of blackmail if this continues."

Another pause, and then Willie spoke again, sounding more deflated. "Look. We both got what we want, right? Can we just put this to bed?"

It was quiet for several seconds after that.

What had *that* been about?

I rolled my shoulders and decided there was no time like the present to confront Willie. I hated the thought of kicking a man when he was down, but in this case, I might be able to use the information I'd just overheard from the phone call as leverage.

Stepping into the main corridor, I rapped on the door to Willie's office three quick times.

"Come in."

I opened the door to find a disheveled Willie scrubbing his hands over his face. He caught sight of me and frowned. "Can I help you?"

"Leigh Notrap." I crossed to his desk and extended my hand. "We've met several times. I'm a friend of Emma's."

Willie shook my hand. "Right. I know who you are."

I swallowed a pang of panic, reminding myself that he didn't *really* know who I was—he just knew of me in association with Emma.

"What are you doing here?" Willie eyed me warily.

"I came to make sure you'd heard about Emma's trouble."

"Heard about it!" Willie scoffed. "The police dragged her out of here during prime operating hours. Not exactly great for business."

I frowned. What a jabroni. This guy couldn't be bothered to even ask how Emma was doing. Instead, he was more worried about the potential fallout for the Banta Bowl.

"Wow, I guess I see where your priorities are." I couldn't keep the condescension out of my voice.

Willie's gaze shot to mine. He looked momentarily stunned at my forward assessment of him, but then he shook his head. "This business is my priority, and since Emma somehow got herself mixed up in Cal's death, I'm having a heck of a time trying to run this place by myself. So, if you'll excuse me, I should get back to it."

"Emma had nothing to do with Cal's death," I seethed. "But you probably know that."

Willie rolled his eyes. "I know no such thing. Not for certain, at least. That's exactly what I told the detectives."

I made a humming noise and took a seat in the chair opposite Willie's desk. He scowled, but I kept talking, refusing to give him a chance to kick me out before I figured out what was going on here. "Did you also tell the detectives about the fight that went down here the night of Cal's death?"

Willie's mouth dropped open. "What ... no! I didn't say anything about that!" He narrowed his gaze at me. "Did Zac send you here? Because I've held up my end of the bargain."

I blinked.

Well, that was easy.

I leaned forward and clasped my hands, resting them on the edge of Willie's desk. "Zac didn't send me here. I came on my own. I'm trying to figure out why you were so worried that the police would find out about an argument between Zac and Cal when it had nothing to do with you."

"Why would I be worried about that?" Willie shifted his gaze.

"I overheard you saying as much to your lawyer the morning after Cal died. The whole time, I thought it had been you that had been arguing with Cal in here"—I pointed to the office space—"but it was Zac Geffadab, wasn't it?"

Willie's eyes widened to wild proportions. "Who told you that? How do you know?"

I waved a hand. "I have my sources. So, tell me, Willie, what's it to you?"

Willie groaned and let his head fall back. "This is a bloody mess, I tell ya. None of this would have happened if I hadn't overheard Cal's fight with Zac."

I nodded for Willie to go on. The sweat beading on his forehead had me guessing he wanted to unburden himself of whatever secret he was carrying.

"Cal had been compiling information that would have tanked Red Vector Music Group if it got into the right hands."

"The hands of the media?" I guessed.

Willie shrugged. "More or less, I think. Cal told Zac that he was engaging in unethical business practices. Zac was arguing that he didn't force anyone to sign with them ... them being Red Vector. But Cal said that he was preying on green talent who didn't know any better. Zac kept saying that Cal couldn't touch him because he hadn't done anything illegal, but Cal said he'd expose Zac and he'd be found guilty in the court of public opinion. Cal said he'd be thrilled when Zac's empire crumbled. That's how their conversation ended."

Willie was silent, and I digested his words. "That sounds a lot like motive for murder if you ask me."

Willie's sharp inhale made me realize I'd spoken out loud. "You really think Zac killed Cal to keep him quiet?"

"It fits," I said. But did it? Could Zac have gotten access to Cal's tea in the time it took Cal to go get some fresh air? Whitney had followed him outside. Autumn had been tied up across the hall with Phil, and I knew from Emma that she'd disappeared to check on the bar after overhearing Cal in Willie's office. Cal's dressing room would have been empty.

If Zac felt like he had no other option, he could have snuck into the room, slipped the drug into the drink, and snuck out with no one the wiser. It would have meant he came prepared with whatever drug he used to poison Cal, but it wasn't out of the question. Hopefully the police knew what that drug was, and they could figure out if Zac had access to it.

I turned my attention back to Willie. "Where do you fit in all of this?" He looked away from me. "Oh, come on, Willie. I know Zac is threatening you. He's obviously not happy that you overheard his conversation with Cal. How did you overhear it, by the way?" If Whitney had been in the alcove I'd hidden in, where was Willie?

"I was in the bathroom," he all but wailed, pointing his finger to a closed door in the far corner of the room. At my raised eyebrows, he threw up his hands. "All of our offices were outfitted with private restrooms just like the musicians' dressing rooms.

I ducked in to relieve myself—like *any man should be allowed to do!*" He spit the words out with added emphasis. "I did not give Cal or Zac permission to use my office, but next thing I know, I'm taking a leak and hearing raised voices. I admit, I was curious, and I hardly thought it wise to interrupt, so I stayed put. Bad decision."

"Zac discovered you?"

Willie nodded. "After Cal stormed out, the toilet flushed automatically. Stupid thing has been on the fritz and decided that *then* would be a good time to actually work. What are the chances? I came out to find Zac fuming mad. He told me if I told anyone what I'd heard, he'd personally see to it that the Banta Bowl and any of my future establishments were blacklisted in the industry. He swore he wouldn't let any RVR singers take gigs at my venues. He said Cal didn't know what he was talking about."

"So you agreed to keep your mouth shut? Willie! This is information the police need. Zac could be a killer!"

Willie's face turned stony. "You don't know that. I don't know that. What I do know is I need to keep the Banta Bowl name clean. Zac has way more clout and power in this town than Cal ever did. I told him I didn't want any trouble."

"Let me guess. He hasn't left you alone."

Willie shifted.

"I literally just overheard your conversation, Willie. If you think Zac's threats are going to end there, you have another thing coming. How long are you going to let him have power over you? If he killed Cal, he could come for you next!"

Willie looked physically pained. "I don't want more trouble. Cal up and dying on my property is bad enough, for crying out loud."

I really didn't like Willie. The man was spineless. Emma would be much better off on her own, and I would tell her that as soon as I managed to get her out of jail.

"You need to go to the police." I shot to my feet. "I'll walk you to your car."

Willie let out a sharp breath. "What? Now? No! I've got an operation to run."

"Bless your heart, Willie, if you don't tell the police what you just told me, then I'm going to tell them. How do you think it'll look for you when it comes out that you've withheld relevant information from authorities? Think about your reputation then."

Willie spluttered.

"Besides, I have a feeling the truth about Zac Geffadab is going to come to light sooner than he thinks. Believe me when I say you want to be on the right side of this thing."

I waited by the door, holding eye contact with Willie.

Finally, he cursed, kicked his chair back, and stormed out of his office.

I bit back a triumphant grin and followed him to the parking lot.

28

I decided we may have better luck at police headquarters if we didn't pile on while Willie was there. After all, now Bobby and I had sent Whitney and Willie to the detectives. They were either going to be thrilled with us or annoyed.

I sat in my car in the parking lot of the Banta Bowl and fired off a text message to Bobby, explaining what I'd learned from Willie and proposing we postpone our own police department errand until later in the afternoon.

His response was immediate.

Bobby: Impressive, Leigh. What time should I meet you there?

Leigh: One o'clock? That should be enough time for Willie to come clean.

Bobby: Yeah, sounds good.

Leigh: Headed for a quick swim first. Promise you won't follow me there and scare the living daylights out of me again?

Bobby: You're no fun.

I smirked as more bubbles popped up onto the screen, waiting to see what else Bobby had to say.

Bobby: But if you insist. No more tailing you.

I laughed outright at that.

Leigh: Whatever you need to say to me, you can say to my face from now on.

Bobby: Deal. See you soon.

I tossed my phone in the passenger seat and drove to Hooks High. The school was quiet, and I made quick work of shedding my clothes and pulling on my swimming suit. I felt like I was rocketing through the water as I started on my usual laps, the adrenaline from my meeting with Jace and then Willie propelling me forward. I couldn't help but think that everything was heading in the right direction. Emma had to be released soon. She *had* to be. If the detectives didn't think so, I was prepared to stay at police headquarters and make a giant fuss until they saw reason.

I kicked off the far wall and focused on my breathing, a song idea popping into my head. Hopefully I could tease it out with Jace.

After another thirty minutes of swimming and dreaming, I pulled myself out of the water. In my haste to get in the pool, I'd left my towel in the changing room, so I hustled across the slick pool deck to dry off and get changed.

Bobby was waiting when I showed up at Headquarters. We approached the desk, and I introduced myself and told the officer I had pertinent information on Cal Dutton's case. "Could I please speak to the detectives in charge?"

"I'll see what I can do," the female officer said.

We took a step back from the counter as she picked up her phone. Bobby fished a file out of his messenger bag.

"What's that?" I asked.

"I figured that to prove we were serious about Cal tipping me off at"—he glanced around before whispering—"the PAP, I'd have to show some proof."

I pressed my lips together. "You're willing to let the police know that you're the man behind that operation?"

Bobby shrugged, tucking the file folder back into his bag before meeting my gaze again. "If it helps, it'll be worth it. Besides, they have no reason to out me to the public. If anyone is going to find out my identity, I figure the police are a safe bet."

The female officer hung up the phone and waved to grab my attention before I could tell Bobby that he was being very selfless and upright, and it sort of made me feel like crying. So many people I knew would have acted differently.

"Detective Yance said to wait here. He'll be right out," she informed us.

"Thank you so much." I smiled, focusing on her and not how weirdly emotional Bobby's actions were making me. I refused to blubber.

Ten minutes later, Detective Yance's imposing figure appeared from the hallway. He nodded at me. "Ms. Notrap. Right this way."

Bobby and I followed him into the bowels of the building. I kept my eyes peeled for Willie, but most of the doors were shut. Detective Yance led us into a small conference room. The walls were blank, and there was an oval table in the center of the space. I spotted one of those gadget-looking cameras in the corner, and it reminded me to ask him if he'd heard from Whitney. Hopefully she told him she planted the cameras in Cal's condo.

Detective Yance sat and motioned for us to do the same. He retrieved a pen from the inside pocket of his suit and tossed a pad of paper down on the table. "Alright. I'm listening."

I took a deep breath. "First of all, you have the wrong person in custody. Emma didn't kill Cal."

Detective Yance let out a sigh. "Save your breath, Ms. Notrap. Your friend will be released this afternoon. We don't have enough to hold her on."

"Thank you, Jesus."

Detective Yance arched a brow at me. "You calling me your Lord and Savior, Ms. Notrap?"

My cheeks flushed impossibly hot. Next to me, Bobby's shoulders shook.

"Sorry. No. I didn't realize I'd spoken out loud. It was more of a general prayer." I grimaced. *Pull yourself together, woman!* I coughed. "Anyway, that's great news. Thank you for telling me. We came to talk to you about information we found out about Cal's contentious relationship with his record label."

Bobby and I took turns outlining what we'd learned. Bobby shared his information on the tip he'd received, and I found myself offering up another prayer of thanks that Detective Ottom wasn't here to grill him on his position at the PAP. Detective Yance just took it all in with an unchanging expression.

I supplied information about what Emma and I had learned about Cal's watch and the hidden compartment.

"All of that, taken together with the warnings Cal was giving to everyone connected to Red Vector, the fight Whitney Allerow overheard between Cal and Zac just before he died that I'm hoping you just had verified by Willie Davis..." My voice rose in question.

He inclined his head, and I took that as a good sign.

"All of that paints a clear picture of discord between Cal and the music group," I concluded.

Detective Yance scribbled a note and stared down at his paper. I decided to press my luck.

"Have you found anything incriminating on any of Cal's personal computers? Anything that points to the bomb he was going to drop through the Printer's Alley Press?"

"I can't share details of an ongoing investigation, Ms. Notrap."

"But..." Bobby pitched his voice in a buddy-buddy way, and I fought back a grin.

Detective Yance stared between us, his mouth a thin line, before finally relenting. "All I will say is that we're backed up. We haven't had a tech specialist available to do a deep dive into Cal's deleted files. On first glance, there's been nothing in his email correspondence or saved on his laptop or phone that proves your theory."

I cocked my head to the side. "That just adds more credence to the idea that he was being secretive about it. Maybe we need to turn his apartment inside out and see if we can find a hidden flash drive or something."

Detective Yance rubbed the back of his neck, the corners of his mouth dipping downward.

"It's a long shot, I realize that," I amended, feeling suddenly foolish for being so forward.

"But it might be your only shot," Bobby spoke up.

I aimed a grateful look in his direction.

Detective Yance stared us down before his shoulders rolled forward ever so slightly. "Was there anything else that you needed to share with me today?"

I asked about Whitney and was pleased to hear that she'd come in.

"Did you find the hidden cameras in Cal's ductwork?" I asked.

Detective Yance grimaced. "I sent an officer over to Cal's apartment directly after she told us. He took the cameras down. We have them here."

"Can you access the footage? Maybe you'll see Cal hiding something. Or maybe you'll see him in an argument with someone other than Emma?" Bobby leaned back in his chair.

"And you can use the footage to figure out who broke in before Emma and I got there to get Cal's stuff," I added.

"Perhaps," Detective Yance conceded. "But for now, please let us do our job."

Bobby and I rose when Detective Yance did.

"Will you be in touch if you do go to search Cal's apartment?" I asked. "We could join you. A couple extra sets of eyes never hurt anyone."

Detective Yance sighed. "Don't count on it. Look, I know you're just trying to help, but you've got to cool it."

I held up my hands in surrender. "That's fair. We'll stay out of your way."

Detective Yance led the way back into the lobby. Before turning us loose, he faced Bobby. "If you wanted to run an article that put some pressure on Zac and RVR, I wouldn't stop you. Since it's an anonymous news outlet, I doubt anyone else would be able to stop you either."

Before I could process that, Detective Yance disappeared.

"Did Yance just give you permission to run with this story?" I turned to find Bobby smirking.

"Like I needed permission," he said with a sly grin. "I was going to tease a story tonight either way. Hopefully the cops find the concrete evidence Cal had soon, and I can follow up with that."

The doors to the station opened. Emma's parents hurried inside. Sandra spotted me and rushed forward, wrapping me in a hug. "Oh, Leigh. They just called us. They're letting Emma come home."

"That is the best news." I hugged her back until a door whooshed open behind me.

We turned, and Emma, looking pale, with her usually styled hair hanging limp, appeared. She shot us a wry smile as the officer at the front desk handed over her personal belongings.

Sandra and Gregory scampered across the room and engulfed their daughter in a hug.

Tears pricked at the corners of my eyes. "Thank you, Jesus," I said, not even caring who heard me this time.

"I can let you all have a moment." Bobby motioned across the waiting area to where Emma and her parents stood. "I'm gonna go and get started on my article."

I nodded. "Thanks for being willing to stick your neck out to clear Emma's name."

He shrugged. "It's nothing."

"It's something to me."

Bobby scuffed his shoe against the floor, and I stood there, not knowing exactly what to say next. Finally, I settled on, "I'll watch for a PAP update."

Bobby's eyes lit up at that. "Should go live just after dinner tonight."

I grinned back. "Be in touch."

"I won't be able to stay away from Java Flo's. That place has the best food in the Village."

"Don't I know it."

Bobby waved, and I joined Emma and her parents. I hugged my best friend, gripping her so tightly she let out a chuckle. "Easy, Leigh. It's okay."

"Are *you* okay?"

Emma shrugged. "I will be. After a long, hot shower, some of Agnes's French toast, and an early bedtime."

"Are you sure we can't convince you to come home with us." Sandra fussed with Emma's hair, brushing it away from her cheek.

"You know we'd take great care of you. Pamper you a bit," Gregory added.

Emma smiled at her parents. "Thank you, truly, for the offer, but what I really want is my own bed. And you guys live way out of the city. I plan to get to work bright and early tomorrow to sort out the mess Willie has made in my absence."

"I'm parked right outside. You can ride home with me," I offered.

Emma nodded, shooting me a grateful look. Turning to her parents, she said, "I'll come for dinner one of these nights. It's just a little crazy with the Country Music Festival, but I know we still have to go through photos for Cal's funeral, and I promise I'll help with that."

Sandra swallowed hard and Gregory shifted his weight, looking beyond where Emma and I were standing to some fixed point in the distance.

"We're so glad you're heading home, Em." Sandra pulled her in for another hug, and Gregory followed.

Five minutes later, I was flying down the interstate toward home, filling Emma in on all Bobby and I had learned in her absence.

"So who killed Cal?" she asked in conclusion. "Zac and his cronies at RVR, or Autumn and Phil in some sort of fit of romantic insanity?"

"That's the million-dollar question."

Emma leaned back in the passenger seat, drawing in a deep breath. "I want to close my eyes, but I feel like I should force them open to take in the outside world. I was afraid for a minute there I'd only be seeing the inside of a jail cell. I was so shocked when they found those eye drops in my desk, I didn't take a proper look around on the way to the station in case it was my final chance."

"Oh my gosh, don't even joke about that," I scolded. "So, it was eye drops?" I added after a second.

Emma swallowed and shivered. "Yeah. The killer left them there, and then must've anonymously tipped off the police or something. Fortunately, the detectives realized I was being framed."

"I wonder why eye droplet bottles were such damning evidence," I murmured, saying a silent prayer of gratitude that the detectives did their job and my friend was free.

"Apparently, the same drug in the belladonna tincture Cal was supplementing with, atropine, is an ingredient found in these eye drops. Ophthalmologists use it to dilate pupils. Detective Yance gave me the whole lowdown when he was walking me out of the jail cell. It was the least he could do after subjecting me to that terrible food and cardboard mattress, not to mention, you know, imprisonment." Emma shuddered. "Anyway, there were three bottles of this specific eye drop solution stowed in my desk. If someone dumped all those bottles into the tiny kettle of Cal's tea, then that would have done the deed."

I gripped the steering wheel. "Thank goodness Autumn didn't take a sip. She would have met the same fate."

"Maybe she knew better than to get anywhere close to the tea."

"Because she poisoned it herself?" I filled in.

"Could have been," Emma said.

"Or," I countered, "it could have been someone else. No one knew Autumn was going to be with Cal. Remember, she said she'd changed her plans last minute. Whoever drugged the tea likely thought Cal would be drinking alone."

"Autumn's either the killer or supremely lucky." Emma grimaced. "We could have been dealing with an accidental double murder."

I parked on the street near Java Flo's. When we walked inside, Agnes wrapped Emma in a fierce hug. She immediately set Dot to work on French toast. "Completely on the house, and I'll even run the food up to your apartment."

Emma thanked her and went to take a shower.

I fed Phelps and sat down in my chair, tucking my feet up beneath me. As the water turned on in the bathroom, I closed my eyes, letting the steady hum of rushing water soothe me. I blinked and side-eyed the piano, a little song about homecoming ready to spring forth.

That's Home by Leigh Notrap

It's chamomile tea
In the middle of the night
A low familiar voice
Saying it'll be alright.
No matter where I roam
There's a light on just for me.
And that's home.

It's Friday movie snuggles
Sitting in the dark
A no-words conversation
A Sunday at the park.
Down the block or cross-country
It's still where I want to be.
And that's home.

Life can take you
All directions
Sinking
Swimming
Pulled in two
But it don't matter
All that matters
Is getting back home
To you.

It's the beat of your heart
My head, your chest
Warm strength shepherding
Deep soul-level rest
I'll be there for you
You'll be waiting there for me.
And that's home.

29

I made it to the Saturday night vigil Mass, so I let myself sleep in on Sunday, but I awoke to rapid-fire incoming text messages. I groped for my phone, where I'd wedged it under my pillowcase. I pulled it up right in front of my face and cracked an eye open to read my new texts.

They were from Bobby, and I jolted upright.

Bobby: A tip just came into the PAP that the police are swarming Cal Dutton's condo.

Bobby: Where are you?

Bobby: I think we should go over there, don't you?

Bobby: Maybe the detectives are searching for that evidence.

Bobby: Based on our suggestion!

Bobby: Sorry for all the messages.

Bobby: I do this when I get excited. My fingers fly faster than my brain.

Leigh: No worries. Good morning. We should definitely go there. Drop me a pin with your address, and I'll pick you up.

I was tripping my way out of bed and shimmying into a pair of jeans when I felt the vibration of Bobby's location ping my phone.

"Emma?" I called out, banging open the door to the main space of our apartment.

One look around told me she wasn't here. The toaster was out, which meant she was in too much of a rush to wait for food at Agnes's. I spotted a loose-leaf sheet of paper on the counter.

It was old school, but Emma and I would leave notes for each other, sharing our schedules and plans. It was our attempt to take back a modicum of control from the digital age. I grabbed the note from the counter.

Hey Leigh,

I'm headed to work to assess the situation there. Lunch downtown? I should be able to get away by that point. Text me where you're at.

Em

I got myself ready in record time and was out the door within twenty minutes. The Village streets were still pretty quiet since it wasn't quite nine o'clock, and after a late night, everyone was slow to get moving.

I called Emma from the car and filled her in.

"Meet you there," she said with excitement tinging her voice.

"Drive safe," I told her and ended the call.

I was able to find Bobby's flat with no problem. He let himself into my truck and reached over and grabbed for his seatbelt. "Hey. Thanks for the lift."

I caught a glimpse of today's t-shirt, which simply read, "Elementary," with a screen-printed image of a smoking pipe.

"Nice." I nodded to his chest before turning my attention back to the road.

"Figured it was a good day to break out the Sherlock Holmes."

"Let's hope our detectives have as much success as Holmes, eh? What did your tip say again?"

"Not much other than there was a large police presence at Cal's place."

"You think it's legit?"

In my periphery, I caught Bobby nodding. "They left their first name and claimed to be a neighbor. I can't imagine why anyone would lie about that. Guess we'll see."

"Yeah. I called Emma, by the way," I said. "She's at the Banta Bowl, but she's going to meet us at Cal's. She still has the key from her parents' house, so she'll be able to get us inside to see what's going on."

"Brilliant. I knew teaming up with you two was the right call." Bobby shoved his glasses up the bridge of his nose before clicking around on his phone.

"The RVR article was great, by the way," I offered.

"Really?" He sounded surprised.

My eyebrows shot up. "You're an extremely talented writer."

Bobby glanced down at his lap. "You're just being nice because we're on the same team."

I shook my head. "No, I mean it. I was a PAP fan well before I knew you were the brains behind the operation. Why would you doubt that?"

Bobby shrugged. "When I was younger, I had a teacher tell me I'd never be a good writer."

I flinched. "That's appalling."

He shrugged again. "Reading didn't come easy to me as a kid. I'm bilingual."

"What? Really?" Was there anything Bobby couldn't do?

"Yeah. Spanish and English. My parents spoke Spanish to me and my siblings at home, so I can speak it fluently. I think it messed with how quickly I was able to pick up on English semantics and stuff. Anyway, who knows. I'm sure the teacher didn't mean anything by his offhand comment, but it still stung."

I scoffed. "Well, just look at you now. Making a living by writing news stories *and* song lyrics."

Bobby laughed, but it sounded forced. "Yeah, except nobody knows it's me. That's what I get for writing under a pen name, and of course, the whole anonymous thing."

"Do you think you'll ever go public?"

"I don't know." He shrugged. "Some of the allure of the PAP is its secrecy. I really don't mind. But it is nice to know you think it's good stuff."

"I do."

We slipped into silence, and I mulled it all over. A soft spot in my heart was forming for Bobby. I'd love to figure out a way to help him prove himself.

First things first, though. We had a murder to solve.

I parked as close as I could get to Cal's condo. There were several squad cards outside.

"Guess you can trust this tipper," I mumbled.

"I can trust most of them. Just not Whitney Allerow," Bobby said.

"At least she came clean."

"There is that."

We got out of my truck. From the other direction, a car came flying toward us. Bobby jumped up onto the curb as it blew by.

"That'd be Emma." I smiled.

Bobby blew out a breath. "Thought someone was trying to kill me for a minute there."

I chuckled, and my phone chimed in my pocket. I silenced it without even looking at the screen. Whoever was calling would have to wait. We met Emma on the sidewalk where she'd parked illegally right outside the door to Cal's building.

When she noticed me eyeing her park job, she shrugged. "What are the police going to do, take me *back* to jail?" Emma waved Cal's key fob in the air, and Bobby and I followed her into the building. "Shall we?"

We bypassed the elevators and took the stairs to Cal's floor. When we opened the door to Cal's corridor, the mood was ... not good.

Next to me, Bobby looked around, taking in the opulence of his surroundings. Emma charged forward. My gaze locked onto Detective Ottom's. His expression was sour, and when he spotted us, it curdled.

"Excuse me," he said to the uniformed officer he was speaking with. In two heavy strides, he had headed Emma off. "What do you people think you're doing here? How did you get in?"

Emma went toe-to-toe with the detective, and despite him being triple her size, didn't bat an eye. Once again, she held up Cal's key. "I'm allowed to be here, Detective. What's going on?"

Emma tried to look around the detective as Bobby and I joined her. I craned my neck to see into Cal's condo, but Detective Ottom's size was working to his advantage.

"That's none of your business," he said.

Emma shook her head. "You're wrong there. My parents are going to be even more distraught if something happened at Cal's place. Tell me what you're doing here."

"Are you searching for evidence against Red Vector?" Bobby asked.

Detective Ottom shot him a disdainful look. Before he could say anything, Detective Yance joined our huddle.

The younger detective's eyes widened when he spotted us, and a twinge of what I'd like to consider amused respect flashed across his pupils before he schooled his features. "We can't find anything of consequence, and fingerprinting is going to be useless at this point."

"Fingerprinting? Has there been another break-in?" I asked.

"Again, that's none of your business. We're in charge here," Detective Ottom bellowed.

"Of course you are." I held up my hands. "I was just thinking that Emma and I were likely the last people in the condo. We might be able to provide some information on the state of things before we left."

Emma nodded vigorously next to me.

Detective Yance ran his hand behind his neck. "I wish you could help," he muttered.

Detective Ottom shot him a frustrated look, but Detective Yance just shrugged. "Someone trashed the condo. It's like they were looking for something."

Bobby, Emma, and I exchanged a glance.

"Incriminating evidence?" I suggested.

Detective Yance tipped his head from one side to the other. "Perhaps."

"You don't have any idea if they found what they were looking for?" Bobby put in.

"Afraid not."

"Can we at least see the condo?" Emma asked.

"I'm not sure that's a good idea, Ms.—" Detective Yance cut himself off when Emma pinned him with a fierce look. "I suppose that would be fine, don't you, Detective Ottom?"

The older man just shook his head, but he let us pass.

Bobby and I hurried behind Emma.

"Oh my gosh," Emma said and gasped. "What a mess!"

That was an understatement. Every drawer and door in the condo was open, and the contents spilled out. Cal's couch pillows were slashed, and the stuffing spewed onto the floor. Certain areas of plaster were banged in, as if whoever was here had been looking for hidden compartments in the walls.

I couldn't help but think it was a blessing that Emma and I had gotten in and out with her parents' list when we did. Had we waited, we wouldn't have been able to find anything. Or worse, what her parents wanted to remember Cal by might have been destroyed.

I wandered into the condo behind the others, careful not to touch anything. I was drawn to the piano, which remained mostly untouched. The top was open, but it didn't look like the insides were damaged. Maybe whoever was here had a healthy respect for music.

It followed.

Who else would have wanted to trash Cal's condo but Zac Geffadab or one of his cronies?

"This building has to have security cameras, right?" Bobby asked from where he stood in the kitchen.

Detective Ottom scoffed as he surveyed the scene, his hands on his utility belt. "Of course. But the people who snuck in here wore dark-colored clothes with hoodies pulled up over their faces. Nothing that would give anything away to us."

"That sounds familiar," Emma mumbled to me.

I nodded. We'd likely interrupted the same intruder when we were here collecting Cal's things. Why had he or she waited to return until now? And with a partner?

"Two people?" I clarified.

"That's what eyewitnesses told us," Detective Ottom confirmed. "They had a key card. We're working to figure out when it was issued so we can trace it."

"Too bad Whitney's cameras got taken down. Bad timing," I added under my breath.

Detective Yance spun his sharp gaze my way. "Did you tell anyone about that?"

My eyes flared at his harsh tone. "No. Of course not." I hadn't even mentioned to Emma that it was Whitney who had filmed her fight with Cal using hidden cameras the crazed fan had rigged up in the ductwork of his condo.

"Whitney might have told someone, though," Bobby suggested. "She was more than happy to unload her grievances and feelings about Cal to Leigh and me. We got more than we bargained for when we ran into her at the Banta Bowl."

Detective Yance and Detective Ottom exchanged a look.

"I'll reach out to her." Detective Yance strode toward the doorway.

Bobby checked his watch. "I need to be getting back, actually."

"You can take my truck," I offered, and then had a moment of panic. Did I really just say that? What was going on with me? I didn't usually trust people enough to share so much as a recommendation for my favorite sandwich, much less my vehicle.

Bobby picked up on my panic. "Are you sure? I can get a rideshare."

"No, it's fine." Maybe this was good for me. A turning over. A metamorphosis. "I'll ride with Emma, and she can drop me off to get my truck on our way home."

I fished out the keys and handed them to Bobby. We said our goodbyes, promising to be in touch soon, and he walked out of the condo as Detective Yance was walking back in.

"We can get—" I was about to say *out of your hair*, when Emma's hand landed on my forearm.

"What did you learn, Detective Yance?"

I glanced between my best friend and the detective. How Emma knew that the detective knew something, I couldn't quite figure out, but she was staring at him unflinchingly, so I kept my mouth shut.

"I spoke to Ms. Allerow." He ran a weary hand over his jaw. "Before I could even tell her why I was calling, she asked what was going on at Cal's place. At first, I thought she'd seen something on the news, but I've already checked the PAP, and there's been no update. The mainstream media is slow to the draw, too. So, she found out some other way."

"There's still a camera hidden here?" I asked, unable to keep the eagerness out of my voice.

In response, Detective Yance walked over to the piano. He inched his hand along the back of the heavy instrument, behind the stacks of books, until he stilled. He readjusted his grip, pulled, and produced a small electronic device.

"That's a camera?" Emma asked, stepping closer to get a better look.

"Not a camera, but a listening device. Whitney claims she forgot to tell us about it until a notification on her phone alerted her to new activity in Cal's condo."

"Do you think you'll be able to get something off of it?" I asked.

Detective Ottom actually looked excited. "Since there were two perps here, I can't imagine we won't get some conversation. Let's listen to it."

Detective Yance pulled out his phone. "Whitney emailed me the link to the program's recording. She swears she didn't listen to it yet, just that she got notified that there was new content." He rolled his eyes at that.

Emma and I exchanged a glance. She was fighting back a smile. "Play it, then!"

"Now I don't know how I feel about civilians being here when we..." Detective Ottom trailed off when Emma stepped in front of him and peered over Detective Yance's shoulder as he tapped around on his phone.

"We're better off bringing this back to the station," Detective Yance said. "To get our tech team on it."

I narrowed my gaze at him. "Isn't your tech team swamped?"

He shifted. "We'll put a rush on this. Or I'll go through the recording myself."

Before Emma or I could put up any more of a fight, a uniformed officer burst into the room. "Sir, we've got a vehicle accident on our hands, two miles down the road."

The officer's radio crackled. "Confirmed one vehicle involved. Tennessee plates, 2149-DTW. Male driver. Initial reports indicate 11-80. Requesting 10-52."

All the blood drained from my face. I didn't know what much of that meant, but I knew that license plate.

It was mine.

"Bobby!" I croaked.

30

"Is he alright? The driver. Is he okay? What are they saying?"

The cop shot me a bewildered look, and I all but growled. I turned my attention to the detectives. "That's my truck. That's Bobby."

Detective Yance moved first. He pulled out his cell phone and put it to his ear.

"Sir, I need to go," the officer said, addressing Detective Ottom. "Are you okay here?"

"We'll secure the scene. I need two of you with me," Detective Ottom responded.

The police jumped into action.

I looked at Emma with panic-filled eyes. "What do we do?"

She reached out an arm and pulled me into a side hug. "Wait and see what Detective Yance says."

The younger detective had turned away from us to make his call. My mind was hurtling toward worst-case scenarios. What if Bobby was dead? What if it was my fault? Did something go wrong with my truck? When was the last time I had it serviced?

After what felt like an eon, Detective Yance turned back to us. "The truck went off the road at a high speed. It sounds like Bobby was able to avoid hitting another vehicle, but he wound up wedged between two trees. According to the person who called the accident in, he was unconscious."

"He's alive, though?" Emma asked the question I couldn't bring myself to.

"As far as I know, yes. 11-80 means potential major injury, and the dispatcher requested an ambulance."

"What hospital are they taking him to?" I asked.

Detective Yance shot me a curious glance. "I'm not sure. How well do you know Bobby Cruz, Ms. Notrap?"

"Not well," I admitted. Now wasn't the time to get into my weird feelings where Bobby was concerned. I wasn't sure if I could explain it if I tried. I just felt a connection to him. I couldn't stop the sob that escaped at the thought that he would just be left alone in the hospital. Did his parents live nearby? What about other friends? The only times I had seen him, he was alone at Java Flo's.

"You wouldn't be allowed up to see him anyway," Detective Yance added. "Not if he's in the ICU. It would be immediate family and approved guests only who will be eligible for visitation."

"He's going to the ICU?" I sucked in a deep breath.

"Leigh." Emma reached for my hand and squeezed it. "Let's go back to the Village and regroup. See if we can do anything for Bobby with Agnes's help. Detective Yance will be in touch when he learns more about Bobby's condition, right?" Emma pinned Detective Yance with another one of her looks.

He nodded without question.

What was going on between these two?

I let Emma steer me out of Cal's condo. Detective Yance walked us to the door, and Emma turned to him before we reached the threshold. "Please let us know what you find out from the recordings Whitney sent over. I'd like to see my brother's killer brought to justice, and I'm hoping that what you hear on that recording is going to shed some light on who is responsible for Cal's death."

"I hope so, too. I'll be in touch with you and your family as soon as I know something."

Emma nodded, thanked the detective, and looped her arm through mine. We walked down the steps of Cal's condo building in silence. My mind was on Bobby. I could hardly bring myself to care about Cal's case anymore.

That wasn't entirely true. I wanted to put the whole thing behind me. But in a weird sort of roundabout way, Cal's death had thrown Bobby into my life, and I wasn't sorry about that.

"You like him, don't you?" Emma said quietly.

"Bobby? Yeah, I guess I do. He's become a friend. It's not easy for me to trust people, as you know."

"Yeah."

"I don't know. With Bobby, I could. He's easy to talk to, and he makes me laugh. He's smart, too." I was so lost in my thoughts that it took me a minute to realize she was staring at me. "What?"

Emma's mouth dropped. "Are you in love with him, Leigh?"

"What?" I flinched. Leave it to Em to go *there*. Good grief. "No! I don't like Bobby in *that* sort of way."

She studied me.

I arched my eyebrows. "Seriously," I added.

"Alright, then." She started the car. "Tell me all about your breakfast date with Jace, then."

I shook my head. I could tell she was trying to act normal—to take my mind off of Bobby's injuries and hers off of the limbo land we were sitting in regarding Cal's case.

"He invited me to write with him."

Emma sucked in a breath. "That's great. Are you excited?"

"Yeah, it should be good. Good experience, for sure." I could barely think about it now. Bobby was hurt, and everything else seemed to fade to gray.

"I'm dying to make a comment about how you guys will probably write a passionate love song and then make out in the studio, but I get the sense you aren't in the mood for my teasing," Emma said.

I glanced over to find her giving me a small smile. I looked to the ceiling of the car.

"You know me well," I said on a sigh. Bobby's situation aside, I couldn't imagine kissing Jace James. Then again, I hadn't really imagined kissing *anyone*—not for a long time. My parents' relationship completely turned me off from the prospect of getting close to someone. All I saw between them was deceit and dysfunction and a selfish, vicious cycle of falling in and out of love. Throw in my dad's unfaithfulness, and it was a recipe for me to be a love hater.

But with Jace, I could see it. We were friends first. We had a lot in common. He was kind and not pushy. We clicked.

I clicked with Bobby, too, but I meant it when I said I wasn't thinking of Bobby romantically. Then again, I really liked his glasses and his rumpled appearance, coupled with his quick mind. I hadn't felt as comfortable in anyone's presence as I did in his in, well, ever.

Bobby and Jace were so different.

I shook my head before swiveling in my seat and facing Emma again. "I'm going to call Agnes and see if she knows Bobby's family and can put me in touch with them. Then I'm going to need to do something productive while we wait for word from Detective Yance, who, by the way, seems to be under some sort of spell where you're concerned."

"I don't know what you're talking about," Emma said, but I spied a blush creeping into her cheeks.

"Sure you don't." I leaned back into my seat, deciding not to press the issue for right now. "Do your parents still need help getting photos together for Cal's funeral? We could go do that."

Emma checked her rearview mirror and merged onto the interstate. "Great idea."

31

"Look at how cute you two were. You could be twins!" I held up a photo of Cal and Emma as toddlers. Cal had a toy guitar slung around his neck, and Emma held a clipboard that was the size of her entire torso.

She glanced up from the stack of printed photos she was shuffling through. We sat on the den floor in her parents' mansion. We were making good progress—especially since we'd heard from Detective Yance. He told us Bobby was stable and coming out of surgery to set a bone in his leg that had cracked in the accident. Detective Yance had also let the name of the hospital slip out, and I had plans to head up there after we were done here.

Emma took the photo from me, and a ghost of a smile formed on her lips. "Cal always knew he wanted to be a singer."

"What were you?" I gestured to the clipboard in the picture.

"He made me be his manager. He always was bossy." Emma made a face, but her expression wasn't malicious—more wistful. "Even at age four."

The mention of a manager brought to mind Phil.

And Autumn.

It was an angle that still wasn't resolved in Cal's case. What were the two of them up to? Were they truly having an affair? Was Cal going to fire Phil? Would Phil have killed to preserve his reputation and clear a pathway for himself and Autumn?

"Speaking of managers," I segued. "You should invite Phil to the Banta Bowl tonight."

Emma's expression soured. "Why would I do that? What if he killed Cal?"

"That's pretty doubtful at this point. Knowing what we know about Red Vector, I'd say all signs point to Zac or one of his minions killing Cal to keep him quiet and save themselves from the fallout of him shining a light on their shady business."

Even as I said it, my stomach felt heavy, like it had been filled with rocks. If Zac would go so far as to kill Cal to keep his business dealings hush-hush, what else would he do?

"So what do you want with Phil, then?"

I sat back on my heels. "I want answers. I'm curious about him and Autumn. I'm also curious if Cal told him anything about Red Vector."

"Makes sense. I don't think I'll have any problem getting him there. Autumn is performing an acoustic set tonight starting at seven. A tribute to Cal ahead of his funeral. Phil is probably planning to be there anyway."

"Okay. Good." I wanted to cover all my bases and get the truth. The police were handling whoever broke into Cal's place, but that left Phil and Autumn's affair—or whatever it was—to us.

"I'll send Phil a text and tell him Willie wants to talk about booking his clients going forward. If he's not planning to be there already, that should get him in the door."

She pulled out her phone and sent the message before getting back to the photos. We worked silently for a couple of minutes before Emma nudged me and handed over a photo. "Here's one of you!"

I glanced down at the frozen-in-time photo. Staring back at me were Cal, Jace, Autumn, a couple of other musicians from music school, and me. Autumn stood between Cal and Jace. They each had their arms around her shoulders, like they were the Oreo cookies to her cream filling. Cal and Autumn were smirking at each other while Jace looked on. He was frowning. Even in music school, he'd mastered the art of the smolder. All you could see was his chiseled profile, but he looked like he was auditioning for the cover of GQ while the rest of us were staring at the camera with big-toothed grins.

"This was right before Cal, Jace, and Autumn graduated," I said. "I remember because I still had a year of school left, and I was so jealous they were headed here to Nashburg to take Music City by storm."

"It's crazy how successful the three of them are. Were," Emma corrected with a wince. She cleared her features. "We should use that photo, too. Add it to the pile."

We went on like that for another hour and half before breaking for lunch. Sandra had prepared us delectable sandwiches. I was happy to see her doting on Emma, and Emma seemed appreciative. I hoped they could mend their rocky relationship—for both of their sakes.

"So." Emma swallowed her last bite and dusted off her hands. "Do you want to come to work tonight so you can hear what Phil has to say for himself?"

I nodded. "Yeah, I'll definitely come. I'll gladly be your backup, and it would be good to get some answers."

"Good. Now what?"

"I'd like to run up to the hospital, but I don't have my own car."

"I'll drive you, and then we can head to the Village before I need to get to the Banta Bowl."

"You're sure you don't mind?"

"Not at all. I'd like to see Bobby, too. I don't know him as well as you do, and I'm more hesitant to trust a Lady Whistledown"—she wagged her brows and I rolled my eyes—"but you're a good judge of character, and I admit that his t-shirts are a mark in his favor."

I smiled at that.

When we got to the hospital, we used what Detective Yance had told us and managed to find Bobby's room. Fortunately for us, he wasn't in the ICU as the detective initially thought, and we were allowed to see him.

I knocked once on his door frame.

"Come in," he called.

I exhaled, a wave of relief coursing through my entire body at the sound of Bobby's voice. I took a tentative step inside the room.

Bobby was propped up by pillows. His leg was in a cast and elevated. His face was purple with bruises, and he was wearing a pair of glasses that weren't his usual Harry Potter-style ones.

"Hi," I said, trying to mask my grimace at his appearance.

"I know, I know," Bobby said, then coughed. "You're dazzled by my good looks."

I cracked a grin, and Emma chuckled from behind me.

"Admittedly, the hospital gown is a far cry from my favorite t-shirts. The Sherlock Holmes one will have to be permanently retired." Bobby casually shrugged, but there was a weight behind his words.

"Thank God you aren't permanently retired," I said before I could stop myself.

"Jeeze, Leigh. Morbid much?" Emma came to stand next to me. "Hey, Bobby. Glad you're alive."

Bobby smiled. "Me too. You can come in. Take a seat." He indicated the plastic chair on one side of his bed. I sat down there, and Emma pulled another chair over from the far side of the room. "It was nice of you both to visit."

"Of course. We wanted to see how you were doing. Do you need anything?" I asked.

"Nah. I'm alright. Grateful to be alive and with it. My friend brought some things from my apartment, and I spoke to my parents. They're going to drive from Atlanta to stay with me for a bit. Until I get back on my feet."

I resisted the urge to make a ridiculous "ba dum ching" sound effect and settled for a nod. I was overwhelmed with how relieved I was to be sitting here, talking to Bobby.

"Sorry about your truck," Bobby said with a frown.

I waved him off. "The least of my concerns. I'm just glad you're okay."

"Yeah, it was touch and go there for a little bit. Sort of terrifying."

"What happened?" I hated to ask and make him relive the accident, but I needed to know.

Bobby closed his eyes, keeping them shut for a long moment. "It was the strangest thing. I drove away from Cal's condo like usual. I'd driven a couple of miles and went to tap my brakes, and nothing."

Emma leaned forward, and her chair creaked. "The brakes just stopped working?"

Bobby nodded.

Guilt ripped at me. "Bobby, I'm so sorry. I didn't know. I should have had the truck serviced or something. I'm just"—I bit the inside of my cheek to stave off tears that were forming in the corners of my eyes—"I'm so sorry."

Bobby shook his head and then stopped himself with a wince. "It's not your fault. It could have happened to anyone."

"Actually, that's what I'm here to talk to you about."

I whipped my head around at the sound of Detective Yance's baritone voice. He stood in the doorway of Bobby's hospital room, Detective Ottom in tow.

"Can we come in, Mr. Cruz?"

"Um, sure." Bobby glanced around. "Sorry, I can't offer you beverages or a comfy spot to sit, but you're welcome to my humble abode."

Emma giggled at Bobby's awkward joke, and my heart squeezed. I wanted to wrap him in a giant hug.

"Standing's fine with us," Detective Ottom grumbled as he wedged his way into the room, nodding at Bobby. "Glad to see you're doing alright."

"Thanks." Bobby dipped his head. "What's this all about?"

"We came with an update and with some questions." Detective Ottom shot his partner a sidelong glance. "Detective Yance seems to think that you all should be brought up to speed on what we learned about the break-in at Cal Dutton's condo."

Emma and I exchanged a look. "Go on," she said.

"The recordings we collected from Whitney were crystal clear. The voice was a match to Zac Geffadab. We just got done speaking to him."

I sat on my hands to stop myself from making a circular *get on with it* gesture. This was it. They were going to tell us that Zac confessed to everything. Not only the break-in, but the murder. I'd finally know what was going on with Red Vector.

"When faced with the evidence we had in the form of the recordings, along with the eyewitness statements from the night Cal died, Mr. Geffadab folded and admitted to the break-in. You were right, Ms. Notrap." Detective Yance nodded at me. "He was hunting down the dirt Cal had on Red Vector."

"And what was that dirt?" Bobby asked.

I grinned at him, feeling lighter than I had since the moment I heard about his accident. He wasn't going to let a broken leg, some bruises, and a head contusion stop him from getting this scoop and having the PAP be the first to report on it.

"Exactly what Willie Davis said. Shoddy contracts. Gag orders restricting current artists under the label from explaining what a rotten situation they were trapped in. Nothing that's technically against the law. Zac maintains he never coerced anyone into signing with Red Vector. He claims they all knew what they were getting themselves into."

"But he was preying on their hunger. Their desperation for a record deal," Emma put it.

Detective Yance squinted. "That's not technically against the law."

"Murder is," I said, throwing up my hands in spite of myself. "Did he admit to killing Cal to keep him quiet?"

I didn't like the look the detectives shared.

"He swears he didn't murder Mr. Dutton," Detective Yance said. "He admitted to being an underhanded businessman. Admitted to trying to save his butt by covering up whatever evidence Cal had compiled against him, but he says he isn't a killer."

"And what, you believe him?" I couldn't keep the exasperation out of my voice. "That's ridiculous. He had the motive and opportunity. I'm sure if you do a deep dive into his ophthalmology history, you'll find he had means, too. A man like Zac could have easily swiped the eye drops needed to poison Cal."

Detective Ottom frowned at me. "Please don't question how we do our jobs, Ms. Notrap."

I pressed my lips together, rubbing at the remains of the lip gloss I'd applied before we came up to visit Bobby. "But—"

Detective Yance held up a hand. "I followed the same logic as you, Ms. Notrap. That is, until Zac made a goodwill offering."

I raised my brows.

"He turned over the flash drive he and Quentin found in Cal's condo when they ransacked it. He said that's all they cared about, and they didn't need to kill to get it. We also re-confirmed his alibi. He was with someone the whole time he was at the Banta Bowl."

My entire body felt like that sound effect producers use when all the music dies out. Deflated. "But ... but what about Quentin or one of Zac's underlings? Couldn't someone else have done his dirty work?"

It had to be. If Zac didn't kill Cal, then who did?

"We heard from the crime scene techs at the site of Bobby's wreck." Detective Yance's abrupt conversational pivot snapped me to attention.

Bobby's mottled face paled. He swallowed hard. "Okay?"

"Can you walk us through what happened?" Detective Ottom asked.

Bobby glanced at Emma and me before repeating the story he'd shared with us.

"So the brakes worked fine when you were starting your drive, but then they gave out?" Detective Yance clarified.

"Yeah, exactly."

Detective Yance squeezed the skin behind his neck and swung his gaze to me.

I shifted uncomfortably in my seat, a sudden awareness coming over me ... the other shoe was about to drop.

Detective Ottom clasped his hands behind his back. "Someone tampered with the truck."

Bobby knitted his brow. "What? Why?"

"Someone was intentionally trying to cause a crash."

Emma's eyes widened. "So the accident wasn't an accident?"

"Afraid not," Detective Yance said. "Someone tampered with the brake line. It wasn't a full cut—just a small slice. Enough that the brake fluid would drain slowly, allowing for the driver to get going along fast enough to cause maximum damage."

Bobby sat unblinking in the hospital bed.

"Can you think of any reason why someone would want to harm you, Mr. Cruz?" Detective Ottom asked.

I could think of several. The article he published last night would have gone a long way in ticking off Zac Geffadab and the Red Vector heads. They claimed they hadn't killed Cal, but would they have come after Bobby? Hadn't I been wondering earlier what lengths they'd go to in order to ensure their reputation was salvaged?

But that didn't make any sense. No one knew that Bobby was the mastermind behind the PAP. I hadn't told a soul. I was sure Detective Yance wouldn't have. Emma had been behind bars, so unless she let something slip at work this morning, which I doubted, then his secret was safe with all of us.

And it wasn't even Bobby's truck.

I sucked in a gasp before clamping a hand over my mouth.

Detective Yance shot me a look and held up his hand, preventing Bobby from answering Detective Ottom.

"You're asking the wrong person that question," Detective Yance said.

Detective Ottom cocked a brow. "What do you mean?"

"It wasn't Bobby's truck that was tampered with. It was Ms. Notrap's. Bobby just happened to be driving it."

"Bobby wasn't the target." I gulped. "I was."

32

"I'm never letting you out of my sight again." Emma fluttered around her office, her nervous energy manifesting itself in the shuffling of papers and endless talking.

"That's a little dramatic. I'm fine. Bobby's fine. Everything's fine."

Emma huffed. "Easy for you to say that now. Someone tried to kill you, Leigh!"

I held up my hands, the dull pounding in my head intensifying by the minute. "I know."

We'd been around and around this conversation since leaving Bobby's hospital room. The detectives had pressed Zac about messing with my truck, but he swore he hadn't cut my brake line. He said he didn't even know that I was digging into Cal's death and RVR's dealings. I didn't buy it. I talked to Quentin about the staff writer position before it was posted. I'd brought up Cal at that meeting. He could have figured out Cal was my contact and told Zac. I was enough of a realist to know it was a stretch, but I wasn't ready to let go of my hunch that RVR was at the heart of Cal's murder. Not yet.

No one seemed to know *when* someone had messed with my truck. According to the mechanics, it was a slow leak, so the line was likely tampered with at some point last night. I hadn't noticed any fluid under the car when I'd left to go pick up Bobby, but I'd been in a hurry and not looking for it. Since my dashboard was always lit up with a cacophony of lights, including the check engine and brake warning indicators, I had no way of knowing that there was actually something amiss.

Emma insisted she drive me to the Banta Bowl and that we stick together until Cal's killer was brought to light. Not that I had much of a choice. My truck was totaled, and I really wanted to hear what Phil McMann had to say for himself.

As much as I didn't trust Zac, I was trying to keep an open mind about possible other suspects. I needed to keep my guard up, now more than ever.

Emma stacked a couple of files on top of each other. "Oh!" she exclaimed. "Look." She reached down and grabbed a box off her desk. "I meant to tell you about this earlier, but it kind of got lost in the events of the day. I picked up Cal's watch from Lyle this morning on my way into work."

I took the box from her and opened the cover. I lifted out the timepiece, letting the gold links of the band slide through my fingers. I carefully flipped it over and studied the backside. "It doesn't work anymore?"

"Not to tell time. But press the turn piece on the side."

I did as Emma instructed, and the entire backside of the watch sprang open. "I'll be darned."

"Lyle did a good job. Cal would have been pleased, I'm sure." Emma shuffled through some more papers before sitting down behind her desk.

I set Cal's watch back into the box. "I'm sure your parents will be glad to have this back."

"Yeah." Emma was noncommittal—distracted. She checked her own watch. "Hopefully Phil shows up soon. I've got to get back out there."

"He'll be here," I assured. "Your message was very convincing."

Emma had texted under the guise of having openings in their schedule where Cal had been slotted to perform. She said she was reaching out as a courtesy to Phil to see if he had any other musicians in mind who'd like to fill the vacancies.

Emma drummed her fingernails on her desk. "Autumn goes on in an hour." She glanced at the door. "It can't be easy being backstage here again. It's only been a week since ... you know."

"Let's go see her, then." I stood up, and Emma followed me to the door.

"We put her in the room as far away from Cal's as possible." She directed me toward the far side of the hallway. We passed by Willie's office door, which stood open. He was on the phone, but he waved to us as we walked by.

The sounds of a banjo and other strings reached my ear from the mainstage out front, but it was quieter as we rounded the corner for Autumn's dressing room. The door was open a crack.

The hair on the back of my neck stood up, and I had the wriggling feeling in my stomach that I was being watched. I glanced left and right as we made our way to Autumn's room.

"What's wrong?" Emma's voice came out strained. She eyed me warily.

"Nothing. I just got a weird feeling."

She peeked over her shoulder. "Don't like that. Not one bit."

I shook my head. "I'm sure it's nothing."

I stopped in front of Autumn's cracked-open door. The sound of hushed voices met my ears. I leaned forward and peered through the crack. Autumn and Phil were sitting hand in hand. Phil was talking, but I couldn't make out what he was saying.

I leaned back and knocked on the door. "Autumn. It's Leigh and Emma. Can we come in?"

Autumn cleared her throat. "Yeah. It's open."

I pushed the door wider, and Emma and I stepped into the room to find Phil standing off to the side of the couch. He'd been quick to vacate his cozy position next to Autumn. Up close, I could see tears on Autumn's cheeks.

"We just wanted to check in on you. Are you okay?" I leaned against the counter in the small kitchenette.

Emma crossed the room and pulled out a small chair from underneath a table positioned next to the bathroom.

"I'm fine," Autumn said. "This is just overwhelming, you know? It's all hitting me ... being back here. The last time I was here, I was with Cal, and he was alive, and then he wasn't." Autumn choked on a sob.

I nodded, trying to show my understanding, but I didn't know what to believe. How did Autumn really feel? Was she a love-sick woman who'd recently witnessed her boyfriend's death? That's how she seemed tonight, but on more than one occasion since Cal's murder, I'd seen her look cool and unaffected, finding comfort in another man's arms already. It was time to get some answers.

I rounded on Phil. "How are you doing, Phil?"

He bowed his head, but not before he shot a look at Autumn. "I'm doing alright. Cal was incomparable. The whole industry will feel the reverberations of his loss for a long time to come, but people like me and Autumn, who were close to him both personally and professionally, are dealing with a different sort of trauma."

I tried my best to look somber and unsuspecting—not like I was trying to ask leading questions. "On top of losing a friend, it must've been hard for you to lose your top client with no warning."

Phil nodded solemnly. "Talent like Cal's doesn't come around every day."

I hummed. "You probably weren't too happy that he was thinking of firing you for a new manager, then."

"Yeah, exactly, I— Hey! Wait a minute." Phil narrowed his eyes at me. "Who told you that?"

I waved a hand in the air. "Does it really matter? Water under the bridge at this point, isn't it? Then again, I'm curious whether or not you knew about Cal's plans *before* he died."

"Seems like it would have been the sort of information that would have made you mighty angry," Emma added.

Phil's gaze bounced back and forth between us before he focused on Autumn. "Did you tell them about this?"

She blinked. "Me? What? No. Why would I?"

"Well, somebody must've." Phil pointed his finger at me. "I don't like what you're implying."

"Tell me what I'm implying, Phil. Because from my perspective, you were on the cusp of a major loss. Cal leaving you for another manager would have left you in the lurch, much like his death did. But his death was much more convenient for you. Because it spared you the embarrassment of having to answer for why the two of you parted ways."

"Did you kill my brother, Phil?" Emma asked.

Ballsy, direct question from my best friend, but I had to give her props for going for the jugular.

"Are you insane?" Phil hissed. "Of course I didn't kill Cal! I would never put so much onus on my career. Yeah, he talked about letting me go and seeking representation elsewhere, but that was only because he wasn't happy with the deal I worked out for him with Red Vector. He had something up his sleeve, I think. We talked on the phone early last week, and he said he wanted to handle RVR himself. He had some sort of grandiose plans to start his own label. He was going to try to get artists who were unhappy with Red Vector to come on board with him."

I considered this. The timing of the call Phil described lined up with what Lyle the watchmaker overheard, so I had to believe he was telling the truth.

Had I finally figured out what Cal was up to? What he wanted to bring Jon Campbell in on? Maybe Cal hoped I'd write for *his* artists and that's why he was trying to keep me away from Red Vector. Something settled inside of me. It felt good to have an answer.

Phil continued his explanation. "I was mad that Cal was going over my head, sure, and that he wanted to try this new endeavor without me. But I'd never kill him over that."

"Okay." I conceded the point, but pressed on, feeling more self-assured than I had in days. "If it wasn't over that, then what about over Autumn? Would you have killed him to clear a way for your relationship with her?"

Phil's cheeks turned scarlet, and he spluttered. "I … how … what? Where are you getting your information?"

Autumn buried her face in her hands.

Emma's phone chimed, and though I kept my focus on Phil and Autumn, I saw her check it out of the corner of my eye.

Outside the door of the room, the band that was playing ahead of Autumn wrapped up their show. Applause reached my ears, and it must've triggered something in Autumn.

"This is all a huge mistake," she wept.

I crossed the room and sat down next to her on the couch. "What's a mistake, Autumn? Were you cheating on Cal?"

Autumn let her head fall back. "I hate that word. I hate that it's true! It only happened one time! I loved Cal. I did." She looked pleadingly at me. "But sometimes he got moody, and he was tough to be around. He was going through a lot of stuff in the lead up to his"—she swallowed—"death, and he was pushing me away. I hated that. All I wanted was to be there for him. But it's hard not to feel needed, you know? And Phil made me feel valuable."

"So you cheated on Cal," Emma said, her tone more of a statement than a question, even as she shot another glance at her phone.

Autumn started to cry. "I'm so sorry, Em. Like I said, it was a mistake. It only happened once, and I told Phil never again."

"Autumn—" Phil started, but Autumn shook her head.

"No, Phil. I *told* you never again. That doesn't change just because Cal is dead."

"But what about in your trailer at the benefit concert? We saw the two of you," I said.

Autumn's jaw dropped, and she pinched her eyes shut. She cursed before blinking wide eyes open. They flashed with anger. She swung her gaze between Emma and me. Emma wasn't looking back. She nibbled on her lip and stared down at her phone.

"I'm guessing you saw Phil plow into my trailer and try to kiss me, but I swear, I told him to stop." Autumn swallowed. "I put my foot down."

"For no good reason!" Phil growled. "Think about it, Autumn. We *could* be together now. Of course, the circumstances aren't ideal, but I have real feelings for you."

Autumn shook her head. "No, Phil. Please don't."

"Um." Emma waved her phone in the air, and we all turned her direction. "I don't know if this complicates things or makes you feel worse, Autumn, but I think it's your right to know."

Autumn frowned. "Know what?"

Emma turned her phone's screen so it was facing the room. "My parents just got this package courier delivered to their house. It was addressed to Cal. They opened it and found this."

Emma stood and walked over to Autumn, angling the phone in my direction so I could see the photo first.

It was a picture of an engagement ring.

Autumn's hands flew to her mouth. "Cal was going to propose." She choked out the words and started bawling.

Phil stood off to the side of the couch, wringing his hands.

"You didn't know?" I asked when Autumn calmed herself after a few moments.

Autumn shook her head. "No. I had hoped, but like I said, Cal was so distant the past few months. It felt like he was pushing me away."

"Did he know you cheated?" Emma asked.

"I may have had words with him about it," Phil admitted, his reluctant words slicing through the thick silence in the dressing room.

"I wish you wouldn't have," Autumn wailed. "You should have let me talk to him first. I'll never forgive myself."

I stared at Phil, trying to figure out how he fit into this whole mess. Was he desperate enough to clear a way for himself to be with Autumn to kill Cal?

"What did Cal say when you told him, Phil?" Emma asked.

"I don't know that he believed me. It's not like I had proof beyond the feelings in my heart and the memories of the night we spent together."

"Please. Don't." Autumn held up her hand.

Phil firmed his lips. "I came here the day Cal was murdered to talk to Autumn."

I nodded. We'd known that from Whitney.

A knock sounded on the dressing room door. My heart rate spiked, and I spun around.

"Detectives." Autumn rose from the couch at the sight of Detective Yance and Detective Ottom, the latter looking none too pleased to see us. "What brings you here?"

"We have some follow-up questions for you and Mr. McMann," Detective Ottom said.

"I have a show in less than thirty minutes." Autumn looked between the pair. "My legal counsel also advised me not to speak to you alone."

Detective Yance nodded. "We'll wait until you're finished on stage. Why don't you call your lawyer to meet you here. Or we can do this down at the station. We'll start with Mr. McMann. Can we use this room?" Detective Yance directed the last question to Emma.

"Sure." Turning to Autumn, she added, "You can come with us and get yourself cleaned up before you go on stage."

Autumn grabbed a tote bag and followed Emma out of the room.

"Autumn, baby, wait." Phil reached for her hand, but Autumn yanked it away.

"I'm no one's baby, Phil. It's done. We're done. We never should have begun." With that, she spun on her heel and marched out behind Emma.

I held back my applause, but I did give a little internal cheer for Autumn. Phil seemed like a whiny brat to me. Not someone who deserved Autumn. Cal had his faults, to be sure, but at least theirs seemed to be a true partnership.

I slipped out the door behind Autumn and followed her and Emma in silence. Emma stopped at a vacant dressing room a couple doors down, unlocked it, and motioned for Autumn to enter. "I can come back and get you when it's time."

Autumn took two steps inside before spinning around. "Look, I know it doesn't seem like it, but I loved Cal. I made a huge mistake and I told him as much when everything came out. He said he needed time, but I have to believe he would have forgiven me. The alternative is—" Autumn's voice broke and she took a moment to collect herself. "Anyway, I hope you'll forgive me for what I did to your brother," she said to Emma.

Emma shook her head. "There's nothing to forgive. I don't think you killed him. You didn't, right?"

Autumn shook her head. "No. I didn't."

"Cal obviously loved you," I said softly, finding myself wanting to offer some comfort. In my periphery, Emma nodded. "He was still planning to propose, even after finding out about you and Phil. I think it was going to be a grand proposal, too, don't you, Emma?"

"I do." She nodded. "After the show, I'll let you see Cal's watch. He had it outfitted with a special compartment. We thought he was going to hide something business-related inside, but now that I see the photo of the engagement ring, I'm certain that's what he wanted to keep close to him at all times."

Autumn smacked her forehead with her palm. "His watch," she whispered. "He was going to keep the ring in his watch?"

"It sure looks that way," I said.

Autumn closed her eyes. "I'm going to love you until my time runs out."

"What's that?" Emma said, arching her brow.

"It's a lyric to a song we were working on. Cal was obsessed with that watch and with the idea of time and making the most of it and all the phrases that went along with it."

I nodded, recalling some of my conversations with Cal. "Well, it makes sense then. I think he meant that lyric. No matter what mistake you made, he still loved you."

Autumn reached forward and hugged Emma and then me. "Thank you," she whispered. "Thank you for telling me this."

I stepped out of her embrace, feeling good about what we'd learned for Autumn and the closure we were able to give her.

Phil, on the other hand, was still a wildcard.

"We'll let you get ready," Emma said. "I'll be back in"—she checked her watch—"ten minutes."

"Thank you." Autumn slid the door shut.

Emma and I walked together down the hallway before she paused. "I've got work to do before I get Autumn. Are you good?"

"Yeah. I'm going to head out and find a spot near the stage. I'd like to watch Autumn's set."

"I'll find you after she goes on. Don't leave without me, okay?"

"I won't."

We parted ways. I wove through the hallways, past the yellow police tape still affixed to Cal's dressing room door. I swallowed down a pang of grief mixed with fear and kept going. The Banta Bowl was packed for Autumn's performance. I had to inch my way to the bar and flag down the bartender.

"Vodka soda, please," I said.

He nodded and got to work. When he handed me my drink, I paid and found an open spot toward the back of the crowd. I tuned in to snippets of conversation. Cal's name came up several times. One particularly loud group was talking about how Cal and Autumn's love story met such a tragic end, but they would always be one of country music's *it* couples.

I shook my head. If people only knew the half of what went down behind the scenes and behind closed doors.

"Someone said they spotted Jace James!" An excitable woman squealed that proclamation at the same time someone knocked into my shoulder.

My drink sloshed over the edge of my cup, and I bit back a curse.

"We've got to stop running into each other like this."

The melodic lilt of Jace's voice lightened my mood, but only for a moment. I flashed back to our first run-in here at the Banta Bowl. Something poked at the corner of my brain, but I couldn't place it. I tried to summon a smile, but he clearly wasn't buying it.

Jace had his hat pulled down low over his brow, but he cocked his head to the side, studying me. "Yikes. Why so glum?"

I sighed. "I don't even know where to begin."

"Start at the beginning." He smiled at me, turning my body so his back was to the crowd. It was a sweet gesture and made the large performance venue seem more intimate. I found myself anxious to spill my guts—to talk about all that had gone down and get it off my chest.

"The police don't think Zac was behind Cal's death. Though he is an unsavory businessman." I made a face. "I don't think I'm going to go ahead with the job at Red Vector after all."

Jace arched a brow. "Okay. Let's circle back to that. What else is bothering you?"

"Everything," I confessed. "The police seem to be at a dead end with Cal's case. They're backstage right now interviewing Phil McMann."

Jace nodded. "Do they think that Phil found out Cal was going to cut ties and was spurred to murder?"

"That, or that he was in love with Autumn and killed Cal to get her all for himself."

Jace's expression darkened underneath the brim of his hat. "Phil and Autumn? That was legit?"

I nodded. "They had a one-night stand. Phil wanted more."

Jace's hands clenched at his sides, and his nostrils flared.

"Easy there, cowboy." I let out a slight chuckle and patted his upper arm. "Autumn shut that down."

Jace relaxed. "Of course she did. Autumn is a smart woman. Way too good for Phil."

The way Jace spat the manager's name made me wonder if there was some history there. Before I could ask, he prodded me to go on. "What else you got?"

"Someone's after me." I shook my head. "Me, of all people."

Jace screwed up his mouth. "How so?"

"My friend got in an accident driving my truck. It turns out it was tampered with."

Jace let out a low whistle. "Is your friend okay?"

"Yeah, thank goodness. But it was serious."

"And you think you were the target?"

I shrugged. "The police do. It was my truck."

Jace's face was etched with concern. "This is serious, Leigh. You need to be careful. It's one thing to play Nancy Drew, but someone cutting your brake line ... you could have been killed!"

"I know."

The music pulsing through the loudspeakers overhead shifted and hushed, and the deejay's voice boomed out, announcing Autumn's arrival. She strode out onto the stage.

"She looks good," Jace commented. He was right. Her face was clear of any emotion, but I hardly noticed. I stared straight ahead at the stage, not really seeing. All at once, several facts hit me, and the piece of the puzzle that had been floating around in my head clicked into place.

My skin prickled with unease, and I shifted my gaze around the room, looking for someone—anyone I recognized.

I had just figured out who killed Cal.

33

"I need to go, Jace." I set my drink on the nearest table and made a move to cut toward the backstage entrance, figuring my best bet was to get to the detectives. I could only hope they were still holed up with Phil.

Jace snaked a hand out and grabbed my upper arm. "Where are you off to? You need to stay and watch Autumn. She's magnificent."

I looked up into his eyes, barely able to see them beneath the brim of his ball cap. I tried to wiggle my arm free, but he tightened his grip.

"Jace," I said slowly.

He angled his head so he made full eye contact, and what I saw in his expression turned my blood to ice. "Dang it, Leigh. I didn't want it to come to this." He tugged me closer to his chest, and I felt a cold ring of metal poking into my side. "If you say one word to anyone, I'll shoot you right here. Now move." He nudged me with the barrel of the hidden gun toward the exit.

I bit my lip. Things didn't look great, but I needed to minimize collateral damage. If Jace opened fire inside the Banta Bowl, any number of innocent people could be injured, or worse. He directed me outside, and I needed to go with it. Hopefully, I could get someone's attention or escape once we were out in the open.

That, or I was about to die.

I blinked several times in quick succession.

"Tell me why," I muttered—and somewhere in the back of my head, I appreciated that I was paying homage to my favorite Backstreet Boys hook.

I had a feeling Jace's answer had something to do with heartache, too. Which really was icing on the freaking cake.

"Did you know Cal was going to propose to Autumn?" Jace spit the words out directly into my ear. If anyone was observing us, they probably thought we were a lovesick couple off to have a little tête-à-tête somewhere private.

I nodded. "The ring arrived at Cal's parents' house today."

Jace scoffed. "Cal told me all about it. How he was ready to finally commit to Autumn. The fool. He took her for granted. They were all wrong for each other." He bobbed his chin ahead. "Now, push the door open casually. Don't draw attention, or I'll shoot the bouncer."

I gulped and did as I was told—for now. I needed to buy myself some time. "Let me guess, *you* were right for her."

"Of course I was. Autumn and I have a deep, soul-level connection. We've both known it for years. My career has gotten in the way to this point. Obviously I've been much more successful than Cal was. Than Cal would ever be. But I expected more from Autumn. She should have waited for me."

Jace was delusional. As far as I knew, he and Autumn had never dated. She'd always been with Cal. "Did Autumn tell you she had feelings for you?"

Jace huffed. "We don't need words to solidify our connection."

"Except for the chorus of your new song, right? Those words that you sang at Cal's memorial? Those were for Autumn."

The lyrics hit me like a sucker punch.

All these years spent living so close but still apart have torn me up inside / Because I've held you close to my heart in secret, waiting for a chance to show / You love, my true love, and now you know

How could I have been so stupid, thinking they were intended for me? Jace was completely obsessed with Autumn Silver. I should have recognized the photo evidence in the picture we'd found at Emma's parents' house. He wasn't smoldering. He was ticked off that Cal got the girl and he didn't.

"The two of us are going to be a power couple. We're going to take the industry by storm. Think about it, Leigh. Now we have the same label. We can coordinate tours. It's going to be the start of our happily ever after. I just have to tie up this loose end." He dug the barrel of the gun deeper into my side, and I winced.

"Why me?" I squeaked.

"Because you couldn't keep your nosy nose to yourself. I didn't want it to go down like this, but you kept sifting around for more information. Why couldn't you have just left it alone? It would have been easier for everyone."

"So what, because I was asking questions and trying to get justice for Cal, you're going to take another life?"

Jace shoved me forward instead of answering my frantic hypothetical question, which, I realized, was less hypothetical than I'd like. "Just keep walking," he growled.

I did as I was told while trying to figure out a game plan. My head felt fuzzy. Everyone assumes that, at the end of your life, when you know death is coming, things move in slow motion and you get all sorts of clarity. That was not happening to me at the moment. I thought about my parents, and there was a slight twinge in my chest. If I lived through this—somehow—maybe I should try to make amends.

I stumbled, and Jace almost lost his grip on me. "Watch it," he hissed.

As he jostled my arm, my spirits revived. I was not out of this yet. I had songs to write. Goals to meet. A life to live. I just had to figure out a diversion or catch someone's attention, and then I could break free. If I could get back into the Banta Bowl, I could find one of the detectives.

"That's good, pet. Let's keep going. We're going to go and do this somewhere a little less messy." Jace's warm breath against my ear made my skin crawl. And the endearment of "pet" was perhaps the worst insult of all. Did I look like anyone's pet?

Anger built up in my chest. I tamped it down. I needed to stay rational. I couldn't be blinded by my rage.

"Where are you taking me?" I asked.

"Closer to the river."

I let out a mirthless laugh. "So you can dump my body?"

When Jace didn't respond, I added, "How very Taylor Swift of you." He said nothing, so I rolled my eyes. "'No Body, No Crime'? Come on, it's a masterpiece."

"Shut up, Leigh. I wouldn't think you'd want to spend your last moments quoting Taylor Swift lyrics."

"What else am I supposed to do?" I muttered. "Besides, her lyrics are practically tattooed on my mind." I was blabbering, but that was my goal. If I could irk Jace, he'd do something stupid, and then I'd make my move. "You know, Cal thought pretty highly of you."

Jace grunted and shoved me forward.

"I'm serious. He complimented 'Heartbreak High' the last time he and I wrote together. He said he wanted to write something that triggered as much nostalgia as that song did. So did you have a lady friend back in the day who you wrote that about?"

Jace scoffed. "I can't even remember. Every other woman faded away when I saw Autumn for the first time."

I tried not to gag. I needed to stay alive to warn Autumn that Jace was a stalker. There was no telling what his delusions would lead him to do next. "You could have killed Autumn, you know. By poisoning Cal's tea with the eye dilation solution you stole from your eye doctor and then conveniently ditched in Emma's office."

I couldn't believe I didn't put it together until now. Jace had mentioned going to get his eyes checked when I bumped into him the night Cal died. I wanted to slap myself for not making the connection sooner.

"You think I don't know that?" Jace seethed. "Why do you think I was so distraught when we got to Cal's dressing room?"

I remembered Jace's face vividly. He'd been pale-faced and shocked. I assumed it was because of Cal, but he'd really been worked up at the sight of Autumn—at the realization that he could have inadvertently poisoned the woman he was desperately trying to have for himself.

"She wasn't supposed to be there," Jace continued on a whine. "It would have been her fault."

He was partially right. Autumn had rearranged her schedule to go with Cal that night. She was lucky to be alive.

If I wanted to stay alive, I needed to keep Jace talking. "You know, I thought you had a thing for me."

Jace let loose a chortle. "Yeah, no. You're fine and all, Leigh, but no one is on Autumn's level."

"Right. I'll take that delightful compliment with me to the grave," I deadpanned. Apparently, when faced with my death, I became all sorts of dry.

I scanned my surroundings. The city was quieter here by the river. Jace was leading me toward a tree-lined knoll. I knew the place, having come down here as a child when I was trying to escape my parents and their antics. It was almost a full circle moment for Jace to bring me here to die.

But then I saw something that made my heart beat fast. Movement in the trees. Lots of it.

The police. The police had somehow found me. My spirits soared. I just needed to put myself in a position to let them handle Jace. I did not want to be used as a human shield, so I was going to need to think fast.

"I can't believe I'm missing Autumn's show for this," he grumbled, dragging me along.

I shot another glance toward the trees, and if I wasn't mistaken, my eyes landed on Detective Ottom's oversized frame. I couldn't make out his expression—had no idea if he tried to mouth any sort of directions to me. I looked straight ahead so as not to draw attention to the law enforcement, but I really could have used some sort of sign. How were they going to play this? I was running out of ground between me and the river.

"Let's make this quick." Jace pulled me in front of him and pushed me toward the rushing water, holding the gun directly at my chest. "You're going to back up until you make it to the edge of the bank. No funny business, Leigh. I will hunt you down. Do as I say."

I held up my hands and walked backward, keeping my eyes trained on Jace, whose hand holding the gun at me didn't tremble.

A sense of calm came over me. This was it. I knew what I was going to do. I could only hope the element of surprise was in my favor and would buy me enough time to escape.

"Any last words?" Jace asked.

"Only this," I said when I reached the riverbank. "I'm not a big ole wuss."

He arched his eyebrows at me.

"It's a song lyric, Jace." I sighed dramatically. "It's like you don't even know me at all."

With that, I turned and dove right into the water.

34

Brad Paisley's cheeky tune, aptly titled "Water," floated through my head as I swam deeper into the murky river. All my time swimming was about to pay off. I could hold my breath for longer than most, and if I could cover enough ground, Jace wouldn't know where to shoot when I finally did come up for air.

That, and hopefully the police would have taken him into custody by then.

I braced myself for a barrage of bullets that never came. I stayed submerged for a solid two minutes, if I had to guess—until my lungs screamed for oxygen. I wasn't exactly sure how far I'd gotten, and I tried to make my ascent as stealthy as possible.

I broke through the surface and blinked the water from my eyes. In the distance, I heard yelling.

"You can't do this to me," Jace screamed. "You have to understand. Where's Autumn? This was all for her! Everything was for her."

I exhaled, my body shaking with relief. It was over. It was all over. I flipped to my back and floated, hardly believing what had happened. Had I actually just been held at gunpoint by Nashburg's biggest star?

A laugh bubbled up, and as I tried to gulp for air, I inhaled some water and sent myself into a coughing jag, effectively giving away my position in the river.

"Ms. Notrap? Leigh? Is that you?"

"Yeah. I'm right here," I croaked, coughing hard and clearing my lungs.

"You alright?" It was Detective Yance.

"All good." I started swimming back toward him. I pulled myself up onto shore with the help of his outstretched hand.

"That was some dive," Detective Yance said by way of greeting.

I shrugged as a uniformed officer hurried over and held out a towel for me. "Kinda felt like my only option."

Detective Yance stared me down, his expression blank as usual. But then I swore his lips ticked up on each end. "Glad you're alright."

I gave him a broad smile in return. "Me too. You arrested Jace?"

"Yes, ma'am. We're going to need to take your full statement. He mostly confessed, but I'm sure he'll pull out all the stops to try to get himself off the hook here. Hopefully, his god-complex will actually come back to bite him."

I nodded, suddenly unsure how I ever found myself attracted to Jace James. I'd rather not think about that. "How'd you find me?" I asked instead.

"You can thank Whitney Allerow for that."

"What?"

Would wonders never cease?

"She was coming into the Banta Bowl as Jace was leading you out. She ran into us just inside the door, and she was complaining that you'd left with Jace James. She said it was crazy that you didn't seem happy about it. I think her exact words were, 'That woman should appreciate the famous men she keeps company with. First Cal, then that hotty Bo, and now Jace.'"

I shivered at the mention of Bo, aka Bobby. Or maybe that was just from my dip in the river.

"Emma was with me," Detective Yance continued. "She asked Whitney what she meant, and Whitney told us you were scowling. Emma demanded we go and find you. She said it wasn't like you to leave the building when you'd promised her you'd wait for her. We all realized at once that Jace was here the night of Cal's death. We set out and picked up your trail pretty quickly, though we couldn't get close enough to hear everything. Once we spotted the gun, we moved into position."

I trembled under the towel, closing my eyes in a silent prayer of thanks that I was still here. Alive. "Thanks for coming to my rescue," I said out loud.

Detective Yance nodded. "Let me get you back to Emma."

He put his hand out and motioned me forward, but I paused. "Speaking of Emma, you have her phone number, right? In her file."

Detective Yance knitted his brows. "I suppose so, yes."

"Is it legal for you to get the number from her file and use it for, say, personal reasons? Like to ask her out on a date? Or would you like me to give it to you directly?"

At that moment, the unflappable Detective Yance—whose stoneface rivaled the statue of David—blushed.

I let loose a delighted laugh. I was totally going to write a song about this.

Emma gripped me in a bone-crushing hug the second we walked in the back doors of the Banta Bowl. Autumn was still on stage, oblivious to the fact that Jace James had killed Cal Dutton because he was madly—literally—in love with her.

"Thank God you're alright, Leigh. I was terrified."

"Thanks for sending the police after me. I'm not sure we would have had a happy ending without them." I trusted my swimming skills, but I would have panicked if I hadn't seen law enforcement on the scene. Jace could have just kept shooting at the river if left to his own devices.

I blinked away those thoughts. "Are you about ready? I could really go for some pancakes. Think Agnes'll make some for me this late at night?" All I wanted was to get back to our cozy apartment in the Village. To take a steaming hot shower, and then go downstairs and sit in the kitchen of Java Flo's, and stuff my face with food.

Emma slung her arm around my shoulder. "After we tell her what happened, I think she'll make you whatever you want. Let's go."

She led me out to her car, and I slid into the passenger seat. Once she was behind the wheel, I asked her for her phone.

"What do you need it for?" she asked.

I didn't answer, just pulled up the anonymous tip page on the PAP's app. I gave a rundown of what happened tonight for Bobby to read and do with what he would. He deserved to be among the first news outlets to break the story. I left out the details of my involvement. The idea of having my name and picture all over the press made me feel like I was going to break out in hives. I'd tell Bobby the full story in person. For now, I signed my tip *Your partner in crime*. He'd understand.

"All done." I set the phone down on the console and leaned against my seat.

Emma started the car, and Carrie Underwood's "Ghost Story" blared through the speakers. Before the song even got to the bridge and the best line about letting love die and carving it in stone, I slipped into a dreamless sleep.

35

"Please," Bobby begged.

"No. No way."

He stared me down. "But that is epic. Like next-level epic. You're a superhero. A real-life Aquaman. Aqua-*woman*."

I scoffed. "Hardly."

I sat in the uncomfortable chair next to his hospital bed the day after my river swim and Jace's arrest. I attended Cal's funeral earlier in the day, but when the public ceremonies were complete, I left Emma with her family.

I didn't want to be alone, so I popped up to the hospital.

I had just finished filling in all the details of Jace's arrest for a wide-eyed Bobby, and now he was badgering me to let him tell the complete story to the PAP's followers.

"Well, if you change your mind and want your fifteen minutes of fame..." He clicked his tongue and pointed his thumbs at himself. "I know a guy who can make that happen."

"Don't count on it."

"Fine. What else? I'm going stir crazy in here. I've never watched so much television in my life." He motioned to the TV mounted on the wall across the room.

"Let's see." I shifted in my seat, grabbing for another one of the homemade cookies Agnes had sent along with me when I left Java Flo's. "These will heal him up right quick," she had said, and I told her I hoped she was right. She'd arched her eyebrows, wagging them playfully at me, but I ignored her. I didn't have a thing for

Bobby. Not like that. I still didn't do love. Look at what a mess I'd almost gotten myself into thinking Jace could be interested in me. Good grief.

But I couldn't deny that I missed seeing Bobby and his t-shirts when I went downstairs for my morning coffee.

Instead of focusing on that, I told him about Emma. "She doesn't know if she wants to use the life insurance money Cal left her to invest in her next property. She says it just seems wrong. But it looks like she won't have to worry about it. An investor approached her last night while I was swimming for my life. They have a meeting on the calendar to discuss Em's vision, so that's exciting."

"I'm so glad for her." Bobby smiled.

I quirked a brow. "What? What's with that grin?"

Bobby looked down at his lap. "I just ... I think I know who Emma's meeting with, because I may or may not have put a bug in someone's ear about her plans."

My jaw dropped. "Who?"

When Bobby said the name of a famous female Nashburg singer, I gasped. "You know her?"

"Sure." He shrugged. "She'd be a good investor."

I laughed. "That's an understatement. How do you have all these connections?"

Bobby fiddled with the blanket on his hospital bed. "I grew up in this town."

"So did I, but that doesn't mean I have people like *that* on speed dial."

"Don't you?" Bobby quipped, though he looked me dead in the eye.

I laughed him off, but it was slightly forced. There was a time in my life when I probably could have gotten a hold of a lot of famous people—through my parents, at least. I had shoved aside the sentimental moment I'd had about them by the river, chalking it up to my near-death experience. In the light of day, I really didn't want to talk to them any more than I had to.

The TV blared the intro music to *Nashburg Insider*, a local show describing town happenings, and the kitschy tune stirred me from my thoughts. I was grateful for the distraction.

"Man, I can see why you're tired of this." I reached for the remote to silence the noise, but I sucked in a breath and my skin broke out in goosebumps when I caught the lead-in to the top story.

"Local radio legend Sonny Smith just announced a new podcast endeavor. He stopped by our studios to share more."

The show cut to a clip of the radio deejay, smiling into the camera as one of the *Nashburg Insider* correspondents held a mic in front of him.

"My goal is to do a deep dive into notable Nashburg families," Sonny said. "The good, the bad, and the ugly. Everything's not all sunshine and roses around here, now is it?" He winked at the camera.

The interviewer agreed. "Who do you have teed up for your podcast?"

"Well now, you'll have to tune in to find out." He chortled. "But I have my sights set on a juicy conversation with Pita Paige and Penn Stewart, for starters."

A picture of the country music duo popped up on the screen as the interviewer gave some closing remarks and then the *Nashburg Insider* reporter moved on to the next story.

I sat frozen in my chair. Was this some sort of joke? Some sort of publicity stunt?

"Are you okay?" Bobby asked quietly.

I turned my gaze toward him, and he was staring back at me.

"You know who I am?" I whispered.

He looked almost sheepish, but then he shrugged. "Penn Stewart and Pita Paige are your parents, right? Your real name is Presley Paige Stewart."

His words crashed into me with the weight of a tanker truck. No one had said my given name in years.

"That's me," I told him weakly, but then I cleared my throat. "Or at least it used to be. I had my name legally changed."

Bobby nodded. "Leigh has a nice ring to it. I'm guessing 'Notrap' is a nod to Dolly."

I blinked back tears. In all the time since I'd adopted an entirely new persona, Bobby was the first person to put it together. The last name I chose for myself is 'Parton' spelled backward.

"Is that what gave me away?" I said through my tears.

"I'm a journalist, Leigh. Research is sort of my thing. But now ... what are you going to do about this?" He motioned to the TV.

"I don't know." I blew out a huge breath. "My relationship with my parents is ... terrible."

"Figured as much."

Bobby might have figured, but he didn't know the half of it. My dad had been missing in action from my life since I was no longer cute enough for the press, only popping back in when it was advantageous for him. My mom wasn't much better. I did *not* want a light shined on my family. I wanted to make a name for myself, separate from Pita and Penn.

I massaged my temples, wishing I could go back to five minutes ago.

"What do you need?" Bobby asked gently.

"I guess I should call them." I let a hiss of air escape from between my teeth. It was the absolute last thing I wanted to do, but if Dolly could write "Jolene" *and* "I Will Always Love You" in one day, I could woman up for this.

Here went nothing.

Be sure to tune into Leigh's next adventure in Dead Beats, *the second book in the Songwriter Sleuth Mysteries.*

Acknowledgements

All glory to God, now and forever.

Trying something new is intimidating and scary sometimes, but I have the best readers in the whole world. Thank you to everyone who trusted me enough to join me on this new endeavor. Whether you're a fan of the Larkspur Library Mysteries and made the jump to Nashburg or you're a romance reader who was willing to give a cozy mystery a try, thank you from the bottom of my heart. You continue to make my author dreams come true. I hope you loved Leigh and the whole Nashburg/Village crew. I can't wait for you to get to know them more as the series progresses.

Independently publishing a book means I get to work with a whole host of amazing professionals. For this project, I'd like to thank Caitlin at CM Editorial who took me on as a new client and lent her editing expertise to *Trebled Waters*. You helped mold this story into what it is, and I'm so grateful. Melody Jeffries (@whimandjoy), I'm so glad you agreed to team up with me for another cover. I put you through the wringer with my off-the-wall ideas for this one. Once I finally figured out our direction (how many pages of emails did I write to you?!), you came through big time. This cover is everything. You brought Leigh's songwriting nook to life, complete with a Dolly Parton rendering. Is there anything you can't do? Thank you!

While I was researching for this book, I had the pleasure of speaking with Garrett Thorn, a singer and songwriter living in

Nashville. Garrett, thank you for your time and for sharing insight into a world I am not a part of but hoped to write in a realistic and true way. You helped me to do that. Any mistakes in this vein are my own. P.S. Everyone, Garrett is the coolest guy and uber-talented. Go check out his music!

There's a very real chance this book would still be sitting in my draft folder if it wasn't for the early encouragement of fellow author, Sarah E. Burr. Sarah, thank you for reading a baby version of this manuscript and yell-texting me your enthusiastic response to the twists and turns of Leigh's adventure. I have the messages saved because they are that good! Your endless support and cheerleading mean so much. Thanks for being a trusted sounding-board and an all-around great friend.

To the Inky Fingers, who let a hybrid romance/mystery author into the critique group and put up with me on the months I'm talking about characters falling in love instead of characters solving crimes. I value each and every one of you and look up to you all as writers and people.

To the local librarians and booksellers in Northeast Wisconsin as well as the online bookish community, thank you for all you do to champion books and authors. A special shout-out to the Kimberly Public Library crew. My home-turf library will forever be my favorite place to pop in so I can surround myself with good books and good people.

No book of mine would exist without the support of my family and friends. I'm blessed with the best of the best on both counts. Thanks to my cousins for brainstorming titles for this book with me. We managed to come up with not only *Trebled Waters*, but also the titles for the next three books in the series, so I guess I better get writing!

To my Well Read Mom book club, thanks for sharing your hearts as we discuss books and life. Ditto to my Saturday Morning bible study ladies. THE book club gals: I love laughing with you and crying with you and being together each month. Game Night crew...you are my very favorite people. So glad we get those dates scheduled six months out...I know the guys are glad too! I love you all.

Mom, Dad, Luke, Bailey, Fr. Ben, thanks for everything. I love you guys.

Miriam, Lyla, Ellen, Francis, and Arthur: you stretch my creativity and my heart in the best possible ways. I love you more than you'll ever know.

Nick...always. You see all of me and you love all of me, and for that there won't ever be words enough. I love you madly.

About The Author

Leah Dobrinska is the author of the Songwriter Sleuth Mysteries, the Fall In Love series, the Larkspur Library Mysteries, and the Mapleton novels. She earned her degree in English Literature from UW-Madison where she was awarded the Dean's Prize and served as a Writing Fellow. She has since worked as a freelance writer, editor, and content marketer. Leah lives in Wisconsin with her husband and their gaggle of kids. When she's not writing, handing out snacks, or visiting the local library, Leah enjoys reading and running.

www.leahdobrinska.com

Instagram: @whatleahwrote

Printed in Dunstable, United Kingdom

74442955R00160